THE RISING

Brian McGilloway was born in Derry, Northern
Ireland, in 1974, and teaches English at
St Columb's College, Derry.

Also by Brian McGilloway in the Inspector Devlin series

BORDERLANDS

GALLOWS LANE

BLEED A RIVER DEEP

BRIAN McGILLOWAY

THE RISING

PAN BOOKS

First published 2010 by Macmillan

This edition published 2011 by Pan Books
an imprint of Pan Macmillan, a division of Macmillan Publishers Limited
Pan Macmillan, 20 New Wharf Road, London N1 9RR
Basingstoke and Oxford
Associated companies throughout the world
www.panmacmillan.com

ISBN 978-0-330-46085-9

1 3 5 7 9 8 6 4 2

A CIP catalogue record for this book is available from
the British Library.

Typeset by Ellipsis Books Limited, Glasgow
Printed in the UK by CPI Mackays, Chatham ME5 8TD

Visit **www.panmacmillan.com** to read more about all our books
and to buy them. You will also find features, author interviews and
news of any author events, and you can sign up for e-newsletters
so that you're always first to hear about our new releases.

For Carmel, Joe and Dermot

Friday, 2 February

Chapter One

I should have kissed Debbie and the kids goodbye before I left the house.

But the call-out came through at 4.30 a.m., while she lay sleeping, our youngest child, Shane, nestled behind her in our bed. I stumbled across the bedroom to answer my mobile, which rumbled dully as it vibrated against the dresser.

'Inspector Devlin?' The voice was young, eager.

I squinted at the display on the alarm clock beside our bed. Grey light leaked around the edges of the curtains, suffusing in stillness my wife and child where they lay.

'Yes?' I managed dryly.

'We've had reports of gunfire on Jackson Road at Carrigans, sir. The Super said you're to investigate.'

I pulled on my clothes and stepped silently down the stairs. Increasingly, following my supposed promotion, I'd been getting such call-outs at night, to the point that I no longer woke Debbie to tell her where I was going. Often the calls were for nothing, and I was back in our bed before she woke.

The drive to Carrigans took me five minutes, the roads being empty of traffic. As I neared the village, I could see an orange glow low on the horizon, which I initially took to be the aura of street lamps over Derry, the city just across the border. But Derry lay to the north: the illumination I could see was smaller and more localized, and lay to the west.

I cut down Jackson Road, heading towards the light. Within minutes I realized that it was coming from a farmhouse out-building, off the road to my left. At the foot of the laneway leading up to it, stood an old woman, her nightgown pulled tight around her, the lapels twisted in one hand, the other flailing to get my attention.

I stopped and got out. She was in her sixties I guessed, the thinness of her face accentuated by the shadows gathered around us.

'My husband,' she managed, pointing towards the out-building, an old barn, where already I could see thick flames through the shattered glass of a side window.

'Is he in there?'

She nodded, her face twisted in terror. 'The boy's in there too. Sam went in for him.'

Despite the recent rain, the ground around the barn had already dried with the burgeoning heat. I could feel it radiating off the corrugated walls even as I approached, removing my jacket and wrapping it around the lower half of my face to protect against the smoke.

The door was slightly ajar and I pushed it further open. It was not hung properly and the bottom edge screeched against the cement floor.

Inside, the barn was bigger than I had expected. The fire was in full blaze along the back wall already and, glancing up through the smoke, I could see flames twisting around the rafters. The air was acrid with the smell of burning plastic and wood. As the smoke was densest at head level, I stooped to see beneath it. I scanned the floor quickly, trying to locate either the man or boy that the woman had mentioned. The floor space consisted of a number of stalls, empty but for a scattering of rotten straw smouldering on the floor.

To my immediate right something moved. I approached, squinting against the glare, my throat already burning with the heat of the smoke that had made it through the covering of my jacket. An old man, his nightshirt pulled over his mouth, lay against the wall of the second stall. His shirt was streaked with blackness, his back shuddering as he coughed onto the ground. He was struggling to make it to his feet, trying desperately to claw his way upright, his hands grappling for purchase against the smoothness of the wall.

I went to him quickly, reaching under his armpits and hoisting him to his feet, though in doing so I had to drop my jacket from my face. He flailed blindly, cuffing me on the side of the head with his arm. I grabbed him more roughly than I

5

had intended and tried to pull him towards the door. I could sense his resistance as he tried to stumble towards the back of the barn.

He shouted something, though the roar of the flames moving towards us made it difficult to hear. My eyes stung with sweat and I twisted round to see a section of the rafters to our left collapsing.

Feeling as if the lump in my throat was about to burst, I took a quick breath, sucking in air through pursed lips. Immediately I regretted it. My lungs spasmed and I released my grip on the old man.

He tried to make his way into the barn again. Clasping my arms around his waist, I pulled him back towards the door, and out into the coldness of the night.

His wife stood, the whiteness of her clothes illuminated by the flames. My vision shifted and the ground seemed to slope beneath us as I fell, dragging the old man down with me. I coughed involuntarily until I began to retch, while the old woman thumped my back.

I wanted to shout at her to stop, but my mouth wouldn't work properly. I managed to drag myself into a sitting position and became aware of a high-pitched keening. In the distance I saw a flickering blue light cutting through the trees and then I heard the wailing of sirens.

'The boy's still in there!' the old woman shouted, pulling at my arm to get me onto my feet.

I struggled to do so, tugging off my shirt. I dipped it in a puddle of dirty water and, wrapping it around my face, went back towards the barn. The whole structure screeched and groaned like some ancient beast in its death throes as I went in through the doorway once more.

The fire had spread the length of the building, the roaring of the flames terrifying above the cracking of the wood and the screaming of metal. But the hole in the roof caused by the collapsing rafters had allowed some of the smoke an escape and it was a little easier to see, although the heat was now almost a solid presence and I had to exert all my strength to keep moving.

I made it halfway down the length of the barn, keeping an eye on the rafters above my head, when I saw the 'boy'. In reality, he was more likely a young man, from what I could see – his upper half was obscured behind the partition of the final stall. Denim-clad legs and workman's boots, badly scorched, lay just past the wall.

As I looked, I thought the legs moved, though I could not be sure that it wasn't a trick of my vision, distorted by the super-heated air round me.

I called out to him, looking for some sign of response, but my very words seemed to ignite the instant I uttered them. If he heard, he did not react.

I tried to push against the wall of heat in front of me. Just then I heard something crack, like gunfire inside my skull. I became aware of the heat on my back. Something rammed into me and I felt the ground shift suddenly sideways beneath me.

As I tried to catch my breath and steady myself, I sucked in more and more smoke. I thought of Debbie and our children, thought of Shane's softness as he shifted in the bed beside her.

The cement floor rose to meet me as my vision dissolved into blackness.

Chapter Two

My face was pressing against something cold and wet. I tried to open my eyes, but could see nothing. I thought I felt pressure build behind in my skull. I tried to breathe but again something prevented me. As I tried to raise myself up slightly, I found that I was lying face down on the ground outside, my face pressed against wet clay.

'Are you OK?' I heard a voice say.

I turned myself around as best I could to see the soot-smeared face of a fireman loom out of the darkness, the paleness of his face seemingly suspended in mid-air, his breathing apparatus hanging loose around his neck.

'There's someone in there,' I said, trying to stand up and failing. I felt as if my back was on fire and tried to reach around to check. I could feel the charred edges of my vest, then touched too tender skin and the rawness at my left shoulder blade caused me to swear.

'Don't touch it,' the man said.

'There's someone . . .' I attempted again.

He nodded. 'It's too late. Nothing we can do now.'

I pushed myself onto my knees, looked around. I could taste the mud off the ground in my mouth. Two fire tenders were parked at the entrance to the property beside an ambulance, its blue light twisting the shadows of the trees to our left. A team of men struggled to hold the writhing fire hose as it spewed water in through the hole in the roof of the barn.

Closer to the roadway, I could see the old woman. Her husband lay on the ground on his back, an ambulance man kneeling in the dirt beside him, holding an oxygen mask to the old man's mouth.

'Is he all right?' I asked.

The fireman nodded grimly. 'Hopefully.' He glanced down at me. 'You saved him, apparently.'

I nodded once. 'I couldn't get the other one though.'

The man shrugged kindly. 'You did your best, mate.'

I looked at him, a single tear of sweat running down his cheek, drawing a ragged line in the soot.

The journey to the hospital was torturous. As the ambulance manoeuvred its way along the country roads to Letterkenny, the pain of the wound on my back intensified with each shudder of the vehicle. I lay on my side to take the pressure off the burning sensation but to little avail. I glanced over my shoulder, trying to see the wound, but could not. The paramedic rested a gloved hand on my shoulder again.

'Is it bad?' I asked him.

He smiled lightly. 'Does it feel bad?'

'Jesus,' I yelped, as the ambulance took a bend too sharply and my back touched the cold steel side-bars of the stretcher.

'That'll be a yes,' he said. 'It'll hurt for a day or two. But you should survive.'

'That's reassuring.'

'All part of the service. The price of being a hero.'

I did not respond to him. Nor did I feel heroic. I thought again of the man in the barn, his legs visible behind the partition. Over and over I replayed the scene, trying to discern whether his legs had twitched, or I had imagined it. I could not shake the feeling that by pulling the old man out, I had allowed the other to die. And while, rationally, I understood that I had done the right thing – it didn't feel that way.

I must have been drifting in and out of consciousness, for the next thing I knew I was in a hospital bed. I could no longer feel the pain in my back though and, strangely, a wave of elation flushed through me. Gripping the side-bars of the bed I tried to heave myself into a sitting position.

A woman's voice, as light as the touch of her hand on my arm, stopped me.

'It's morphine,' she said. 'You feel better than you are. Stay in bed.'

Her face appeared at the edge of my vision. Thin, pale blonde hair tied back severely into a ponytail, her eyes brown and wide.

'Rest,' she said.

The morphine had worn off by the time I woke again and my back ached like hell beneath the coldness of the cream in the compress they had applied.

Debbie stood at the end of the bed now, with my superintendent, Harry Patterson, beside her. Both looked at me with expressions of long suffering, as if I were a recalcitrant child confirming once again my waywardness.

Debbie came and sat by me, taking my hand in hers. Patterson stood awkwardly beside her.

'You're up,' he said.

I nodded unnecessarily. 'How're the kids?' I asked Debbie.

She looked at me quizzically. 'They're fine. We wondered where you were. You didn't tell me you were going out.'

I tried to speak but my lips felt cracked and dry.

'He was too busy being a hero,' Patterson said, aiming for humour but missing.

'I'm sorry,' I managed.

Debbie squeezed my hand lightly, her eyes glistening, but she did not speak.

'How's the old man?' I asked.

Patterson coughed lightly into his hand.

'Not so good,' he said. 'He took in a lot of smoke. He's in ICU.'

His comment hung there for a moment.

'What about the dead man?' I asked finally.

Patterson shook his head. 'We're waiting for the fire brigade to clear the scene. They haven't let us in yet. Won't even let us near the cottage until they have the fire in the barn out.'

'Any names?'

'Possibly. A Martin Kielty owned the cottage. His motorbike is parked outside it.'

'Does the name mean anything?'

Patterson shook his head. 'Not to us. I've contacted your friend in the North, Hendry, to see what they have up there. I'll speak to the old couple, the Quigleys, in a while, and see what they have to say – assuming the old fella pulls through.'

'I'd like to see them myself, too,' I said.

Patterson nodded agreement, though was unable to hide the grimness in the set of his mouth.

That meeting did not occur. The old man, Sam Quigley, died at 4 p.m. that afternoon.

When I learned of his death, I disconnected the monitors to which I'd been attached and shuffled my way down to the elevator. On the ICU floor, I found Nora Quigley standing, dazed, at the end of the corridor, her shoulders stooped, her hands hanging limply by her sides. To her left, in the room where he had been since his admission, her husband lay unmoving on the bed. His face was drawn and waxy already, his jaw hanging slack, his mouth open. A white hospital sheet had been pulled up to his chest.

'I'm terribly sorry, Mrs Quigley,' I said, approaching the woman, my hand outstretched.

She looked at me, her eyes glassy with tears, the loose skin of her jaw shaking visibly. Ignoring my proffered hand, she came towards me, moving into the circle of my gathering arms.

Her embrace was light, the bones of her back brittle and sharp beneath the fabric of her cardigan. The smell of talc and rosewater drifted between us when she moved back from me again, still gripping my hand awkwardly in her own, the skin blotched with liver spots.

'I'm so sorry,' I said again.

The old woman looked up into my face, her features drawn with loss.

'I tried my best,' I found myself saying. 'I tried to . . .'

Nora Quigley shushed me, patting my arm lightly as if it were I, and not she, who was the grieving relative.

'I tried my best,' I repeated.

Against the wishes of the doctor, I discharged myself that night. Debbie and the kids called to collect me. Shane was effusive when he saw me, jumping up for me to lift him, despite Debbie's protestations that it would hurt my back. He clasped my hand in his as we shuffled out to the car, interlinking our fingers and smiling up at me.

My daughter, Penny, was a little quieter. Indeed, on the drive home, I glanced in the vanity mirror and realized she was watching me, her eyes searching the reflection of my face, as she bit at the skin at the side of her thumb. She had stretched over the past year or two, her face thinning, her hair growing longer. She smiled when she realized I had seen her, but the expression did not make it as far as her eyes, which retained a hint of melancholy.

In that moment, I recognized that my daughter was growing older, and with a pang I sensed that she had realized the same about me. Neither of us seemed happy with this knowledge.

'What's up?' Debbie asked, patting my knee with her free hand as she drove, stealing a glance across at me.

'I'm getting grey,' I said.

She looked at me again, quickly, her eyebrows raised.

'Maybe you should take things a bit easier then,' she said. 'Starting today. Get to your bed when you get home.'

I glanced again at Penny, but she had turned her attention to the window, her reflection spectral against the darkness beyond her.

Saturday, 3 February

Chapter Three

The following morning, I could not easily dismiss the thought of the two deaths I had witnessed. I spent the morning with Debbie and the kids, but she could sense that there was something bothering me and we skirted around increasingly fraught conversations as I tried to reason my way through the guilt I felt at having failed to save either of the dead men.

I was sitting at the window in the back room with a mug of tea, looking at the cherry tree at the top of our garden, its bare branches springing in the light wind. Debbie came in and stood beside me.

'Are you OK?'

I nodded.

'Penny has something to ask you.' She waited a beat for me to speak, then continued. 'She wants to go to a disco on Wednesday night.'

'She's eleven,' I said.

'The school is running it. She wants to go with all her friends.'

'I think she's too young.'

'There'll be *a* boy at it. Someone she likes.' Debbie smiled as she told me this.

I thought I felt something crack inside me. My stomach twisted so forcefully I had difficulty in swallowing my mouthful of tea.

'She's too young for boys,' I stated.

'Wise up, Ben,' Debbie said, laughing lightly. 'She's eleven. I'd be more worried if she *didn't* like boys.' It was a mother's logic. 'I told her she'd need to ask you.'

'We'll see,' I said, aware of the fact that, having enlisted her mother's support, Penny had ensured that the decision had already been made. 'I'm going out for a drive,' I added, ignoring Debbie's look of concern.

I pulled up to the laneway that led to Martin Kielty's house. A number of squad cars were parked haphazardly along the roadside and a single fire tender still stood at the end of the lane, though the fire was now extinguished.

An ancient oak demarcated the line between Kielty's property and Quigley's and it was here that I laid the two bunches of flowers I had bought. I stood in the silence, conscious of the sharp scent of burnt wood carried downwind from the barn, and whispered a prayer for the two men, and asked their forgiveness for my having failed to save them.

'You should be home.'

I looked up and saw Harry Patterson at the entrance to the old barn, his bulk exaggerated by the blue paper Forensics suit he wore.

'I couldn't settle,' I explained as I approached. Patterson and I had got off to a bad start when he took over as Super. Over the course of the year since, we had established an uneasy sort of truce, led in part by his decision to move to Letterkenny and leave me in Lifford with responsibility for an almost defunct station.

'We've only got in this morning. There were traces of accelerant all over the barn. The bloody thing kept re-igniting.'

He glanced past me to where the flowers I'd laid rested at the foot of the oak.

'You heard about the old man, then,' he said.

'I spoke to his wife. I couldn't ask about Kielty though.'

Patterson waved aside my comment. 'I spoke to her myself after I saw you. She was the one who called the fire in; said they were woken by loud bangs just before three. She confirmed seeing Kielty here earlier that night. She also saw an old blue car outside the cottage around 8.45. Old-style Volkswagen Beetle with an orange door, apparently.'

I nodded. 'That should be easily traced.'

Patterson nodded. 'We also got reports of a white builder's van here around 2 a.m. Milkman saw it – tinted foil on the windows of the rear doors, peeled off on one side. We have bulletins out on both.'

I nodded absent-mindedly and turned towards the barn.

'Is he still in there?'

The charcoaled remains of the roof rafters crunched under our feet, and the dry air, coupled with the unmistakable stench of burnt flesh, made remaining inside the barn difficult.

The body lay to the rear of the building, in the corner. The medical examiner, John Mulronney, was squatting beside it as we approached. The upper torso and face were severely damaged by the fire, the features impossible to distinguish. The lower part of the body, though scorched, had not been burned quite as deeply. The clothes had been burnt away and the charred shreds scattered beneath the body. It was evident that, regardless of identity, the victim was male.

Mulronney used a long thin piece of wood, more commonly used for throat examinations, to angle the head. He did not acknowledge our presence until he had finished.

'He's dead, obviously,' he said, standing up. 'It appears he was stabbed in the chest. There's a deep wound near the sternum. Might have killed him before the fire – might not. Hard to tell.'

'Any gunshot wounds?' Patterson asked.

Mulronney shook his head.

'Are you sure?'

'As much as I can be,' he said, a little irritably. 'Why?'

'The old couple heard shots,' I explained. 'That's what brought me here in the first place.'

'No gunshot wounds that I can see,' he repeated. 'Unless the state pathologist finds them.'

'Anything else?' I asked, as we started to move back out into the freshening air.

'Nothing obvious; the state pathologist will check his lungs to see whether or not he was alive when the fire started.'

We stepped away from the ruins and I took out my cigarettes and passed one to Mulronney. One of the fire crew, still sifting through the debris, shouted to us.

'Put those bloody things away. We've just got this out.'

I raised my hand in apology and pocketed the packet. It had been an impulsive act anyway, for I certainly didn't feel like smoking.

'You'll need dental records to confirm ID,' Mulronney said, placing his unlit cigarette in his breast pocket and making his way back to his car.

To our right, outside the door of Kielty's cottage, sat a Kawasaki motorcycle, the helmet hanging from the handlebar. As we approached, Patterson gestured once more to the flowers I had brought.

'You'd have saved your money if you'd seen inside,' he said.

*

The hallway of the cottage was lit by an arc light, and trapped smoke from the barn still swirled through the lamp's illumination.

I followed Patterson through a doorway to our left, into a room I took to be the living room. Against the right-hand wall sat an old threadbare sofa. A stained hearthrug took up most of the middle of the floor, and on it stood a small coffee table. On its surface lay scattered a mixture of syringes and spoons and the stub of a candle, squatting amidst thick veins of hardened wax. A number of empty beer cans, bent double, lay on the floor. One had been cut open; the metal of its base scorched into a rainbow pattern through frequent heating. Also on the floor lay a mobile phone, its screen and casing cracked. A group of Forensics officers had marked each of these objects and a photographer was moving around taking shots.

I went into the next room, a bedroom. The wall was papered in a pattern of large pink roses, the boarded-up window framed by tattered pink satin curtains. The only furniture in the room consisted of a stained mattress against one wall and a single shelf running across the centre of the opposite wall. On the shelf lay an empty cigarette packet and several broken filters. Beside that was the empty foil wrapping of a condom. As I moved around the room, I could feel the resistance as my feet pulled against the stickiness of the carpet.

The back room was a small kitchen. An assortment of crockery was piled up in one of the cupboards. The worktops were empty, save for a block of knives, the uppermost one absent. On the floor by the sink, arranged in order, were several empty vodka bottles and a black bin bag, spilling beer cans onto the floor. The room stank of stale water and the sweet yeasty smell of beer.

'Look at the state of this place,' Patterson said, surveying the room with disgust. 'Imagine thinking your kid was living here, sticking some filthy skag needle in their arm.'

I glanced around him, grateful that I was unable to imagine my own children in such a place.

'Have we any next of kin for Kielty yet?' I asked.

'Your pal, Hendry, is meant to be working on it,' he said. 'I'm surprised he hasn't been in touch – he was asking about you earlier.'

I patted my pockets and realized I had left my phone in the car. Sure enough, when I went out to retrieve it, Hendry had left a message for me. He had located Kielty's girlfriend, in Plumbridge.

Chapter Four

I met Jim Hendry and a young female officer, whom he intro-duced as WPC Tara Carson, just over the border. He had offered to take me to Plumbridge, a small village a few miles out of Strabane. Patterson had initially been reluctant for me to go. Finally he relented, sensing that I felt I should be the one to see Kielty's partner, having been witness to his death. Before leaving, I contacted Burgess in the station and asked him to send one of our uniforms, Paul Black, to come to the barn to assist the Scene of Crime team.

On the way to Plumbridge, Hendry, having asked in his own gruff way about the fire and my injury, filled me in on all he had learned about Kielty.

'Drugs Squad know him fairly well. He's a low-grade dealer. Or he was. Word is he was trying to make a name for himself. Operated mostly over here until the paramilitaries warned him off. He's done time twice – first for aggravated assault when he was eighteen, then for burglary when he was twenty-two.

He broke into an old woman's house outside Donemana. Threatened her with a syringe full of his own blood. Took over four hundred pounds she had in her mattress. The woman was so terrified she wouldn't leave the house again. She died from heart failure a few months after, though they could never link it to Kielty's break-in. He's stayed out of trouble since then.'

'Until now,' I said.

Kielty's girlfriend's house was at the end of a row of terraced houses. A lone hydrangea bush, its spiky branches bare of leaves, sat in the centre of the small front lawn, the thin skin of the petals translucent in the weak sunlight.

From inside the house I could hear the raised voices of an American daytime chat show. The front door was white PVC with two narrow panels of frosted glass, through which we could see someone moving about. Hendry rang the doorbell then stepped back. We could see a figure approach the door, heard the grate of the key in the lock.

The girl who answered looked around eighteen. She was soft-featured, with a rounded face framed by brown hair cut in a long bob. Her eyes were clear and bright green, her nose thin and her full lips parted, as if she were expecting someone else. She smiled quizzically as she shifted the weight of the baby girl she held in her arms from her left to her right shoulder. The baby must have been no more than a few months old.

'Yes?' she said. A question, not the statement of greeting common in the North. I thought I could discern an English accent.

'My name is Detective Inspector Jim Hendry,' Hendry said. 'We'd like to speak to you about Martin Kielty.'

Her expression remained one of mild bemusement.

'Is something wrong?' she asked, then shushed the baby who had stirred at the sound of her voice.

'Might be best if we come inside,' Hendry said, nodding gently towards the house next door. An elderly woman's face peered at us through the front window, without even a pretence of subtlety.

I smiled at her and she scowled in return.

Kielty's girlfriend introduced herself as Elena McEvoy. She brought us into the living room and invited us to sit as she laid the baby in a Moses basket. She wore a dress patterned with roses, and as she sat she swept her hand beneath her to ensure the dress covered her legs. There was a sense of dignity and decorum to the gesture which made me reassess my original assessment of her age. She rested one hand on the edge of the basket, which she rocked gently as we spoke.

'What's she called?' Tara Carson asked, looking in at the infant.

'Anna.'

'She's beautiful. What age is she?'

'Three months,' Elena McEvoy replied, smiling at her with pride.

Hendry looked at me and winked.

'So, is something wrong?' McEvoy asked. Clearly she was used to policemen calling at her home. Her question also told me something about the body in the barn. If it was her boyfriend, then she was used to going days or nights without seeing him, for she did not seem to connect our presence to his absence. Nor, it appeared, had she reported him missing.

'There was a fire, at a property outside Carrigans, over the border,' I explained.

She stared at me levelly, holding my gaze, one hand resting lightly on her knee, the other still rocking the basket.

'We believe the property belongs to your boyfriend, Martin Kielty? Is that right?'

'Yes,' she said. 'Was anyone hurt? Is Martin OK?'

'I'm afraid we've found human remains at the scene. We haven't been able to identify the victim yet. We were hoping that you might be able to tell us where Mr Kielty is.'

Her expression did not change, though I noticed a shift in the rhythm of the rocking. So too did the child, for she mewed mildly, causing McEvoy to lift her. She stood, swaying gently from side to side, whilst regarding me over her daughter's shoulder.

'I don't know where he is. He hasn't come home.'

'When did you last see him, ma'am?' Hendry asked.

She shook her head. 'Thursday, sometime. Late afternoon, maybe.'

'Yet you haven't reported him missing,' Hendry commented.

She glanced at him. 'He's often away for a day or two at a time.'

'We suspect that your partner was involved in drugs,' I said, finding it hard to place this woman alongside a drug pusher. 'Is that the case?'

She nodded, her mouth a thin defiant line.

'Would you have any reason to believe that someone might want to hurt Mr Kielty?' I asked. 'That's not to say that he has been hurt, of course. It's too early to tell.'

'He was assaulted in the pub a month or two ago. Told he'd have his knees done. He was terrified.'

Though not terrified enough to stop selling drugs, I thought. 'Where was that?'

'Doherty's,' she said. 'In Strabane.'

'I know it,' I said. 'Was there any follow-up on the threat?'

'He was sent a Mass card with a bullet in it a week or two after it,' she continued. 'That terrified me.' She shuddered involuntarily and rubbed away the shiver in her arms. Having been at the receiving end of such a threat myself in the past, I knew the effect it could have.

'Any idea who might have sent it?' Hendry asked, glancing at me. The threat was one commonly associated with the paramilitaries during the height of the Troubles.

She shook her head. 'Martin binned it, said it was nothing.'

'He should have contacted us,' Hendry said.

'As if you'd have done anything. They signed it the Rise or something.'

'The Rising?' Hendry asked. He nodded lightly at me to let me know he would explain later.

McEvoy nodded once, curtly. 'That sounds like it.'

'That's very useful, ma'am,' Hendry said.

'Anyone else your partner would have dealt with who might be able to help us?' I asked, sensing that our interview had reached a natural conclusion.

'He mentioned someone called Lorcan Hutton,' McEvoy answered, her jaw set. Hutton was a well-known pusher on both sides of the border, though he had settled in the South. I'd had experience of Lorcan Hutton before, though would never have considered him to be violent. Then again, violence and drugs tend to be easy bedfellows.

We asked a few more questions regarding Kielty's movements. McEvoy was unable to tell us anything more about the threat made to him. She did not know where he might have kept lists of contacts or phone numbers; he had his mobile with him, she said. I suspected it might have been the one I'd seen lying broken on the floor of his cottage. McEvoy denied using drugs herself. As she spoke, she smoothed down her daughter's hair softly with one hand. The child in turn gripped her mother's dress in her small fist, twisting the cloth in its grip.

'Does Martin have any other family?' I asked. 'Any blood relatives?'

'His mother lives in Derry. In Galliagh,' McEvoy said. I could tell from her tone that their relationship was not a good one.

'We'll need to contact her.'

She nodded sharply, tossing her head a little to the left.

Finally, I asked for a photograph. I needed to put a face to Kielty's name. Plus, of course, he was still technicelly a missing person. Elena McEvoy went into the next room and I heard the sliding of a drawer. She returned with a single colour photograph of Kielty reclining on a bed, smiling, his infant daughter comfortable in the crook of his arm.

'This was only taken a few weeks ago. I hope it's OK,' she said.

'It's fine,' I replied. Then added, 'I'm afraid I'm going to need the name of Martin's dentist too.'

Her face twisted with revulsion as she realized the implication in what I had said.

Back in the car I called Patterson and reported back. He promised he would have someone go out to Kielty's mother while I retrieved the dental records. When I finished the call, I asked Hendry about the group he had named, The Rising.

Ten minutes later, in his office, he handed me three photographs. The first image focused on a youngish-looking man pictured coming out of a house, his thick head covered in a bennie hat, his fists shoved in his coat pockets.

'Charlie Cunningham,' Hendry said.

I flicked to the next image. An older man, the shape and size of a club bouncer, his hair cropped short. He had a spider's-web tattoo on his neck.

'Tony Armstrong. Did time for shooting a policeman during the Troubles.'

Another picture. This time the man was in his forties I guessed, his head completely shaven. His brow was heavy over hooded eyes and he was looking directly at the camera. I thought I recognized him.

'Jimmy Irvine.' He tapped the picture. 'All three are ex-paramilitaries. All three have done time for murder. All are hardliners pissed at the political process. Fed up with being told they had to stand down, the war was over.'

'What's the connection?'

'They've started an anti-drugs organization called The Rising. Small fry really, but they've learned one good lesson from their previous allegiances: you want political clout in a community, you give the people what they want. They reckon if the local communities see them 'dealing' with the drugs problem, they'll gain some electoral support.'

'How are they "dealing" with it?' I asked.

'Mostly punishment beatings so far: that's why I didn't imme-diately think of them for Kielty. They haven't killed anyone yet. They tried to shoot a dealer in Derry about two months ago, outside the cinema, but they made a balls of it.'

I recalled the case. A young couple walking out of the late night screening of a movie were shot at from a passing car. The girl had been hit in the arm.

'Bit amateur, to be honest. If you're going to shoot someone, get them when they're stationary at least, right?'

'I'm not sure if it's the same racket,' I said. 'Kielty was stabbed in the chest and set on fire. It looks like a spur of the moment killing, not something planned.'

'Don't dismiss this crew. They tarred and feathered a young fella in Galliagh in Derry a few weeks ago, and then kneecapped his business partner. They're not afraid to evolve – change their methods.'

'You don't think they're just trying to control drugs in the area themselves?'

'Apparently not,' Hendry said. 'The word coming to us from the street is that these guys are thugs, but they don't have the money to invest in product. They seem to be purely political. All they want is public support. Get people behind them on the anti-drugs thing, get their feet under the table in a few areas, then introduce some of their more extreme political ideologies bit by bit. They're not the first to try it – I doubt they'll be the last.'

*

After leaving the station, I made my way into Strabane to the dental surgery Elena McEvoy had named. It was a Saturday and the surgery was closed but Hendry had called the dentist at home instructing him to meet me there. He had also offered to contact the Drugs Squad again and ask them to keep a look out for Kielty and to follow up on Lorcan Hutton if he ventured north of the border.

The dentist was waiting for me when I got to the surgery, clearly a little piqued at having to open up on his day off. Still, he handed me a small, A5 slip-wallet in which were a batch of white cards and a few X-ray sheets.

When I got back over the border, I drove up to Letterkenny to leave the dental records in the General Hospital where the post-mortem was to be conducted on Monday. I was getting used to driving again, turning my body a little to one side in the seat to avoid putting any pressure on my left shoulder blade.

On my way back home, Patterson phoned me. He had spoken to Kielty's mother himself. She hadn't seen him in a few days, she claimed. Patterson told her that a body had been found and that he would keep her informed. He did not comment on how she had reacted to such news.

'I've had Technical check out that phone,' he added. 'It seems to be Kielty's. A lot of incoming calls, which suggests he was a dealer rather than a user. None were answered after 10.15 on Thursday night.'

'Yet the fire was after 4 a.m., which suggests he was dead six hours before the fire was started.'

'Technical identified one number which was used by Kielty a lot, earlier last month, as belonging to Lorcan Hutton.'

'Hutton. The girlfriend mentioned him too.'

'Might be worth bringing him in; see what he has to say,' Patterson suggested.

I drove round to Hutton's house in Rolston Court, on the off-chance I might catch him on the hoof. The problem with bringing him in for questioning was that he tended to lawyer up very quickly. His parents were both doctors and spared nothing in their treatment of him – even continuing to support him when he began peddling drugs to the teenagers of the borderlands.

In the end, his house was empty, which was probably just as well, for it was approaching seven, I hadn't been home all day, and my back was aching again.

I radioed through to Central Communications, asking for a bulletin to be issued directing all local guards to be on the lookout for Lorcan Hutton.

Then, praying for a quiet evening, I headed back home.

Sunday, 4 February

Chapter Five

Following Patterson's relocation to Letterkenny, I had been left in charge of Lifford station. In reality, this 'promotion' meant having to take every call-out that occurred this side of Letterkenny, regardless of the time of day. That night, I had hoped that Patterson would allow me some leeway because of my injury. It seemed I was wrong.

I snapped a terse greeting when I answered the phone at 3.30 a.m. the following morning, assuming it to be Letterkenny station.

Instead, a female voice answered; a voice that was somehow familiar. 'Hello?'

'Yes. Who is this?'

'It's Caroline Williams, sir,' the voice said.

'Caroline!' I said, squinting at the bedside clock to make sure I'd read it properly. 'Is everything OK?'

'I'm sorry to phone; I need your help. It's Peter.'

*

Within half an hour I was dressed and on the road. Debbie was unhappy about my leaving again, and the stinging ache of my back meant I would happily have stayed in bed, but I felt I could not refuse.

Peter, Caroline's son, had been almost nine when they left Lifford for Sligo, after Caroline's resignation from the force, which put him around fifteen years of age by now. Apparently, Peter and one of his friends had gone camping near Rossnowlagh, an Atlantic beach situated a few miles north of Bundoran, at the furthest reach of Donegal County. According to his friend, Peter had gone out of his tent to go to the toilet at around two in the morning and had not returned. He had phoned his father, who in turn had contacted Caroline to tell her Peter was missing. She had contacted everyone she knew in the area to assemble a search party. And then she had called me.

An hour later I stood with around a dozen other volunteers on the headland overlooking Rossnowlagh beach, where Peter's tent was pitched, my coat buttoned against a bracing Atlantic wind. The edge of the headland was fenced by paired steel poles running horizontally, supported by concrete bollards every twenty yards or so. It was a basic affair, but enough to prevent someone falling over the edge accidentally.

Caroline came over to me when she saw me, her arms stiffly

by her sides, her coat sleeves pulled down over her hands. Her face was flushed, her eyes raw with tears. Her hair, now curly, hung in straggles around her face. She hugged me fiercely, then stepped back.

'Thanks for coming, sir,' she said. 'I didn't know who else to call.'

'I'm sure everything will be all right,' I said, trying as best I could to sound sincere. 'Anything I can do?'

Caroline nodded over her shoulder at an elderly man speaking to a group carrying torches. I recognized him as Caroline's father; he had come to collect her and Peter when they had moved from Lifford. 'Dad's taking care of everything,' she said. 'He's been great.'

Looking down towards the beach, where the tide rushed the sand, I could see an inflatable approaching the shore, its spotlight raking the beach. Within the hour, I knew the coastguard helicopter would likewise be sweeping the shoreline.

'What about Peter's friend?' I asked.

Caroline groaned lightly. 'Cahir Murphy. Peter told me that a group of them would be here. If I'd known it was just Murphy I'd . . .' The sentence faded into the wind.

'He's over here,' she added instead, leading me over to where the tent had been pitched. Circular pools of torchlight projected the silhouettes of its two occupants against the canvas.

At the entrance to the tent stood a middle-aged Garda

officer. He watched us approach, rubbing one eye with his middle finger as he did so. His breath carried the smell of coffee and cigarettes, and breath mints.

'DI Devlin,' I said by way of introduction.

'Dillon,' he replied. He pointed into the tent where his partner squatted, talking intently to a teenager I took to be Cahir Murphy. 'He's McCready.'

'I'm here as a friend of Ms Williams,' I said.

He looked at me levelly for a moment, then turned his attention to Caroline. His gaze settled on her chest and did not waver.

Cahir Murphy sat cross-legged on the ground inside the tent, his unzipped sleeping bag wrapped shawl-like around his shoulders. In one hand he held a cigarette, in the other an empty beer can, which he was using as an ashtray. The whites of his eyes were laced with blood vessels, though he appeared in control both of himself and the situation in which he found himself. He looked up at me as I peered in through the tent entrance.

'Who's he?' he asked.

The young Guard in the tent with him twisted to face me. He looked to be in his late twenties. He wore his uniform neatly, his tie knot tight to his throat. He was thin, his face newly shaven despite the hour.

'Benedict Devlin,' I said, deliberately omitting my title in case the presence of a third Garda overwhelmed the boy. I needn't have bothered.

'You're the Guard?' Murphy said.

'That's right,' I replied.

'Peter said his mum talks about you *all* the time,' he said.

I glanced around the interior of the tent. It was big enough for four at least. 'Sorry for interrupting,' I said.

The young Guard turned towards Murphy again. 'Anyone drinking this evening, Cahir?'

'Nah, no drink,' he said. 'Coke and Fanta and stuff, just.'

'Apart from that beer can you're using as an ashtray,' I pointed out.

Murphy looked at the can in his hands, then dropped his own butt into it where it extinguished with a hiss.

'Maybe one or two,' he said. 'Nothing much. He wasn't drunk, like. He'd only had a can.'

'What do you think happened to him?' I asked.

Murphy looked at me a little defiantly. 'I don't know. He just vanished. One minute he was standing here and then he was gone.'

I turned to Caroline, only to realize that she had moved away from the group and stood alone at the edge of the head-land. She cupped her hands around her mouth, and began howling her son's name, forlornly against the prevailing wind, the word almost indecipherable beyond the anguished tone of her cries. To the east, someone else took up the cry of the boy's name. As I exited the tent, I found myself doing likewise, our voices rising together into the chilled night air.

A quarter of an hour later, the young Guard approached me, a plastic bag in his hand.

'Can I have a word, sir?' he said.

'What can I do for you . . .?' I couldn't recall what Dillon had called him.

'McCready, sir. Joe McCready,' he said, extending his hand.

'Good to meet you, Joe McCready.' I shook, feeling the wet and grit off his hand.

'Sorry, sir. I've been looking through the bins. I forgot to wash my hands.'

McCready saw from my expression that some further explanation was necessary.

As he spoke, I noticed his partner sauntering over towards us. He winked at me conspiratorially, then nodded towards McCready.

'What did you find?' I asked.

'Thirteen cans, sir, all the same brand and same bags. The fourteenth is being used as an ashtray by Cahir Murphy.'

The older Guard looked at me, his mouth bleary with lack of sleep. 'So they were drinking. So what?'

'It's not the drinking,' McCready said, 'so much as the lying about it. What else is he lying about? Fourteen cans seems excessive even for two young fellas; especially considering Murphy's not that well on. He doesn't strike me as the kind to tidy after himself either.'

'Where did you find them?'

McCready led Dillon and me to the edge of an adjoining field where a large plastic wheeled bin had been left for campers to dump their rubbish. It was empty now.

Looking up, across the field beside us, I could see a small caravan park, the vehicles sitting symmetrically in rows. The park was in darkness; most of the caravans would be empty at this time of year.

'It might be worthwhile taking a look over there,' I suggested.

Chapter Six

The caravans were parked in nine rows, so we took three rows apiece. I took the furthest three rows from the entrance, which were also the closest to the headland where Peter had been camping. I walked along the first row, glancing under each caravan before checking the doors. As I reached the end of the first of my rows, though, the constant stooping caused the wound on my back to start aching and I decided to settle with checking the doors of the caravans themselves.

It was on the turn to the third row that I noticed something odd about the caravan to my immediate left. The outer flange of the door had been bent backwards slightly, the deadbolt exposed by my torchlight. I found that, with minimal force, the door opened. I called out before entering.

'Hello?'

Silence. I raked the torchlight across the interior. The

vehicle smelled musty, as if it had not been used in a while. The ceiling was low, the interior cramped with furniture.

'Anyone here?' I called.

Somewhere further back in the vehicle I could hear the dripping of a leaky tap. I stood a moment, the torch held down by my leg, allowing my eyes to become accustomed to the gloom, waiting. Finally, I heard the laboured suspiration of one releasing a pent-up breath, the sound low and soft enough to cause my skin to prickle with goosebumps. I moved towards the back of the caravan, the torch low. Then, as I passed the table at the seating area, I caught a glimpse of something red beneath it.

'Hello?' I said again, more speculative this time.

I approached the table, angling the torch beam to better see what was beneath the table.

'Peter?' I said, quietly, suddenly aware of the silence around us.

No response. I stooped slightly to look more closely. Just as I realized it was a rucksack, the door of the toilet cubicle behind me flung open and someone shoved past me knocking me flat on the floor.

I scrabbled after the figure. He wore jeans and a puffy blue jacket, his build slight. I grabbed at his leg, managing to grip his ankle. He turned and kicked viciously backwards several times, the sole of his trainer connecting with my temple. Having forced me to release my grip, he stumbled to the doorway and fell out onto the grass.

Blundering out after him, I shouted to Dillon and McCready.

I could see the two of them scanning the caravan park trying to locate the cause of the disturbance. In the middle distance I heard more shouting from the headland and saw the bobbing of torchlight across the field as they ran to join us.

I looked around but could not see my assailant. Dropping to my knees, I leant down and shone my torch under the caravans. My wound reacted angrily to the movement and I had to swallow back the bile that rose with the pain. Nothing.

Moving on to the next row, next to Dillon, I repeated the manoeuvre. There, four caravans up, I caught a flash of blue as the boy tried to squeeze under the vehicle.

'There,' I shouted to Dillon, as the man lumbered towards the caravan.

Seeing his approach, the figure struggled all the more, and managed to make it to the other side before Dillon had a chance to grab him.

Cursing the man's inefficiency, I called to McCready as I ran up the next row. I went as quickly as I could, but my lungs felt ready to burst, my throat burning with each gasp of air. The boy was much faster than me, sprinting past each caravan, closing constantly the distance between him and the low wall at the top of the park.

He glanced around once at me, gauging the space between us, his expression one of sheer terror. He was about ten feet from the wall, his pace increasing as he prepared to vault the boundary, when McCready blindsided him, appearing from around the side of the last vehicle, rugby-tackling him to the ground.

The boy struggled for an instant but McCready soon subdued him and by the time I reached them, the boy lay face down, his arm twisted behind his back.

'Peter?'

He turned his head to me, grit stuck to the side of his face as he began to sob.

Behind me I heard the others arriving. Caroline Williams pushed her way through them, her face alight with expectation. She ran to the boy lying on the ground, dropped to her knees before him, and gripped his chin in her hand, raising his head slightly as if to examine it. Her expression darkened.

'Adam!' she snapped. 'Adam.'

Her shoulders began to shudder as she lifted her fists and began to hit the boy around the head, cursing him for not being her son.

The boy continued to cry, his face a smear of tears and dirt. 'I'm sorry. Please don't tell my da,' he pleaded.

Chapter Seven

Adam Heaney sat in the tent with Cahir Murphy now, his rucksack lying forlornly on the grass outside, where Guard Dillon had discarded it.

'Please don't tell my daddy,' Heaney repeated for perhaps the fourth time since we'd caught him.

'What the hell did you run for?' I asked him, angry that he had wasted our time, that he had caused me to hurt my shoulder again, and that he had dashed Caroline's hopes.

'I told my da I was staying with Peter,' he explained. 'He'd have a fit if he knew I was . . . here.'

He glanced at Murphy quickly before finishing the sentence. Murphy scowled. Clearly, Heaney's father shared Caroline's view of Cahir Murphy.

'So, was anyone else here or just the three of you?'

Murphy laughed without humour. 'No, that's the lot.'

Heaney shuddered involuntarily, then tugged his jacket tight around him.

'What happened to Peter tonight, Adam?' I asked, squatting down level with the boy.

Again he glanced at Murphy. 'He got up to go to the toilet. We never saw him after that.'

He tried to hold eye contact, but could not.

'Was he drunk – don't look at him, Adam,' I said. 'Look at me.'

The boy's gaze shifted sharply from Murphy to me, but fell around my chin.

'No. He might have had a can or two. That's all. Nothing happened.'

'Told you,' Murphy said behind me.

I stood outside the tent with Caroline and Joe McCready. Caroline had settled herself a little now, though her eyes were raw with crying.

'They're lying about something,' I said. 'The problem is Heaney's so scared of his dad finding out he's here, we're not going to get anything out of him.'

'His dad is a bit of a thug,' Caroline commented.

I nodded to McCready. 'Take them home. Let their parents deal with them whatever way they want. Once that's out of the way, bring them in again, separately, and make them go into detail. Look for anything out of place.'

McCready nodded earnestly. Dillon, by contrast, yawned

loudly into his fist then squinted against the early morning sun cresting the headland to the east.

By noon, the search party had moved from the headland to a wider sweep of the beach and currently was combing the edges of the grass-covered sand dunes to the north. Search teams had also been dispatched to the fields running away from the beach, among which whitewashed holiday cottages caught the watery rays of late winter sunlight.

Caroline was part of one such team, making its way through the thick meadow grass of a field bordered by a drainage ditch that ran alongside the main road. She wore jeans and a heavy jumper several sizes too big for her, which I suspected one of the men had given her. Her hair was tied back from her face, her eyes puffy with tears or lack of sleep, or both.

I joined her team and walked alongside her, scanning both the ground in front of me and the ditch to my right.

'You holding up OK?'

She shook her head. 'I keep hoping he is going to phone me. I've called his mobile all day but it kept ringing out. An hour ago it stopped ringing and went straight to the answering service. Do you think maybe he turned it off?'

She glanced at me and I could see in her expression both the hurt that her son might choose not to answer her call, and the hope that he had been able to make such a choice at all.

'Maybe,' I said. 'Maybe his battery died.'

She nodded her head vigorously. 'Maybe,' she said.

We walked in silence for a moment, before Caroline spoke again.

'We . . . we argued before he left,' she said. 'He wanted to go camping and I'd said no. His friends were going surfing, he said, and he wanted to go with them.'

Murphy had told McCready a different story; he had claimed thcy were there for his birthday. And there had been no sign of surfboards in the tent.

'I refused and he said he was going anyway. I couldn't stop him.' She looked at me a little plaintively. 'He was right. There was nothing I could do. I . . .' She began to speak, then seemed to choke on her words.

'What, Caroline?' I said.

She shook her head. 'He was right,' she repeated. 'Do you think he's doing this to punish me?' she asked, suddenly.

'Peter's a good fella, Caroline. We'll find him.'

'He changed, Ben. As he got older – he changed.'

'They all change,' I said. 'Penny's looking to go to discos, for God's sake,' I added with a laugh.

'No. Peter's become very angry; judging me. He blamed me for his father leaving. His moods were all over the place for a while there, he wasn't sleeping, he was tying himself up in knots. The doctor actually put him on medication for depression, though he only took it off and on. He kept casting up the fact that I chased his father away from him. I think it was easier for him to blame me than to accept that Simon hadn't wanted to see him.'

'You had no choice there, Caroline. You had to do it for Peter's sake as much as your own.'

'He doesn't remember that. He said it was my fault.'

'Kids say things, Caroline.'

'I should call his father,' she said, decisively. 'He deserves to know.'

'Whatever you think is best,' I said.

Simon Williams, Caroline's estranged husband, had beaten her frequently. Only the intervention of our old boss, Superintendent Costello, had convinced Simon to leave Caroline and Lifford.

'Maybe Peter will think better of me if he knows I called his father.' She looked up into my face hopefully, as if the act of contacting Simon Williams might in some way precipitate the return of her son.

'Maybe,' I said. We walked in silence for a few more minutes, scanning the ground around us.

Then she spoke again. 'I told him not to come back,' she said, matter-of-factly. It took me a moment to realize that she was talking about Peter again rather than Simon. 'That was the last thing I said to him: "If you go camping, don't bother coming back."'

'We all say things, Caroline.'

'I told him not to come back, Ben. That's what I'm being punished for.' She stopped walking and looked directly at me. 'What if I deserve it?'

As the sky darkened we headed back to the hotel where the manager had offered tea and sandwiches to all involved in the search. The hotel itself was quiet, operating with a skeleton staff throughout the winter to cater for the handful of tourists and surfers who visited the beach this early in the season.

Caroline and I were standing at the table of food, when Joe McCready approached us. Removing his cap, he nodded to Caroline. 'Ma'am,' he said. Then he turned to me. 'I spoke to the boys again, sir. After their parents arrived.'

I glanced at Caroline, who was listening intently. 'Grab yourself something to eat, Joe.'

We took a seat by the bay window facing out on the shoreline. During our conversation I could see Caroline's attention shift if she saw some movement along the beach. On several occasions she stood and stared out of the window, squinting into the middle distance every time a figure moved along the beach.

'Anything of any use, Joe?' I asked.

'The same story as before, sir. They claim they came here for Murphy's birthday party.'

Caroline turned from the window. 'Peter told me they were going surfing,' she stated.

McCready looked at his notebook of notes, then looked up at her blankly. 'Neither of them mentioned that,' he said.

'What else?' I asked.

'Murphy admitted they'd had a can or two each. When I told them I'd found fourteen he denied it. Said they'd not had as much as that.' He glanced at Caroline again. 'He said that Peter had drunk the most. He'd been angry about something . . .' He glanced again at Caroline, then at me.

'Go on,' I urged him.

'He and his mother had had a row, he claimed.' I noticed that Caroline did not turn round at that point, but maintained her silent vigil at the window.

'Heaney continued to deny he'd been drinking at all. Though I . . .' Again he glanced at Caroline, coughed, then continued, 'I told them both that when we find Peter, we'll find out the truth anyway.'

I could understand the delicacy of what he had said. If Peter turned up alive, he could tell us himself. If not, toxicology results would reveal traces of any alcohol taken prior to death.

'Did he mention running away from home?' Caroline asked, turning her body towards us but remaining where she was, her back against the window, her arms folded across her chest.

'None of them said that as such, ma'am,' McCready said.

'Caroline,' she corrected him, before returning her gaze to the shoreline.

*

I left for home at around seven thirty that evening, once the twilight had deepened to night. The road to Lifford takes you through Barnesmore Gap, between Croaghconnelagh and Croaghonagh. On either side of the road, you are enclosed by the sheer climb of the mountainsides, their ridges marked with angular dark-brown boulders, jutting through the soil, their sides flanked with sparse forests of fir trees. The thin black shadows of the trees were elongated by a heavy moon that clung close to the mountaintop.

Just as I was passing through the lowest point of the valley, where the river snakes along the base of the mountain to the left of the road, my mobile rang. It was Caroline.

The proximity of the mountains affected my reception and her message was broken. Yet there was no denying the changed tone of her voice. Between the static and the breaks in reception, I was able to decipher that she had received word from Peter.

I stopped in Ballybofey once I'd made it through the Gap, and phoned her from the car park outside Jackson's Hotel.

'He's OK!' she said, her voice buzzing with elation, as soon as I answered the phone. 'He's in Dublin.'

'That's fantastic news, Caroline. I'm delighted for you. What did he say?'

'He . . . I didn't talk to him. He sent a text message. He's in Dublin.'

'He didn't say why he'd gone?'

'No – that's it. He's in Dublin somewhere. Not to worry about him.'

'That's good news, Caroline.'

'I'm heading down to Dublin, now, Ben. I just wanted to let you know. I . . . Thanks for your help.'

'Not at all, Caroline,' I said. 'It was good to see you, despite the circumstances. I'll contact someone in Dublin – get a bulletin out to the uniforms.'

'Simon is meeting me there,' Caroline said. 'Look, I'll be in touch,' she said. 'Thanks again.' Then the line went dead.

As I drove back towards Lifford, I was a little ashamed to realize that my relief at Peter turning up alive was tempered by the knowledge that I would now be unlikely to see Caroline Williams again.

Chapter Eight

As I passed through Castlefinn on the way back to Lifford, I noticed a number of squad cars parked along the main roadway. An unusually large number of people were walking along the pavements, spilling onto the road as they made their way towards the entrance to Rolston Court, a cul-de-sac of thirty or so small council houses. Several of them had banners and placards. Pulling in, I approached a group of squad cars and was more than a little surprised to see my superintendent, Harry Patterson, standing with some of the men.

'Where were you?' he said.

I explained that I had spent the day in Rossnowlagh with Williams looking for her son.

'How is she?'

'Better now,' I said. 'What's going on?'

'Anti-drugs demo.'

'What are they doing?'

'Someone told them that Lorcan Hutton operates out of one

of the houses up in Rolston Court. They're going to protest outside his house.'

'Why?'

'That fucker on the local radio named him at lunchtime as a suspect in the killing of Kielty. This Rising crew held a meeting about it this afternoon and arranged this.'

'How the hell did the media know? We haven't even got official confirmation that the body is Kielty's.'

'God knows,' Patterson said. 'Your station leaks like a sieve. Speak to that fat sack Burgess about it, find out if he told anyone.'

Your station.

'Is Hutton there?'

'We'd better hope not,' Patterson said, then turned and walked away from me.

After putting on one of the fluorescent vests being handed out to Gardai by two uniforms, I walked back up towards the gathering crowd. I called Debbie to tell her I'd be a bit late home. I'd missed dinner and the kids' bedtime yet again, she observed, before hanging up.

As I was putting my phone away, our desk sergeant, Bill Burgess, approached me. He was usually good-humoured, if not a little sarcastic, but it was clear that Harry Patterson had said something to him regarding the leak of Lorcan Hutton's name.

'I tried calling you several times today,' he started, clearly believing the best form of defence to be attack.

'I was busy. Harry spoke to you, I take it.'

His expression softened a little and he nodded his head. 'Ignorant bastard,' he murmured. 'He accused me of letting slip about Lorcan Hutton and Kielty to the press.'

'Did you?' I asked. Burgess was reliable but was so used to doing things his own way and in his own time, he could have said something carelessly in earshot of the wrong person.

'I did not,' he said, indignantly. 'I don't know who told them, but it certainly wasn't me.'

'Then forget about it,' I reasoned.

'But Harry said—' he protested.

'Don't worry about it,' I said. 'There's no harm done.'

I was fairly certain it hadn't been Burgess who'd leaked the news. But I had lied when I'd said there was no harm done. It had alerted Lorcan Hutton to the fact that we were looking for him, which would probably mean that he'd go underground for a while.

Satisfied that I was convinced, Burgess wandered off, trying to look busy. I followed suit.

I scanned the crowd in front of me as I walked. There were upwards on one hundred present. Two press photographers skirted the body of people. One of them climbed up onto the pillar of someone's garden wall in order to get a shot encompassing the whole crowd. I climbed up on the wall beside him to get a better view of proceedings myself.

'All right,' he said, nodding, his camera poised in front of him. I suspected he thought I was going to tell him to get off the wall.

'What's the story?' I asked, gesturing towards the front of the throng.

'You tell me,' he shrugged. 'We just got word that this Rising crowd were protesting tonight. Do you think there'll be any trouble?'

'I doubt it,' I shrugged.

'Pity,' he replied, then continued taking his shots.

I thought of something and, checking my jacket pockets, found the pictures Jim Hendry had given me the day previous.

'You couldn't do me a favour,' I said, handing the images to the photographer. 'Would you let me know if you spot any of that crew?'

He glanced down at the pictures, flicking from one to the next, committing the faces to memory. At the third he stopped.

'Jimmy Irvine?'

I nodded.

'Shouldn't be too hard to spot that baldy bastard,' he said, handing me back the pictures I'd given him.

I scanned the gathering myself, looking for familiar faces. To the front of the crowd, a cameraman and interviewer were moving slowly backwards while they interviewed someone at the head of the mass of protesters. The cameraman had a light attached to the top of his camera, which silhouetted the heads of those in the front rows, making it difficult for me to see who the interviewer was speaking to.

The lights went out suddenly, as the crew finished filming, and flickers of white light dazzled my eyes as I adjusted to the darkness again. Someone at the front had produced a bullhorn and was starting a chant of 'What do we want? Dealers out! When do we want it? Now!' The gathered crowd soon took up the mantra, their chants growing in intensity.

Finally, the shouting began to quieten and I realized someone at the front had started to address the crowd. It was difficult to hear exactly what was being said, though I could hear something about 'peaceful protest'. I saw, from my vantage point, a figure break from the protesters and walk up to the door of Lorcan Hutton's house. He stopped at the door and pushed a white envelope through the letter box. The crowd cheered and the man with the bullhorn started another chorus of chanting. The crowd stood like that for a further fifteen minutes before those gathered at the rear, disappointed not to have witnessed a lynching, began to break away and make their way back out of the court.

As they did so, the photographer I'd spoken with earlier nudged me. He pointed to our far left, towards a group of men standing distributing leaflets.

'That's the crowd you were looking for,' he said. 'Irvine's not there though.'

'Thanks,' I said, palming him twenty euros.

I made my way over to where the men stood. Some of those they had given leaflets to passed me, dropping the green flyers on the ground as they went. I stopped and lifted a copy.

Under the heading, 'Taking Back Our Community', the flyer boasted a photograph of a man, tarred and feathered, tied to a lamp post. Around his neck hung a sign, though the reproduction quality was too poor to be able to read clearly what was written on it. Under the picture was a lengthy piece of text about the rising drugs problem and the lack of response to it from the police and politicians. It called for 'a new Rising to reclaim our streets'.

As I approached the group, the older man – Armstrong, Hendry had called him – stepped forward, a leaflet held towards me.

'I've seen more than enough already.'

'We're just saying what needs to be said. Someone has to take a stand against the dealers poisoning our children.'

'Fascinating,' I said. 'I'd like to speak with Mr Irvine.'

'He's not here.'

'Where is he then?' I asked.

'Fuck business is that of yours?' Armstrong asked with sudden aggression.

'Someone murdered Martin Kielty. I've been told that your outfit are likely to blame.'

'Then you've been told wrong. We'd nothing to do with Kielty. We're a legitimate, peaceful community organization.'

'Distributing images of fascist street justice?'

'Still justice though, innit?' Armstrong leaned slightly forward on the balls of his feet as if trying to emphasize his point.

'Tell Jimmy Irvine we'd like to speak to him when he has a chance. He can find me at Lifford Garda station any time he feels like talking.'

'We're holding a rally in Letterkenny on Thursday night,' Armstrong sneered. 'You want to hear Jimmy talk, you can come along to that, same as everyone else.'

The conversation reached an abrupt conclusion with the arrival of Harry Patterson accompanied by a handful of Guards in fluorescent vests. He had clearly been shown the flyers.

'What's this bullshit?' Harry barked as he approached us.

'Here we go, lads,' Armstrong said, smirking to the others. He underestimated Harry Patterson if he believed he could intimidate him.

Harry squared up to Armstrong, their faces inches apart.

'Take this crap and clear off back over the border. If I see this bollocks around here again, I'll lock the lot of you up.'

'On what?'

'A whim,' Patterson said quietly, his forehead almost touching Armstrong's.

Armstrong lingered for a few seconds, as if to show his men that he was unafraid of Patterson, though perhaps he also recognized that Patterson was just the type of Guard who *would* have them held for the night on a whim, for he gathered his flyers, dropped them into a bag that had lain at his feet and began to move away. The others followed, their recalcitrance intended to imply that they weren't obeying Patterson's command.

'Prick,' Patterson said. 'What the hell does he think he's at, handing out this shit here?'

'Jim Hendry told me the Drugs Squad in the North thought this crowd were responsible for attacks on dealers over the border. He suggested we look at their head man, Jimmy Irvine, for Kielty.'

'I'll follow it up and see what I hear,' he said. 'Ask around. If yer man shows his face on this side again, lift him. The same for this character Irvine too.'

He moved back into the crowd again. 'Let's move back, men. Make sure there's no trouble on the way out.'

Over the course of the next twenty minutes, more pockets of people broke away from the crowd and wandered back down from Hutton's house. Some of them looked a little bemused by the whole activity, some others seemed to have been fired up by it and spoke animatedly to those around them. It was as I was removing my Garda overcoat before getting back into my car that one such group passed by. As I slammed the door, I looked out through the windscreen. One member of the group caught my eye as he passed and nodded. A narrow face, brown, untidy hair, darkened glasses; he was past my car and had disappeared into the dissolving crowd before I could catch a second glance. The man's identity played at the edges of my mind all that night, but I was unable to place him.

Monday, 5 February

Chapter Nine

I slept late and it was almost ten thirty by the time I made it to Letterkenny, where Kielty's post-mortem was being completed. In fact, I hadn't even had time to contact the station to let them know that was where I would be.

When the state pathologist, Dr Joseph Long, had finished his examination, I went in to speak to him. In the adjoining room the charred remains of Martin Kielty – for identification of Kielty had been confirmed – now lay on a trolley, shrouded in a stained green scrubs sheet. The assisting technician was washing down the steel table on which the post-mortem had been conducted. The dental records I had left at the hospital matched the corpse and, said Dr Long, with no possibility for visual or fingerprint identification, and a lack of hospital records in Letterkenny, would have to suffice for identification evidence.

'The body was very badly burned,' Dr Long stated, washing

his hands at the sink. 'Cause of death though was a knife wound. There was one stab wound, above the eighth rib on the left-hand side of the sternum. The blade passed through the lung causing fatal haemorrhaging. There was no evidence of respiration of soot or ash, as one would expect from a victim in a fire. Nor is there evidence, in the less badly damaged skin, of vital reaction to the burns. He was dead for some hours before the fire started.'

'No gunshot wounds?' I asked.

Long shook his head. 'None.' Mulronney had been right.

I wondered again where, then, the gunfire had come from. Perhaps the Quigleys had been mistaken.

'What about time of death?'

'Very difficult to say. Liver temperature would be unreliable in a corpse as badly burned as this one. I've taken a sample of the vitreous humour to test potassium levels, but even with that, it'll still be an estimate.'

'The fire was reported after 4 a.m. It certainly wasn't burning at two thirty – we have a witness. Kielty's phone hadn't been used since ten fifteen the evening previous.'

'That sounds like a reasonable time frame,' Long suggested. 'I'll not be able to narrow it down any further than that for you anyway.'

'Anything else?'

'I've taken swabs from the victim's skin. The severity of the burns would suggest that he was coated in an accelerant of some sort. Again, when I know more, I'll send on the information to your superintendent.'

I didn't spend any longer than necessary breathing in the stench of the embalming fluids in the autopsy suite. Excusing myself, I headed out to the car park for a smoke. As I leant against my car, I breathed an inward sigh of relief. Kielty had been dead before the fire started; he had not moved as he lay in the flames; I could not have saved him. I realized too, though, with a sudden shock of sadness, Sam Quigley had given his life in attempting to rescue someone who could not have been saved. Still, whoever had killed Kielty and set the fire in the barn was also responsible for the death of Quigley. And I could do something about that.

Kielty had been selling drugs out of his house in Carrigans. I suspected that he was working with – or for – Lorcan Hutton, of whom there was, as yet, no sign. On Friday evening, Kielty had arrived at his house at 8.30 p.m. The blue car pulled up at 10 p.m. when Nora Quigley looked out. Kielty last used his mobile phone around that time too. By 2.15 a.m., the car had gone and a white Transit van was there instead.

By 4 a.m., the barn was burning, with Kielty's body inside, soaked in accelerant. The thought reminded me that I had to chase up the Forensics report from Patterson.

*

Burgess was holding his usual spot at the front desk, a paper-back novel sitting in front of him, its spine bent backwards, and a sloppily filled mug of coffee adding to the collection of coffee rings on the desk.

'Good afternoon, Inspector,' Burgess said when I came in. 'Nice of you to join us.'

'Always a pleasure to see you, Sergeant,' I said. 'Learning to read, I see.'

Burgess snorted. 'That part-timer, Black, wants to know, should he go back out to that house again? He sat outside it for most of his shift yesterday helping the Forensics.'

I'd forgotten that I'd asked him to go out to assist. 'Where is he?' I asked, eager to find out what, if anything, Forensics had uncovered.

'He's doing a border checkpoint. Superintendent Patterson asked for "increased Gardai visibility". For the benefit of the press, what with this whole thing with The Rising going on.'

Paul Black was standing at the end of Lifford bridge, his squad car parked in the middle of the road, while he waved through car after car. I parked outside the old customs post and watched him for a moment and noticed that the only vehicles he stopped were those being driven by young, attractive women. I supposed he was showing some initiative. I parped the car horn a few times and he reluctantly pulled himself away from the small Tigra he had stopped and ran over to join me.

'You're doing good work there, Paul. So long as all our drug dealers are good-looking young women, the streets of Lifford are safe with you.'

'What?' He looked at me blankly.

'Never mind,' I said. 'How did it go yesterday, Paul?'

'Fine,' he replied, though I notice his leg had started jittering up and down. 'The Forensics team were there for most of the day.'

'What did they find?'

'The murder weapon – a kitchen knife.'

'Where?'

'In the shed, close to where the body was. The blade had been cleaned. The handle was plastic and had melted in the fire.'

'Anything of use from it?'

'It was taken from Kielty's house.'

I nodded. I remembered that one had been missing from the set in the kitchen of the cottage. 'Anything else?'

'A lot of fingerprints. A couple of hundred apparently. They're going to have to run through them to cross reference them or whatever you call it.'

'Any of them useable?'

'I dunno,' he said.

'Any bullet casings? I was called out because of reports of gunfire.'

He shook his head.

'What else *did* they find?' I asked with growing exasperation.

'Someone started the fire deliberately. They found traces of accelerant near the back of the barn, and a few melted plastic bags with traces of dope and stuff. And they found a few melted containers they said might have had petrol in them.'

The presence of an accelerant was in keeping with what Dr Long had said following the post-mortem. The containers exploding would probably also have accounted for the reports of gunfire.

'Though they said there wasn't much,' he added, his jittering becoming more exaggerated.

'Much what?'

'Drugs. They found traces just. Lots of bags, but only traces of coke, like he's had his stash there at one stage. They reckoned the coke was high purity though – really good stuff. If you like that kind of thing.' He squeezed his two hands between his legs as he spoke.

'Are you all right?'

'I need a slash and I'm the only one on the border,' he said.

'Jesus, go into the Customs post and go. It'll not matter if you're off the checkpoint for five minutes.'

'I just thought – the Super sent me out. I thought it was important.'

'I'll keep an eye,' I said, rolling down my window and lighting a smoke. 'Make sure no undesirables slip through.'

THE RISING

It was while I was sitting in the car, enjoying my smoke, that Joe McCready phoned me to say that a body had been found on the beach at Rossnowlagh.

Chapter Ten

A bracing wind, heavy with the scent of salt water, had risen somewhere in the mid-Atlantic. It thudded across the heavy-bodied waves that had washed the corpse of Peter Williams onto the beach. A local doctor, acting in the role of medical examiner, was carrying out a superficial examination of the body before confirming death. I watched the breakers rush the shoreline and waited for Caroline and her estranged husband, Simon, who were making their way back from Dublin.

For once, there were no Scene of Crime Officers or journalists present. There appeared to be no crime involved in the death of Peter Williams, beyond the wasted life of a young man who, perhaps in a drunken stupor, had fallen into the darkness and plunged several hundred feet into the Atlantic Ocean below. The headland from which he had most likely fallen was already shrouded in a pall of rain.

An American couple, attracted to the Atlantic coast on the promise of good surfing, had found the body an hour earlier, as they came back to shore after a day on the boards. They were currently in the Sandcastle Hotel, in the company of the Garda Joe McCready, who had accompanied me to the site.

As the doctor, a locum from Sligo, stood up, I approached him. 'Storm coming,' he said, nodding out towards the darkening sky on the horizon.

'Anything unusual, Doc?' I asked, handing him a cigarette, then taking one for myself.

'Nothing,' he said. 'Apart from a fifteen-year-old fella falling off a cliff. Are you sure the parents want to see him?'

I glanced down at the body. Were it not for the clothes, positive identification would have proven difficult. I recalled my last view of him, nestled in the back seat of his grandparents' car, beside Caroline's father. His hair had been soft and blond, his features, like Caroline's, small and neat, his eyes pale blue, his mouth slightly crooked when he smiled. It was one of the most disturbing things I had ever done to look at him now. He was, naturally, taller than I remembered, but his build was impossible to discern by the bloating the seawater had caused, and his skin had swollen and wrinkled, leaving his face distorted. One of his eyes had been removed from its socket, presumably by a sea animal, and chunks of flesh had been torn from his cheeks and neckline.

'Crabs,' the doctor commented, following the line of my gaze. 'It could have been worse.'

'Could it?' I asked.

'I worked in Derry for a while,' he stated. 'We had jumpers

going off the bridges almost every other week. You get used to it.'

'I hope not,' I said.

The doctor nodded past me. 'You might want to stop them,' he suggested with a flick of his head.

I turned around to see Simon and Caroline Williams emerge from the Garda car that had collected them when news of the body's discovery broke. They slowed as they approached us and could glimpse more clearly their son lying on the sand.

I strode up the beach towards them, my arms outstretched in a futile attempt to block their view. Caroline walked slightly ahead of her husband, her arms gathered around her. Her face was drawn and pale, her eyes red-rimmed. She looked at me without speaking, her expression one of pleading, both for news that her son had been found, and also partly the hope that he had not.

'I'm so sorry, Caroline.'

She fell against me, her fists bunched against the side of her face, her thin shoulders hunched in tight knots. Simon continued walking towards the body, seemingly having not heard what I said.

Still holding Caroline, I reached out and put my hand on his arm. He turned towards me and away from his son's body, his eyes glistening with both anger and sheer terror.

'Might be best not to, Mr Williams. Remember him how he was, eh?'

He looked at my hand where it rested on his arm, and

stared levelly at me until I let go. Then he moved past me and stopped.

His cry seemed to die in his throat, as if the sight before him had taken the wind from him. Despite my best efforts, Caroline broke from me and rushed down to her son, stopping a few yards short of the body, her arms hanging at her sides. Simon stood above the corpse, his hands covering his mouth. Caroline inched forwards towards her son and dropped to her knees. She reached out and touched her son's head, her hands barely making contact with his hair. I gradually became aware of a low keening noise building in strength over the rush of the noise of the waves beating against the beach. Finally Caroline opened her mouth and a single, savage shriek of pain seemed to tear itself from her and hang suspended in the air.

I approached them slowly. The Sligo doctor had muttered his sympathies and was making his way up the beach towards the hotel. I nodded to him as he passed, and said I would be up in a while. Simon now knelt on the sand beside Caroline, gulping for breath against the wind, his face smeared with his tears. I knelt to the other side of her and put my arm around her shoulders. Despite her husband's proximity, she leaned against me and I waited with them, while the thick grey Atlantic rushed up the beach towards us under purpled twists of clouds.

Simon placed his two hands in front of his face, as if in prayer.

'I'm afraid . . . I'm afraid to touch him,' he said.

'It's OK,' I said.

'He's my boy and I can't touch him.'

I could think of nothing to say to the man. I knew that Simon had had little time for Peter as a child, indeed had not seen him in almost a decade. Despite my professional and human urge to console a bereaved parent, I found it difficult to look at Simon without the memory surfacing of the injuries he had inflicted on his wife and his emotional neglect of his son.

'I saw him born,' he said, turning towards me, his expression almost one of pleading. 'I had to see him . . . you know.'

I nodded silently, placing my hand on his shoulder. He turned to face Caroline, shrugging away my hand as he did so.

'This is your fault,' he said.

Beyond us, a breaker rose briefly, then exploded against the shore, flecking the body of Peter Williams with its foam.

Soon after, Peter's body was removed by the undertakers to be transferred to Sligo General Hospital for a post-mortem examination. I had asked for toxicology tests to be run; while the boys with whom Peter had been camping had admitted that some alcohol had been taken, I wanted a more accurate assessment of how much he'd taken before he died.

For our part, we moved up to the hotel, where the manager had provided us with a room and a supply of tea and sandwiches. Simon had spoken little on our way up from the beach.

When we got inside, the heat made the sweat break on my

face, even while my skin remained numbed from the wind. Caroline had stopped crying and busied herself pouring tea. Simon stood to one side, speaking into his mobile phone, telling a partner or family member about the discovery. He had not changed much in the past decade. He was a small, squat figure – five eight maybe – carrying excess weight around his gut. He had thinning, sandy hair brushed over to one side to cover his increasing baldness. His arms were heavy, his fingers' stubbiness accentuated by gold rings. He wore glasses with reactive lenses that even now, under the lights of the hotel conference room, were slightly darkened. He returned my gaze without discernible emotion as he continued his conversation on the phone.

'That was unfair – what he said to you. It's not true,' I said, taking the cup of tea that Caroline offered me.

She looked at me, her eyelids dropping slightly. 'He's upset. He doesn't mean half of what he says.'

I waited for her to say something else, but she simply sipped her tea. She sat upright, her legs crossed at the ankles, her shoulders rounded as if she was physically regressing into herself.

The air in the room had taken on an unusual quality, the light seeming to have stilled and greyed. In the distance we heard the first heavy rumbling of a thunderstorm. The windows stippled with heavy drops of rain, which ran grimy steaks in the fine dusting of sand on the glass.

Simon concluded his conversation by snapping his phone

shut, then came over to where we were sitting. He stood above us.

'Where's my tea?' he asked, staring at Caroline.

'I'll get it for you,' she said, standing up so suddenly she spilt some of her own tea on her hand and trouser leg. 'Shit,' she said, trying to find somewhere to place her cup and saucer.

I stood and reached for a handful of napkins from the table for her, but in order to do so, I had to reach past Simon. He continued to stand in my way, until I had to ask him to let me past.

By the time I had gathered a handful and turned to Caroline, she had already wiped her hands dry on her jumper and was pouring Simon his tea. He must have recognized the annoyance on my face as he returned my stare.

'He's still an asshole,' I told my wife Debbie later. I had accompanied Caroline and Simon back to the B&B where they were both staying, though in separate rooms, before coming on home myself to get something to eat. Peter's body would not be ready to be waked until the following day, when his remains would be taken back to his grandparents' house in Sligo.

'He's lost a child, Ben,' Debbie said. She was washing up the dishes while I finished eating. By the time I'd got home, the rest of the family had already eaten and our children, Penny and Shane, were in bed.

'He didn't give a rat's ass about Peter when he was alive.

Caroline was the one who cared for him. She's grieving too, but she's not throwing her weight about.'

'You can't get involved,' Debbie said, putting down the dishcloth and coming over to the table to sit. 'You know how marriages work. You need to stay out of it.'

'I don't like seeing Caroline being taken advantage of,' I said.

'She's a big girl, Ben. She doesn't need you to look out for her.'

'It's not the way I remember her. Caroline wouldn't take shit from anyone.'

'People are different with their partners. Maybe this is her way of grieving. Maybe it's easier on her not to fight. However she handles her husband, you need to respect it.'

She stood up, then added darkly, 'And try to keep your feelings for her under control.'

Tuesday, 6 February

Chapter Eleven

I made it to the hospital before 10 a.m., driving through a rainstorm so heavy that, even on full speed, my windscreen wipers proved ineffective. The remains of Peter Williams were to be released sometime later that day, to be driven to Caroline's parents' home, from where he would be waked. I had promised Caroline that I would see her at the hospital.

She and Simon were sitting in the cafe on the second floor when I arrived. Peter's remains would be delayed for another hour, they'd been told, with the result that they were forced to remain in the hospital together in what seemed an uneasy truce.

I bought a cup of tea and sat with them. Despite having been in Caroline's company on and off since Saturday, I had not had a chance to speak to her at any real length. Our conversations, prior to Peter's body being washed up on the beach, had revolved around the efforts being made to find him. We had not spoken about Caroline's life since leaving Lifford, as if to engage in such a reflective topic would force her to consider also the more recent events and whether the two might be connected. However, with the discovery of his body, I was aware that in addition to the physical post-mortem being conducted, Caroline would be conducting her own private self-examination, fired no doubt by her ex-husband's accusation the day before that she was, in some way, responsible for her son's death.

'Have you been given any word yet?' I asked when I sat down.

'Nothing,' Caroline said. 'But thanks for coming.'

I waved away the comment. 'How have you been since?'

She glanced sideways at Simon before answering, 'Fine.'

'You've asked for blood tests,' Simon said, his tone heavy with accusation.

'That's right. I've asked for toxicology tests,' I said. 'I want to check whether Peter had taken or been given something in the time prior to his disappearance.'

'Why?'

'It's standard practice, Simon.'

'Don't Simon me,' he snapped. 'You didn't ask our permission.'

'He asked me,' Caroline said, though that was untrue. I had simply assumed that they would be agreeable to such a test being conducted. Besides, there was no legal requirement for me to ask their permission.

'That's right,' I said, smiling lightly to show Caroline I appreciated her support.

'There's no need,' Simon Williams continued. 'He was allowed to go off the rails. She couldn't keep a handle on him, didn't discipline him.'

'I'm familiar with your views on discipline, Mr Williams,' I said.

'What's that meant to mean?' he demanded, leaning forward in his seat, the table edge digging into his gut.

'Stop it,' Caroline snapped. 'Both of you. Stop it.'

Simon Williams glared at me and jerked his thumb in Caroline's direction. 'Ask her what he was doing out camping in the month of February.'

Caroline looked at me, seeming to struggle with how best to answer his accusation and clearly questioning herself why she had allowed her son to spend his last night on earth in a tent at the latter stages of winter.

'Look, I understand how you feel,' I said, 'but blaming someone won't help Peter.'

'You couldn't understand how *I* feel,' Simon Williams snapped. 'He was my son. And he needed his father.'

'His father didn't want him,' Caroline retorted, and I saw for the first time since her arrival a flash of the Caroline Williams I knew.

'Watch your m—' Simon Williams began, emphasizing his point with a single podgy finger, but he got no further for I gripped his wrist in my hand and slammed it against the tabletop.

'Mind how you speak to her,' I warned.

'For God's sake,' Caroline snapped again. 'Stop it, both of you,' she added, pleadingly, before getting up and rushing from the table.

I followed and caught up with her in the corridor.

'I'm sorry he spoke to you in that way,' I said, my hand on her arm.

'I'm not fucking helpless, Ben,' she said. 'I don't need you to stand up for me.'

'I'm sorry,' I said. 'I thought—'

'Stop saying sorry. And stop treating me like an invalid,' she said, her voice rising to the point where it cracked a little on the final word.

I took my hand from her arm and stood foolishly, as she rushed down the corridor and through the double doors at the far end.

I called in to Letterkenny station, to meet Harry Patterson and update him on the state of the Kielty investigation, though my focus had shifted slightly with the discovery of Peter Williams's body. Indeed, that was the first thing about which we spoke.

'Bad news about Williams's wee boy.'

'It was fairly horrific,' I said, shuddering involuntarily at the memory of Peter's damaged face.

'A fucking waste,' Patterson said. 'He was always a bit . . .' He struggled to find the right word. 'Sensitive,' he concluded.

'He had an abusive, neglectful father,' I said levelly.

'We all have our sob stories,' Patterson said, belching lightly into his fist. 'Doesn't mean we all take a one-way flight off a clifftop, does it?'

'It's been assumed that he fell.'

Patterson sniffed dismissively.

My feelings must have been evident in my expression for Patterson, his mug paused inches from his mouth, looked at me with bewilderment.

'I've asked for toxicology reports to be done with the post-mortem,' I said.

He put down the mug on his desk. 'Why?'

'A fifteen-year-old falling off a cliff seems a little out of the ordinary. He'd been camping with friends. Maybe someone slipped him something.'

Patterson guffawed. 'Depends what you mean by slipped him something.'

'He was Caroline's son, Harry. Jesus, have a heart.'

'It's a waste of time and money, Devlin,' he said, suddenly serious. 'What's it going to achieve? So what if you find he took something, or someone slipped him something? What do you do then? He went off a fucking cliff. No one pushed him – he fell himself.'

'I'd like to do something; for Caroline's sake.'

'Did you talk to her? Did they have a row? Was it something she said?'

'I'm not sure facetiousness is appropriate, Harry,' I said, standing up to leave.

'Try finding out why the fuck she let a fifteen-year-old go camping on the beach at the start of February,' he suggested, glancing up at me, then turning his attention to the sheets of paper he had started shuffling on his desk. 'Now what's the story with the actual murder you're meant to be investigating.'

'Not much to report. He was stabbed in the chest and set alight. Forensics found traces of drugs in the barn, but little more than that. There does seem to be some confusion from witness accounts. The neighbour saw a blue car parked outside the house at ten. The milkman saw a white Transit van with Southern plates there at two in the morning. The pathologist can't state time of death with any certainty, but it doesn't really matter. Kielty's phone wasn't answered after 10.15 on the evening of his death. I suspect he died around that time.'

'Why did they hang around until two in the morning then?'

'Maybe they didn't. Maybe it was a different person – a buyer maybe?'

'Or maybe they killed him, headed off for a van and came back to lift his stash. There were only traces of drugs found in his barn. If he was selling, where's his supplies?'

'Robbery gone bad?'

Patterson shrugged. 'Maybe. He got what was coming to him, anyway. People choose to live that lifestyle, they take the risks.'

'He didn't deserve to die, Harry,' I said. 'No one does.'

'Spare me the bleeding heart liberal, Devlin. The man was a scumbag.'

'He may well have been, Harry, but his daughter will grow up without her father. Someone needs to answer for that.'

'She'll be better off without him,' Harry muttered. 'Besides, it was probably one of his own who did it, anyway. What about this connection with Lorcan Hutton? Any sign of him yet?'

'None so far,' I admitted. 'I think that Rising thing the other night might have driven him underground.'

'Which reminds me,' Patterson added, flicking through the various sheets of paper on his desk before selecting one and handing it to me. 'The local radio station want to run an interview with one of the local community associations who've thrown their support behind The Rising and a member of An Garda, about the drugs problem in Lifford.'

'There is no drugs problem in Lifford,' I said.

'That's what I like to hear. I knew you were just the man for the job,' Patterson said, smiling disingenuously. 'I've also told Rory Nicell that you'd be calling. He's one of the Drugs Unit for the region. He'll fill you in before the interview; might be able to pull you out with Kielty too. His details are on the back of that sheet, along with the stuff about the interview.'

'Who's the other speaker?' I asked, scanning the sheet which gave details only of time and location: the local radio station at 1 p.m. the following afternoon.

'How the hell should I know?' he said. 'Tell Williams I passed on my condolences,' he concluded, already turning from me as he gestured towards his door with the pen in his hand.

I called Rory Nicell on the number Patterson had given me,

though it cut straight to an answering machine. I left a brief message, explaining who I was and that Patterson had passed on the details, finishing by asking Nicell to call me when he got a chance.

Chapter Twelve

My parents agreed to watch our two children that evening so that Debbie and I could attend Peter Williams's wake. The rain continued for the duration of our journey down, falling in fine needles that careened off the roadway at angles. Debbie was uncharacteristically quiet, looking out the side window as we drove.

'What's up, Debs?' I asked, patting her lightly on the knee.

She took my hand in hers, though did not, at first, look over at me. 'I'm just thinking about Penny and this disco tomorrow. She's so excited about it.'

'I still think she's too young,' I ventured, half joking.

'She's grown up on us without our noticing,' Debbie replied, looking across the car at me.

'She's still a child,' I said. 'She's not looking to get married.'

'This is the start of it. She wants to go because there's some boy in her class she really likes.'

The comment affected me in ways I could not express.

'So you said. Who is he?' I asked, swallowing hard against the words.

'Some new boy. She's got a real crush on him.'

'We'll soon stop that,' I said. Half joking again.

'It's cute,' Debbie said, smiling. 'Her first crush. At least she can tell me about things like that. I'd hate for her to feel she couldn't tell us, wouldn't you?'

'Mmm,' I agreed, though part of me could do without knowing that my daughter had a crush on someone. And the other part of me thanked God, as I approached Peter Williams's wake, that I still had a daughter who was alive and well enough to have a crush at all.

A group of people were gathered outside the wake house by the time we arrived, just ahead of the hearse carrying Peter's remains. I stood to one side as the coffin was lifted from the back of the hearse and a group of men gathered, a little embarrassed, to share the weight of Peter Williams, as they attempted to manoeuvre the coffin in through the narrow front door of Caroline's parents' home. The undertakers shuffled beside them, umbrellas held aloft, though they did little to shield the coffin from the rain, which rattled on its lid. I was surprised at the size of the coffin. I had, I suppose, been expecting something smaller – it being some years since I'd known Peter Williams.

We gathered in the hallway for a few moments while the family said prayers upstairs around the coffin. When the rosary was finished, Caroline's parents brought the priest downstairs again. He was now sitting on one of the hard wooden seats brought in from the kitchen, a cup of tea and a sandwich balancing on his knee. Caroline's father, John, nodded to us and gestured that we could go upstairs.

The stairway was narrow, and we had to stop and stand against the wall as those mourners coming down from the wake room squeezed past us. At the top of the stairs, a middle-aged man I did not recognize, in white shirt and black trousers, nodded to us solemnly and pointed with an open hand towards the room where the coffin had been placed.

The bedroom was tiny, even with most of the furniture removed. Peter's coffin rested on a stand against the wall behind the door. The lid had been left on the coffin, for Peter's body was marked beyond the capability of even the most seasoned undertaker. A batch of Mass cards rested on the lid, to which pile Debbie added the one we had brought. At the head of the coffin, her hand placed lightly on the brass crucifix at its centre, Caroline Williams sat, flanked by two women who introduced themselves as her cousins. Caroline smiled sadly when she saw Debbie, then her face creased in tears. Debbie rushed to her and they hugged. To my left sat four upright wooden chairs of the style I had seen downstairs. Simon Williams sat alone on the furthermost chair, his back straight, his clasped hands in his lap. I approached him and extended my hand.

'I'm very sorry, Simon,' I said. 'It's just terrible.'

'It is,' he agreed, looking at me but not shaking my hand.

'How are you since?'

'What – since this morning?'

I opened my mouth to speak, but the words faltered in my throat.

'I'm Ben's wife,' I heard Debbie say as she came over to us. 'I'm truly sorry for your loss. Peter was a fine boy. We loved him dearly.'

Simon Williams stood and took my wife's hand and thanked her for coming.

I turned to Caroline, who remained at her son's side, her fingers lightly stroking the wood of his coffin. There was something pathetic about the intimacy of such a gesture on cold, varnished pine.

I hunkered down in front of her, my hand taking her free hand, which rested on her lap.

'How are you?' I asked, aware of the futility of anything I said.

She looked at me a little blankly, as if struggling to place me. She had slept little over the past few days. After the terror of Peter's disappearance, she had experienced the false hope of his text message and finally the knowledge that he was dead. I hoped that, at least having got her son back, she could begin to grieve properly. I only worried about what that grief might do to her.

'Anything you need, Caroline. Just ask,' I said, standing up to go.

She attempted to stand and put her arms around my neck, hugging me close to her.

'It wasn't my fault,' she croaked. 'I didn't do this.'

'No one did this, Caroline,' I said, holding her tight against me. 'It was a horrible accident. No one is to blame.'

'I didn't do this,' she repeated, her voice rising hysterically.

'But, Caroline,' I began, moving out of our hug to face her. 'No one's bl—'

She grabbed my face in her two hands, forcing me to hold her gaze. 'I didn't do this. It's not my fault. It's not my fault. It's not . . .' Her words repeated over and over until they became indecipherable from her sobs. She rested her head against the crook of my neck. Her father, clearly having heard the noise from downstairs, appeared beside us, placing his hands on her arms, attempting to disentangle us.

Caroline looked at me, pleadingly, her eyes drawn in terror as her father surrounded her in his arms. Simon Williams sat straight-backed on his wooden seat, staring at the wall opposite, his expression unreadable.

Downstairs, Caroline's mother, Rose, offered us tea before we started home. I noticed, sitting alone in the corner, a cup in one hand, his Garda cap hanging on his knee, Joe McCready.

'I'll only be a minute,' I said to Debbie who was standing with Rose, offering her condolences.

McCready stood up when I approached him and appeared relieved to have someone to talk to.

'Inspector,' he said.

'Good to see you, Joe,' I said. 'What are you doing here?'

He looked around and blushed.

'I felt . . . it was my . . . not my duty, but . . .'

'I understand,' I said. 'Above and beyond the call of duty though, Joe.'

'I could say the same to you,' he said, smiling.

'Caroline's my friend,' I explained as I took out my cigarettes and offered him one. Smoking in a stranger's house is frowned upon on almost any occasion except a wake. I had noticed when I came in a number of the other mourners smoking. Most of them, granted, were elderly men, smoking yellowed twists of Rizla paper loosely filled. I offered one of my own smokes to McCready, but he shook his head.

'I don't, thank you, sir,' he said.

'Clean living for a Guard,' I commented, lighting my own. 'Married?'

'Nearly, sir,' he smiled.

'Congratulations,' I said. 'When's the big day?'

'December, sir.'

'How does . . .?'

'Ellen,' he prompted.

'How does Ellen feel about you doing this?' I said, gesturing around the room, though I meant being a Guard.

'Oh, you know,' he said. 'The same way your wife does, I imagine.'

I stopped myself from telling him that that wasn't necessarily a good thing.

'We have a slight problem, sir,' McCready said.

For a second I assumed he was still speaking about his forthcoming marriage and I demurred from responding.

'The pathologist's report,' he muttered, glancing around.

'Let's step outside,' I said. Debbie scowled at me when she saw me leave the room, though I gestured to her I would only be a moment.

'What's the problem?' I asked, once we had stepped out into the garden. The rain was falling heavier now, in thick swathes that washed up the street, hammering off the roofs of the cars, splintering off the glistening pavements beneath the street lamps. Already one of the drains across the road had flooded and a stream of overflow water rushed alongside the kerb and bubbled in the drains. We stepped in tight against the front of the house, sheltered from the worst of the rain by the eaves.

'The pathologist has put time of death as Saturday night,' he stated. 'I went to the post-mortem. She said Peter died at some stage between Saturday night and Sunday morning.'

'So he couldn't have sent the text message to Caroline on Sunday night.'

'Exactly. I've been thinking about it. I put pressure on Murphy and Heaney. I asked had he been drinking and told them that when we found him, dead or alive, the truth would come out. Then this message comes. Do you think one of them was trying to throw us off the scent?'

Despite the clichés, McCready was right. Someone wanted to stop our searching in Rossnowlagh.

'Anything else come up?'

He glanced around him, then leaned closer to me. 'She thinks he killed himself on purpose.'

'Why?'

'There are no injuries on his hands. She suggested that there should have been laceration, or bruises where he tried to stop his fall, if it had been an accident. Even drunk, she thought, he'd still have tried to break his fall. She reckoned his injuries were more consistent with someone who had jumped rather than fallen.'

'That's speculative,' I argued.

'Isn't most pathology?' McCready countered.

'Maybe. To be honest, his mum told me that he'd been depressed recently. His GP had prescribed him antidepressants.' I was reluctant to betray Caroline's confidence, but at the same time McCready had obviously invested heavily in the investigation into Peter's death. 'They'd argued before he left home. She said he's been out of sorts quite a bit recently.'

'It's a bit extreme – jumping off a cliff, though.'

I nodded as I stubbed out my cigarette and blew the last stream of smoke upwards against the rain.

'Will I cancel the tox reports? The pathologist said she'd have them done as soon as she could.'

'Leave them for now. But I guess we accept that Peter Williams killed himself and leave it at that.'

'What about the text about Dublin? One of the boys must have sent it.'

I nodded. 'God knows why, though. Maybe they wanted to give Caroline a bit of hope. Who knows what goes on in a youngster's mind?'

'When the tox report comes through, I'll send you on a copy, sir,' McCready said, fitting his cap back on his head.

The journey home took almost an hour longer than it should. The roads were flooded most of the way, especially around the Gap, where streams had washed smaller rocks down the mountainside and onto the hard shoulder. The car steered light, and on bends slid towards the centre of the road, even at low speeds. The rain battered against the windscreen and, when we stopped at traffic lights, thudded off the roof.

A wind was rising, coming in from the west, and the forecasters had issued gale warnings overnight. I'd phoned ahead and told my parents we'd be delayed. As a consequence, they decided to stay with us that night rather than risk driving home in a storm.

By one o'clock we were home. Several thick pockets of wind had buffeted the car sideways along the final stretch of road before Lifford, the elms lining the road thrashing to and fro with the gathering gale.

Wednesday, 7 February

Chapter Thirteen

The night had done little to ease the storm, which continued to blow the following morning. Despite the large black umbrella I carried, the lower halves of my trouser legs were dark with rain by the time I made it into the church, at the back of the small procession which heralded Martin Kielty's final journey.

The priest spoke, during his sermon, about Kielty's love for his child, and the pain of his passing for his mother, Dolores. I could see the woman in question, standing in a pew near the front of the church. Kielty's sister sat beside her, her arm around her shoulder, her head pressed against her mother's, both of them crying openly. By contrast, and strangely separate from these two, in the front pew, sat Elena McEvoy. She wore a black trouser suit and white blouse. Around her neck she had tied a polka-dotted kerchief, twisted to the side. Every so often her hand ran up through her hair and flicked it to one side, and I could see the profile of her face, her eyes clear and dry.

On the seat beside her, her daughter slept in a curved baby carrier, her dummy bobbing among the bundle of blankets.

After Kielty's body had been carried out of the church again, and most people forsook the drive to the cemetery, scattering instead to escape the rain, I saw Elena approach Kielty's mother. They did not kiss or embrace, and I guessed that Kielty's mother had not approved of her son's girlfriend.

McEvoy said something, about which the older woman began to protest, but McEvoy gestured towards the baby who was exposed to the rain, beneath the thin fabric hood of her seat, then she turned and strode over to one of the black funeral cars.

Despite the damp, under the cover of the porchway, I managed to light a cigarette, and watched as the remainder of Kielty's family shuffled through the storm into the other car. A heavyset undertaker approached them when he saw them moving, and held his umbrella above their heads.

At one o'clock I made it to the local radio station, 108 FM. The car park was full, so I had to park in the estate across the road. In running across the road at a break in traffic, my umbrella was blown inside out, the spokes snapping against the wind. I made it to the front door and pressed the buzzer. The security man sitting at the reception desk was speaking with someone on his phone and the concept of multitasking seemed to escape him, for he left me standing in the rain until he had finished his call. Indeed, it was only because the water dripping from my hair was marking the sign-in book on the front desk that he offered me a bunch of paper towels he had sitting on the desk beside him to dry myself.

'Wet one out there,' he said, in case I hadn't noticed. 'What are you here for?'

'I've been asked to speak about drugs. *The Afternoon Show*.'

He leaned back in his seat and pointed to a small room to the left.

'The other man is in there already. Get yourself a cuppa before they take you into the studio, if you've time.'

I thanked him and handed him back the wad of wet towels, then went down the corridor to the room he had indicated. The other man was standing at a tea urn, his back to me, making himself a cup of tea.

'Jesus, what a day,' I said.

'It's to get worse,' the man replied, turning to face me. 'Good to see you again, Inspector.'

In the time it took me to formulate my response, I not only placed the man's face, but also realized that I had seen him a few days earlier, nodding at me as he walked past on his way back from the protest outside Lorcan Hutton's house. 'Vincent Morrison?' I hadn't intended it as a question.

Morrison had been the owner of a haulage firm that was involved in the smuggling of military software to Eastern Europe and of illegal immigrants back to Ireland. Despite his involvement in a variety of criminal enterprises, the only thing we'd managed to get him on was fuel laundering. The last time I had seen him, he was standing outside Derry court-house on the day of his trial. Since then he had shaved off his moustache, which made his face thinner and more youthful-looking.

'What are you . . . are you part of The Rising?' I managed finally.

'Not quite. I'm a spokesman for the Portnee Community Association. We're supporting The Rising in their anti-drugs stance. I've become something of a community activist these past few months, Inspector.'

'You're kidding me,' I said. 'That's quite a career change. Have you moved into drugs now instead of smuggling people?'

He smiled and looked past me. The presenter of the pro-gramme, a young man with a mullet hairstyle whom I had seen presenting on regional TV, was standing in the doorway, staring from one of us to the other, presumably having overheard my final comment. 'Are you two here to speak?' he asked. 'Which one of you is the Guard?'

'That'll be him,' Morrison said, gesturing towards me with his polystyrene cup. 'We'll pretend he didn't make that last statement, eh? Defamation of character and all that.'

We were led into a small, stuffy studio. The presenter took his seat behind the main console, and we were directed to a pair of seats on the other side of the desk, positioned around a single microphone.

In order to be heard clearly, we both had to lean towards

the microphone in a manner that resulted in our sitting so close together our knees touched under the desk.

'This is cosy, isn't it?' Morrison observed.

'I imagine this must have been about the size of your cell. Am I right?' I asked, smiling. I was aware of the rising panic of the presenter, Laurence Forbes, who sensed that his interview might be headed in a different direction from the one he'd intended.

'We'll just wait for the news to end, then we'll start. I'll come to you first, Inspector Devine, if that's OK?'

'Devlin,' I said, a little embarrassed. I cleared my throat. 'My name's Devlin.'

'Devlin,' Forbes repeated, nodding. 'And you're Mr Morrison?'

'Indeed I am,' Vincent Morrison said. 'Mr Morrison.'

I heard the producer's voice over my headphones and Forbes held up his hand to let us know we were about to go on air. Just as he closed his fist and the light above the door turned red, Morrison muttered into his headphones: 'My boy's just dying about your Penny.'

The comment was so incongruous that I convinced myself that I had misheard. Still, it took me a moment to realize that Forbes was speaking to me.

'Inspector?' he repeated.

'Sorry,' I said. 'Could you repeat that?'

He looked at me quizzically. 'I said, good afternoon, Inspector. I was afraid your headphones were playing up.' He pulled a face and rolled his hand in the air, encouraging me to start talking.

'Sorry,' I said. 'They're working fine. I can hear perfectly.'

'Maybe we'll start by discussing the drugs problem on the border then,' he suggested.

I ran through the spiel I had already rehearsed. There was no problem as such. The border region has always had some low-level drugs movement, though nothing too extreme. Dealers around the border tend to be small-time crooks. The difficulty was that the people who could help the police were too often those using the product these people were selling and who wanted to ensure that their supplier remained free to keep supplying.

Forbes turned to Morrison. 'If there's no problem, as Inspector Devine says, why does the border area need an organization such as The Rising?'

'Well, I should point out that I'm not part of The Rising. I represent the community of Portnee. We believe that The Rising is taking a stand against drug dealers that needs to be taken,' Morrison said. 'We are simply a group of residents and parents, looking to voice our concerns about the availability of drugs in our schools and towns. The drugs problem in Ireland has moved out of the cities and into the rural areas, now. Our concern is that this has been, and continues to be, allowed to happen.'

'I don't think it's a case of allowing it—' I started, but Morrison continued unabated.

'I suppose when there is a vacuum, something moves to fill it. For too long now, we feel there has been something of a vacuum in the policing of drugs in this area. We aren't suggesting that groups like The Rising should replace the police. As a community group though, we appreciate the opportunity to express our frustration in a focused, non-violent manner. As Inspector Devine says,' he continued, smirking, 'we all know who these people are. We need them to know that they are no longer welcome in our community.'

Before Forbes could say anything, I interjected. 'If I can come in there; the reservation that An Garda has about such things is that groups like this can drive people underground. Recently a protest was held outside the house of an individual to whom we wished to speak regarding recent activities in the area – though I stress at this point that the individual concerned is being sought only to help us with our inquiries. We have yet to locate that individual, perhaps because he has gone into hiding. We would prefer that such people are in the open where we can monitor them.'

'Monitoring them doesn't deal with the problem,' Morrison countered. 'The Inspector mentions a protest. The man in question was named as a suspect in the murder of a drug dealer. He himself is a drug dealer.'

'Allegedly,' Forbes stressed. 'We have to be careful about what we say on air.'

'I don't want such people living in *my* community,' Morrison said.

'Your community,' I commented. 'I understood you lived in Derry, Mr Morrison.'

'I live in Portnee, outside Lifford, not far from yourself, Inspector,' Morrison said, smiling. 'Sure our children are even in the same class at school. So, it is very much *my* community.'

His comments took me so much by surprise that I had little to say in response. Forbes, clearly sensing this, thanked us both and wrapped up the interview before hitting a button on his console which started a Johnny Cash number.

'Thought it was appropriate,' he commented, looking for us to share his assessment of his own sense of humour. 'Thanks, gents, that was . . . umm, interesting,' he added.

We left the studio without speaking. Only when we reached the front door and paused before launching out into the rain again, did we acknowledge that the other was still present.

'Big disco tonight, isn't that right?' Morrison said. 'The kids'll love it.'

'What the fuck are you at?' I asked. 'That bullshit about community. What's the angle?'

Morrison shrugged, as if unaware of my meaning. 'No angle. I want my kids to grow up somewhere nice. Your crowd are doing fuck all to deal with drugs around the borders. I joined a peaceful community group. I did my time, no complaints. I believe in fresh starts, so I'm prepared to let it slide.'

'I don't believe a word of it.'

'That's up to you. Sorry about the "Devine" thing – I couldn't help it.' Then he winked and stepped out into the rain, his hands in his pockets, as if impervious to the elements that raged around him.

Chapter Fourteen

By the time I had finished up some paperwork back at the station in Lifford and made my way slowly through the flood-water that was threatening to make our road impassable, it was already past dinner time. Penny was in our room, trying on clothes while Debbie offered advice and Shane squatted on the rug, playing with his dinosaurs.

When I came up the stairs Penny ran out to meet me, her eyes almost disappearing in the breadth of her smile.

'What do you think?' Debbie prompted, nodding towards Penny. I realized she was dressed in her best clothes for the disco. She wore jeans and a top her granny had brought her from their holidays. I noticed that her cheeks were slightly rouged, her neckline broken with a thin silver cross on a necklace we had bought her for her confirmation. She looked prettier and older than I had ever seen her before and both of those realizations made my heart constrict in my chest.

'You look lovely, sweetie,' I said. 'You'd best get changed though – you can't go to the disco; it's raining too heavily.'

'What?' Debbie asked, before Penny could even formulate the same response.

'It's too rough out. Maybe next time,' I said. 'Let's watch a movie together instead.'

Penny looked from me to Debbie. Redness was already flushing her neckline and cheeks.

'It's not that bad out,' Debbie said. 'If you could get in and out to work, we can get her to the disco. She's been looking forward to it all week.'

'She's not going,' I said, a little more forcefully than I had intended, for I noticed Debbie's jaw set, an expression that was mirrored on our daughter's face.

'That's not fair,' Penny stamped. 'Everyone is going. You said I could go.'

'It's too wet, sweetie,' I said.

'It's not,' she snapped. 'And don't call me sweetie. I'm not your sweetie.'

'Penny,' I warned, my voice rising.

'Maybe we should talk about this, Daddy,' Debbie said.

'Mummy,' Penny said, pleadingly.

'Mummy and Daddy will talk about it,' Debbie said, though with not enough conviction to prevent Penny from dropping onto the top step and beginning to sob into her hands.

I placed my hand on her shoulder, noticed the tiny finger-nails of her hand painted pink. 'Honey, honestly, it's too—'

She shrugged away my hand and spat 'I hate you' before getting up and running into her room, slamming the door behind her.

Shane, sat in the middle of our floor, held aloft a model tyrannosaurus. 'What's wrong with Penny?' he asked in a gruff voice, moving the toy with his hand as if it were speaking.

'What the hell are you doing?' Debbie hissed to me. 'It's her first disco. She was dying for you to come home and see her.'

'I met Vincent Morrison today,' I said.

'What of it?' Debbie asked quizzically.

'His son is in Penny's class. He'll be at the disco tonight.'

'What of it?' Debbie repeated. 'You can bring suspects and witnesses to our house when it suits you, but Penny can't go out to a disco in case someone's eleven-year-old son is there. Catch yourself on. She's going.'

'I said she's not,' I said.

'And I said she is. And she'll love it. And you'll tell her how pretty she looks and sound like you mean it.'

'I know she looks pretty. That's not the point. What if Morrison is trying to . . .'

'Trying to what?'

'I don't know. I just don't trust him.'

'So I heard. You need to start listening to yourself, Ben. Do you know how you sounded on the radio? Petty. And you're being petty now. She's going to that disco, and that's final.'

'I said she's not going,' I started, though my mobile began

to ring, cutting me short. I glanced at the phone. Letterkenny. As I flipped the phone open, one finger held out in a request for a moment's quiet, I heard Debbie mutter, 'Fucking typical. Off you go, back to work.'

Shane's mouth opened into a wide O. 'Mummy said a bad word,' he said.

Distracted, I had to ask twice for the desk sergeant in Letterkenny to repeat himself. Finally I managed to piece together his message. An old-style blue Volkswagen Beetle with an orange door had been discovered, abandoned near Barnesmore Gap.

I said my own share of bad words as I negotiated one pool of water after another on my way first to Ballybofey, then on through to the Gap. Streams had gouged red mud scars out of the mountainsides flanking the road, the water thick with dirt washing onto the road ahead of me. The car slid on one particularly bad corner and my headlights raked across withered bunches of flowers that had been taped to the crash barriers, marking the site of an earlier fatality on this stretch. The rain thudded off the windscreen, the wipers serving little purpose beyond distracting my attention from the road. Finally I spotted the blue winking light of a Garda car and pulled over.

The Beetle had been left in the picnic area of a small forest just off the main road, parked far enough back that only someone driving into the picnic area would see it, which was unlikely to happen too often here in mid-February. In fact, I idly wondered why the Guard who had found it had come in here at all.

Whoever had abandoned the car had wanted to destroy it for the doors all lay open, the interior was burnt, the dash console blackened twists of moulded plastic. The rain though had been so heavy that, despite some tarnishing of the metal of the roof, the bodywork was remarkably clean, which meant that there might be the possibility of prints, though no dusting could be completed on the outside of the vehicle in this weather. There was no doubting that it fitted the description given to me by Nora Quigley of the vehicle she had seen outside Kielty's house on the night of his death.

The rain had also, however, prevented the lower half of the bodywork being too badly damaged and the car's registration plate – and Northern number – was clear. I climbed back into my own car and radioed through to Letterkenny to request a Forensics team. Then I called Jim Hendry.

'It's my night off,' he said upon answering.

'How the fuck do you think I feel? I'm sitting in a hurricane in Barnesmore Gap looking at a burnt-out car – a car from your side of the border.'

'What? Misery loves company, so you thought you'd phone me?'

'I need a registration number run, Jim.'

'Can it not wait till tomorrow?'

'I think it's connected with the murder of Martin Kielty.'

'The dealer?'

'The very one.'

He paused for a second, and I could hear him slurping from a drink. 'Leave it with me,' he said finally.

I gave him all the details, then added, 'Thanks. Sorry to spoil your night off.'

'Fuck it; I'm sitting having a pint in front of the telly. What else have I to be doing?'

I laughed and hung up, then looked out at the storm that was whipping the fir trees on the incline above me. I wondered what I was doing here. Patterson's invitation to run the station had been a poisoned chalice from the start. I needed some support, another full-time detective working the border with me. I had hoped when I'd heard from Caroline Williams that her entry back into my life might extend to her coming back into the Guards, too, but I realized that I had been deluding myself.

I ran across to the other car where an elderly uniform from Ballybofey was sitting smoking his pipe, listening to classical music.

'No one's going to steal this thing tonight,' I said. 'Why don't we head on, get a team out tomorrow?'

The man shifted his pipe to the corner of his mouth, released a billow of pungent smoke upwards and nodded.

'Sounds good to me,' he muttered around the stem of his pipe.

*

I was almost back in Lifford when Hendry called me back with a name and address.

'I've tracked your car,' he said. 'No need for thanks, that's why I'm here.'

'Thanks, Jim,' I said.

'Ian Hamill, living in 38 Tulacorr Heights.'

'Do you know him?' I asked.

'Bit of a scumbag, just,' Hendry said. 'Petty thief, junkie, that kind of stuff. I wouldn't pin him for a killer, but when these guys are off their heads, fuck knows what they're capable of.'

'His car was seen outside Kielty's the night he died,' I explained. 'If he didn't kill Kielty, he must at least know who did.'

'Well, that's his info. I'll follow it up for you tomorrow if you like.'

I hesitated, a little disappointed that he hadn't offered to follow it up immediately, though I was aware that it was his night off.

'That would be great, Jim,' I said. 'Thanks.'

'Go home, Devlin,' he said.

I grunted my agreement and hung up. By this stage I had reached the centre of Lifford. I sat at the roundabout at the bridge. A left turn would take me home; right would take me over the bridge into Strabane and Mr Hamill. It wasn't a hard decision.

Chapter Fifteen

Tulacorr Heights is an estate along the Derry Road on the outskirts of Strabane. The odd sequencing of the numbers of the houses threw me a bit and it took me longer than I expected to find the house in question, which was up along a cul-de-sac near the old Mass Rock.

The house appeared abandoned even from the road. It sat on a slight rise, the driveway sloping up towards the front door. The grass was thick and long, and the flower bed had been overtaken by weeds. I took my torch from the glove compartment and ran up to the front door. I knocked a few times and leant against the door until I caught my breath. Then I knocked again and called in through the letter box. It was fairly clear that Hamill was not home. To the rear of the property I could hear a low thudding sound in the wind.

I crossed to the large window in the front of the house and looked in. Though the blinds were partially closed, I could see through the slats that the house was furnished. The screen of a television reflected the light of my torch, the red standby light beneath it glowing angrily in the darkness.

The side gate screeched against rusted hinges and scraped along the concrete path, forcing me to push against it with my shoulder to overcome the resistance.

The backyard of the house was as overgrown as the front, a rusting barbecue collecting rain, lumps of charcoal floating in the bowl. A plastic patio table had blown over against the garden shed which lay open, the door thudding against the wooden side in the wind.

I checked the back-door handle, in vain. Then I scanned the back windows with my torch. The smallest section of the kitchen window was ajar. Laying the torch on the windowsill, I hoisted myself up onto the dustbin to see if I could reach down and open the main window. I was able to reach halfway down, my fingers brushing the edge of the handle but not making sufficient purchase to allow me to open it completely.

Whether it was because I was too absorbed in what I was doing, or because of the noise of the shed door thudding and the wind whistling along the backs of the houses, I did not hear the figure to my left approaching. In fact, I only realized someone was there when a torch beam shone in my face, dazzling me. I was sure, however, that the squat black object he held in his other hand was a gun.

Instinctively I reached out to get a grip on my own torch, in the hope of using it as a baton. Then a voice I recognized said 'This is a stick up' before the speaker broke into a cackle that dissolved into a smoker's cough.

'Jesus, Jim, you nearly gave me a fucking heart attack. What the hell are you doing?'

Hendry laughed. 'I fucking *knew* you'd be over. You can't help yourself, can you?'

'I thought you were having a pint in front of the telly,' I said.

'I knew you'd be looking for someone to cover your back. Besides, there's fuck all on anyway,' he complained. 'Now, after you break in here, what's your plan?'

I glanced at the window, trying to come up with some excuse for the position he had caught me in but I had none.

'I don't really have a plan,' I said. 'Even the breaking-in part wasn't working so well.'

'That's because you didn't come prepared,' he said, rummaging in his coat pocket and removing a ring of keys. 'One of these should do it,' he said, gesturing towards the lock. 'A gift from a grateful locksmith,' he added, smearing the rainwater from his face with the palm of his hand.

Sure enough, the sixth key I tried unlocked the back door. I entered the house, calling out Hamill's name. Hendry followed me into the kitchen, searching along the wall with the palm of his hand until he found the light switch.

The kitchen was a mess. Dirty dishes lay in the sink. The counter was coated with breadcrumbs and a tub of margarine sat with its lid on the counter beside it and a smeared knife sitting atop the tub. A bowl containing overripe fruit sat to one side of it. Small fruit flies crawled over the blackened bananas. To the other side, a kettle was plugged in and the wall switch turned on.

Hendry went over and opened the fridge. A carton of milk was curdling on the shelf: beyond that sat a half-eaten loaf of bread, the grey furze of mould on its crust clear through the wrapping. A few beer cans were on the bottom shelf with a bowl of something that looked like solidified chilli.

'Untidy bugger,' Hendry commented.

We moved into the rest of the house. The hallway was clear, save for a pile of assorted letters which lay discarded beneath the letter box.

As I had seen from outside, the television in the living room was on standby. The remote control sat on a small coffee table in the middle of the floor, beside which was a half-drunk mug of something on which a scum of mould had grown. A newspaper lay on the floor beside the chair nearest the table. On the chair arm, a filter from a cigarette had been broken off. A few small circles of card suggested Hamill had been making roaches.

'Spliffing up before he goes to kill Kielty?' Hendry gestured towards the chair arm.

'It doesn't look right, does it?'

'It looks like he thought he was coming back, if that's what you mean,' Hendry said.

'So, if he did kill Kielty, it probably wasn't premeditated. If he had been planning it, you'd imagine he'd clean up a bit. Especially if he knew he was going to go on the run.'

'Maybe they had a row.'

'And he happens to have petrol with him just in case? Unless he killed Kielty then went off and got the petrol then went back again.'

'Though you'd think he'd come back here and get some stuff.'

'Maybe he panicked,' I reasoned.

'Maybe,' Hendry shrugged.

The rooms above were in a similar state. There were two bedrooms and a lumber room. One of the rooms – a spare room, we guessed – sat tidy, the bed made. In the other, Hamill's bed linen spilled onto the floor, his nightclothes rolled in a ball in the corner. A pint glass of water stood on the locker beside his bed.

Hendry flicked through the drawers of his dresser, then lifted out a black pouch about the size of his hand. He unzipped it and peered inside.

'Aha,' he said. 'Mr Hamill's stash.'

He threw the pouch over to me. Inside was a syringe and a scorched spoon. A small folded white piece of paper bulged slightly in the middle.

'Would a junkie abandon his stash?' Hendry asked.

'If he'd just stolen Kielty's stuff, then I suppose so.'

But Hendry shook his head. 'Not a fucking chance. Those guys wouldn't pass on a hit, no matter how much they had.'

We had locked up the house as well as we could and Hendry phoned the station, requesting that they put out an alert for Ian Hamill on suspicion of murder. I was climbing into my own car when I saw him running over, gesturing to me to wind down the window.

He ducked his head down level with the window. 'Do you fancy a pint?' he suggested, squinting through the rain.

'I know just the place,' I said. 'I want to check McEvoy's story about Kielty being threatened in Doherty's pub.'

Hendry winced. 'I'm not sure I could step foot in that place. Five years ago they'd have fucking skinned a copper alive in there.'

'New times, Jim: haven't you heard? Besides, we're only going for the one.'

I drove ahead of him to Doherty's pub on the outskirts of Strabane. The pub itself was a single room lounge with an oval bar in the centre. The furniture was mismatched, the faux suede upholstery on the booths matted and stained with cigarette smoke, despite the smoking ban. Old-style yellowed wall lamps provided the only illumination. Despite this, the arrival of a

PSNI man into the bar did not go unnoticed by the other drinkers, even though Hendry was in civvies.

In all the time I had known Jim Hendry, we had never really socialized beyond grabbing cups of tea after an interview. I sensed that he wanted company on a Friday night and, for my part, I was coward enough to want to avoid Penny. In fact, Morrison was the topic of conversation when Hendry sat down with two pints for us.

'Vincent Morrison has reappeared,' I said, supping from my pint, while Hendry swallowed mouthfuls of his.

'Remind me,' he said, wiping the froth from his moustache with his thumb and forefinger.

'People smuggler. That Chechen thing a while back.'

He nodded in recognition. 'So what's he up to?'

'I'm not sure. He's part of a community group supporting this anti-drugs crowd, The Rising. He's living on my side of the border now.'

'And you don't think he's on the level?' Hendry asked, one eyebrow raised in mock seriousness. 'You're so suspicious.'

'I don't trust him. There must be an angle. Have you heard anything over here?'

Hendry shook his head, drained his pint, thumped his chest and belched.

'Excuse me,' he said, placing the back of his hand against his mouth. 'Nothing. I'll keep an ear out, see if the Drugs Squad up here have anything on him.'

'I appreciate it. The fucker's sent his son to my daughter's school.'

'Did he actually send him to her school, or have they just ended up in the same school?' Hendry asked.

'I don't know.'

'How many schools are there in your area?'

'I'll get your pint,' I said, standing up.

He started to laugh. 'How many?'

'One,' I said. 'OK, point taken.'

'I'll have a Smithwick's,' he said, winking at the barman who was already pulling the pint.

I bought myself a Coke. While the barman was pouring the pint I placed the photograph of Martin Kielty on the bar.

'How's it going?' I said, my money in my hand as the barman approached me. He glanced over my shoulder at where Jim Hendry sat then turned and walked down to the far end of the bar without another word. I watched him walk away until I realized I recognized the man sitting at that end.

Patsy McCann perched on the furthest barstool from me, presumably having just finished his shift, for he was dressed in the livery of the bar. The last time I had seen him, he had packed in his work and was panning for gold on the Carrowcreel river, following a mini goldrush in the area.

I walked down to him, only to see the barman mutter something and move away again at my approach.

'Ben,' Patsy said, twisting on his stool and extending his hand to shake. 'Bit off your patch over here.'

'I get around,' I said.

'Your pal's even further off his patch,' he said. 'He's making some of the other customers nervous.'

I glanced around the lounge and realized that the conversations had muted somewhat since our arrival and several drinkers were looking over at Hendry, some with open hostility. If Hendry saw them, he gave no sign of it.

'I'm looking for some information,' I said.

Patsy called the barman over. 'Give these two whatever they're having,' he said. 'They'll not be staying.' Then to me: 'I need to buy some ciggies, Ben.' He nodded very slightly with his head to suggest that I should follow him.

I waited until our drinks were poured, took them back to our table, and then excused myself for a moment. Hendry waved me away as he swallowed the first third of his fresh pint.

Patsy McCann was standing by the cigarette machine when I went out. He had aged in the year since I had seen him, his dark curly hair thinning now, the white of his scalp noticeable through the curls.

'You need to get him out of here before someone arrives,' Patsy said.

'Do you know this man?' I countered, handing him the image of Kielty.

He glanced at the picture then gestured with his chin that I should put it away.

'He used to drink here sometimes.'

'Used to?'

'He's dead, ain't he?'

'How did you know?'

'It's all over the news for fuck's sake.'

'His missus tells us he was threatened in here one night a month or two back. You wouldn't know anything about that?'

'Is this for you or him?' he asked, pointing in towards Hendry.

'Me. He's off duty,' I said. 'He's only here for the drink.'

'He's a brave man coming here.'

'So he told me.'

Patsy glanced at the picture again. 'Martin Kielty. He was in here about six weeks ago, dealing from the bogs.'

'Is that allowed here?'

'Jesus, look around you, Ben. What do you think?'

'So what happened?'

'Three boyos came in. Gave him a kicking in the cubicle. Told him he'd be killed if he came in here again.'

'Who were they?'

'Jesus, Ben: I'll be shot myself.'

I took fifty euros from my pocket and placed it on top of the cigarette machine. 'For your ciggies.'

Patsy licked his lips quickly as he lifted the money, folding the note over on itself several times, as if in making it smaller, he was somehow diminishing the significance of what he was about to say.

'Jimmy Irvine and his crew. They beat fuck out of him.'

'Would you come into the station and make a statement about that?'

'Would I fuck!'

'His crew? Armstrong and Cunningham?'

Patsy nodded, peeling the cellophane off his cigarette packet.

'Thanks, Patsy,' I said, turning away.

'I– I thought it was lousy,' Patsy said. 'Not on Kielty, like – he deserved it, selling his shit. But there were plenty of others selling too, but they only went for him.'

'What do you mean?'

'You think people in there are pissed about your cop friend being here for *political* reasons? Half of them are dealers looking to do some trade. New times, Ben.'

'I was just telling him that,' I said. 'Irvine didn't touch any of the other dealers?'

Patsy shook his head. 'I'm going out for a smoke,' he said. 'Have a safe journey home.'

I told Hendry what McCann had said when I went back to my seat. 'They want us out of here,' I said, drinking down half my glass of Coke and lifting my coat.

'Did I hear that wee girl Williams's kid died?' Hendry asked, having seemingly not heard me.

I nodded. 'Fell off a cliff out camping.'

'Christ, that's rough. Anything sinister?'

Typical cop, I thought. Focusing on the death, not the victim.

'Nothing. Pathologist suggested he might have jumped. She couldn't find any evidence that he tried to stop his fall.'

'How's Williams? I'm sure she must be in pieces.'

'Not good. Her husband's back on the scene too – he's a first-class prick.'

'Jealousy, Inspector?' Hendry laughed.

'Statement of fact. He treated her like shit.'

'I always thought you two would – you know . . .'

I shook my head. 'I'm a happily married man, Jim,' I said.

'She's a lovely girl. Nice looking. I think she had a wee thing for you too, if I remember rightly.'

'I'm a happily married man,' I repeated.

'Which is why you're sitting in the pub with me, pretending to drink, instead of going home to your wife,' he replied. 'You'll be getting me a bad reputation with the boys, sitting drinking Coke.'

'I'm driving,' I protested.

'Jesus, so am I,' he said, incredulously.

It was after eleven by the time I started back home. The rain continued to beat down against the car, the wind catching me sideways on the roundabout. I wondered how Caroline was holding up. In truth, I had missed her as my partner. I missed her friendship, the craic and support she gave. She was solid, in the same way that Debbie was solid.

I also missed having someone to talk to about the cases I

was working on. A fresh pair of eyes might see something I was missing. The evidence suggested that either Irvine or Hamill had been responsible for the killing of Kielty. But I still had to find Hamill. I also wanted to find Lorcan Hutton to see what his connection was. And I couldn't shake my suspicion that, in some way, Vinnie Morrison was involved in this, even though it was possible that he had gone straight, as he claimed. Whatever the case, I knew where Jimmy Irvine was going to be the following night and had enough to at least question him about the killing of Martin Kielty.

I was passing the filling station when my radio crackled into life. It was the desk sergeant in Letterkenny. He needed someone in Lifford. One of my own neighbours, who lived a few miles up the road, had phoned the station to say that a body had just washed into her back garden.

Thursday, 8 February

Chapter Sixteen

Margaret Hunter was still in a state of shock when I reached her home. The house backed against a steep, grass-covered incline down which floodwater could be heard rushing. She stood now in her kitchen, wearing her late husband's wellington boots, which she had retained despite the fact that he had been dead almost six years. I noticed that she had placed rolled-up towels at the foot of her back door, in an attempt to stymie the floodwater. A discarded mop seeped onto the tiled floor beside the door.

'I opened the door to mop out the water,' she explained, handing me a torch. 'I could see it from the back door; it was lying against the fence. Just lying there.'

'You might have been mistaken in this weather, Margaret,' I suggested. 'I'm sure it's nothing. Clothes blown off someone's line, perhaps?'

She regarded me warily, as if insulted that I was suggesting she might have made a mistake.

'It's a body, Benedict,' she stated.

She was right.

A wooden fence marked the rear boundary of her property. The body had come to rest against one of the fence posts, its tattered burial shroud lifted by the floodwater rushing past it. The deceased, however, looked to have been dead for many years. The skinless skull grimaced at me through a frame of tangled yellowed hair, the bones of the arm missing, save for the ulna which seemed caught in the sleeve of the gown. The grass on the incline above the body was flattened down showing the path the body had travelled along, and I guessed it had been washed down from the top of the slope behind Hunter's house.

I shone the beam of the torch up the incline the water was running down. Further up the gradient, I believed I could discern the shape of a second corpse, though the beam of the torch was not powerful enough to allow me to see it clearly.

'I told you it was a body,' Margaret Hunter said, leaning out from her back door. 'Didn't I say that?'

'You did indeed, Margaret,' I agreed. I pointed up the incline with the torch beam. 'What is that up at the top there?'

'That's the old Abbey,' the old woman said, pronouncing the words slowly and clearly, tutting as she did so, that I should have asked such a question.

*

About a mile from our home, a laneway runs down from the road towards the river. At a fork in the path, a turning leads to the east through a field of cattle, along a tributary of the Finn. The western path at the fork, however, leads to the ruins of an ancient abbey that once housed the sanctuary of St Lugadius. All that remains of the old building is a single, crumbling wall. The area is rumoured to be one of the resting places of the treasures of the Knights Templar which, according to local rumour, was hidden at the spot where three rivers meet.

On either side of the Abbey lie two graveyards. The one nearest the gate is the more recent, most of its graves now cemented over, their inhabitants secure beneath the earth. The older graves, though, dating from the eighteenth century, are situated on the far side of the Abbey wall, in rocky ground at the top of a gradient that leads to Margaret Hunter's back door. At the time of their creation, the ground must have been prohibitively rocky, for the graves here, owned by Lifford's wealthiest families during the 1700s, are actually sarcophagi sitting above ground.

The graves had been sealed with heavy sandstone blocks, which over time have cracked and eroded, through environmental damage and the weight of young boys jumping from one tomb to the next. The stonework was already weakened by the time the storm hit.

Over the next few hours it became clear that the continual rain had flooded the ruins of the Abbey. The older graveyard, situated in the bowl of the grounds, filled with the rainwater and held it there, the solid rock of the ground beneath preventing the water from seeping away. The pressure eventually burst through the walls of one of the sarcophagi, washing the remains of the inhabitants out into the open. The flow of the wash drifted the bodies towards the lip of the bowl and then down the slope of the hillside, until they came to rest around the lands of Margaret Hunter.

It took me a few moments to walk the incline up to the Abbey. The muddy ground was sodden and slippery. I also had to keep to the outer edge of the incline to try to avoid treading on parts of any other bodies which might have come down from above.

When I reached the top, the low stone wall around the graveyard was on the point of collapse. A great pool of water had gathered behind it. Even in the torchlight, I could make out three more bodies, floating just below me. One was little more than bones held together by rags, the yellowed death shroud billowing out below it. I could see a copper-coloured skull grinning up at me from beneath a foot of water.

I waded across to the side of the broken sarcophagus, shining my torch in through the demolished wall. Beyond it, waist-high nettles fanned out in front of me and I could see the path the bodies had taken, the flattening of the nettle bed where the floodwater had washed. In the torchlight, I could make out the white patches of clothes amongst the nettle patch, where other bodies had come to rest.

I noticed, to my left, a second tomb which seemed to be

crumbling under the strengthening rain which pattered off the leaves of the undergrowth. The idea of standing in an old grave-yard in the dark while corpses floated around me caused me to shiver involuntarily, and the urgent whisper of running water caused me to bless myself and rub the goose pimples from my arm. Clearing up could wait until morning, when the weather might have improved and I'd be able to rouse assistance. Though I had little doubt that, by morning, more bodies would have been washed from their rest.

The storm raged through the early hours, the wind at times a thudding against the dormer windows of our bedroom, at others a harsh cry whistling along the valley. The rain seemed to fall in fits and starts, at once battering the glass of the sky-lights in our hall, then easing, as if gathering itself for a further assault.

If Debbie heard me coming to bed, she did not show it; instead she lay in silence, with her back turned towards me. Both Penny and Shane woke during the night, calling from their rooms for me to come in and get them. By 6 a.m. both were curled up in our bed, snuggled between myself and Debbie. I lay awake for a while, watching their sleeping forms. I reg-retted what had happened between Penny and myself the night before. I didn't want her being too friendly with Morrison's son. But I was also aware that I couldn't dictate to her who her friends should be. Perhaps I had been unfair in not letting her go to the disco. In truth, I resented the fact that, before long, I would not be the only male with a claim to her heart. And it frightened me that, soon, she would know enough about men and their secret prides and vanities to judge me and find me wanting.

Finally I got up and went downstairs for breakfast. Frank, our one-eared basset hound, lay curled up in his bed. When he saw me, he attempted to get up, though his joints seemed to fail him, for he raised himself on his two front paws, then lowered himself back into his bed, whining softly. Within a minute he was sleeping again, the loose skin of his lips flapping slightly in the path of his warm breath. We had bought Frank when we believed we would not be able to have children. Then Debbie got pregnant with Penny. The two of them had grown up together. With a pang, I realized that, for Frank at least, who was now almost twelve, their journey together was nearing its end. I rubbed the velvet fur on the dome of his head, though noticed that it was tougher than I remembered, his coat aged now.

Standing at our back door, smoking my first cigarette of the day as the wind blew stray drops of rain against my face, I could not easily dismiss the sadness that had settled around my heart.

I arrived back at Margaret Hunter's house after eight that morning. I contacted the local councillor and he had arranged for a number of council workers to help with the recovery of the corpses. I had also phoned our local priest, Father Brennan, who arrived in the waterproofs he usually wore when he went fishing.

I'd asked for help from Letterkenny, but there had been a number of accidents during the night, and there would be no free officers until lunchtime. I did manage to rouse Paul Black, though he had a shift in the hotel where he also worked part-time, starting at eleven. Finally, a local undertakers had offered assistance. With a crew from the local hospital, they were standing, sheltering against Margaret Hunter's gable wall while the rain finally began to lessen in intensity until eventually it was no more than a haze. Still, it was enough to seep through the protective layers of clothes we were wearing, and gather in a mist around the base of the hillock we were standing on.

The body against the fence had already been bagged, following a blessing from Father Brennan. The second form, which I had seen further up the hill, was indeed another corpse, or parts of one at least.

We worked mostly in silence for a further hour or so. One team worked its way up from the bottom of the incline whilst another worked down from the Abbey. Each corpse had to be bagged and blessed. Any belongings or pieces of clothing had to be recovered and, where possible, matched to a corpse. In total we bagged eight sets of remains. I was about to call everyone to head down for a tea break and a chance to warm up a little in Margaret Hunter's house when I noticed one of the council workers stumbling down the embankment.

He had worked his way further up the hill than the rest of his team and he had been cutting back the nettles I had seen from above the previous night. He swore loudly now as he stumbled backwards down towards us. He managed to stop himself, then turned to one side and vomited noisily onto the ground.

I went up to see if he was OK, and to suggest he stop for a while. He was on all fours by the time I got to him. I put my hand on the arch of his back as he continued to retch on the ground.

'Take five or ten minutes,' I said. 'Have a smoke or something.'

He looked over his shoulder at me, his face ashen, his wet hair hanging in his eyes.

'There's a fresh one up there,' he managed. 'In the nettles. A fresh body.'

I stumbled up the incline myself, struggling to find my footing. The body lay about halfway up the gradient, making access to it from either top or bottom equally awkward. I could see why the council man had recognized it as more recently deceased, though 'fresh' was not quite accurate; 'fresher' would have been nearer the mark. Its skin was fairly intact, though it was marbled, the veins unusually visible. The victim's hair, long blond curls, was tied back from his face, which was pressed into the mud. Though the floodwater had washed away the blood the ragged bullet hole near his left temple was clear. His hands were tied behind his back, his wrists bound with something resembling piano wire. The body was still dressed, in jeans and a T-shirt. Having known the man when he was alive, I said a quiet Act of Contrition for his soul, though I suspected his reckoning had occurred weeks past. Then, getting a decent footing against the flow of water still washing around us, I took out my mobile and phoned through to Patterson.

'We can call off the search,' I said. 'I've found Lorcan Hutton.'

Chapter Seventeen

Patterson arrived about forty minutes later, lumbering up the incline in his Garda overcoat and a pair of wellingtons. A second man accompanied him, thin and slight of build, brown hair cut tight against his scalp. I put him in his early thirties and, though he was wearing civilian clothes, I pegged him as a Guard straight away.

I slid down to meet them, using my arms to keep my balance.

'Devlin – this is Rory Nicell from the Drugs Unit. Rory, this is Inspector Devlin.'

'How're you?' Nicell said as we shook hands. 'I got your call. I've been meaning to get back to you, but things are a little hectic at the moment.'

'No hassle,' I said.

We stood a little awkwardly on the incline. The hood of my waterproof kept flapping in front of my face as the rainwater dripped into my eyes from my hair.

'So you found Lorcan then,' Nicell said, gesturing towards the body.

'Eventually.'

'We thought this Rising crowd had driven him underground, to be honest,' Nicell commented, stepping up towards the body.

'He was underground all right,' Patterson said with a smirk.

'Almost. His body was put in one of the sarcophagi in the Abbey grounds. The rain flooded the place, burst the walls and washed the bodies down. If he'd been properly underground we'd never have found him.'

'Foul deeds will rise, isn't that the line?' Nicell said.

'So what brings you out to the arse end of Donegal?' I asked.

'Your Super asked us to put in an appearance, see if we can't help out in some way.' He glanced over his shoulder to where Patterson remained at the bottom of the incline, speaking to some of the council workers. Then he continued in a lowered voice, 'To be honest, we're so fucking stretched at the minute we're just about covering the big players. Hutton's name featured with us a few times, but he was small fry.'

'Small fry? He's been running drugs here for years.'

Nicell stopped and raised a placatory hand. 'Sorry – I don't mean it like that. It's just, there are eight of us to cover the entire county. I know Hutton was a prick, but the actual figures he was pushing were relatively small. There are really only four big players in Donegal and they're all further into the county. The borderlands have been left fairly much to their own devices. I think most of the big pushers didn't want to piss off the paramilitaries who were running the trade in the North and over the borders for years.'

'What about Martin Kielty?'

'The guy who died?' Nicell shook his head. 'Never featured on my radar. I'd heard the name in dispatches. The drugs may have moved out of the cities, but the resources to tackle them haven't.'

'We're looking at Irvine for the killing of Kielty. Seems possible he's to blame for this one too.'

'It does, all right,' Nicell said. 'Again, Irvine's figured more in the North than over here.'

'Kielty's girlfriend told us that Irvine's crew threatened him in a local pub and then sent him a death threat in the post. The barman in Doherty's confirmed it was Irvine. Though he said that he picked on Kielty and ignored other pushers in the pub at the same time.'

'Who knows what these fuckers are thinking?' Nicell said. 'Could be a private beef between the two of them. It sounds likely that he's your man, though. I'll keep an ear out and let you know what I hear.'

We reached Hutton's corpse and Nicell knelt beside him to examine the wound to his head.

'The ME hasn't even arrived yet,' I said.

'Poor bastard,' Nicell said. 'Though the fucker had it coming to him if he was happy enough to keep peddling his shit.'

'If he was small fry, what's your interest?' I asked. I'd already experienced the NBCI arriving halfway through an investigation and sidelining the locals in a previous case. I didn't want a repeat performance from the county's Drugs Unit.

'Honestly? None. Your boss there wants us to show our faces at a press conference he's organized to say that Hutton has been found. This Rising crew have him riled. I think he wants to reassure the public that the "Drugs Unit" is on the case. Pure bullshit, of course. Fucking PR exercise.'

'What's the story with The Rising?'

'Fuck knows. The only thing it has done is drive a few of the dealers underground or out of the county. Hutton and Kielty are just two of a half dozen we know of, stretching to Inishowen, who have upped sticks and moved. Though in the case of Lorcan and Kielty, the move was more permanent.'

'Do you know anything about a guy called Vincent Morrison?'

Nicell shrugged his shoulders. 'Nothing, why?'

I explained my previous encounter with Morrison. 'He's a slick bastard and he got away with murder, quite literally. I'd swear if he's involved with The Rising, there's something else behind it. He's not the community-minded type.'

'I'll ask around and see what I can find,' Nicell said. 'Though I've not heard his name in connection with anything. Whatever else I can do, just give me a bell,' he concluded, handing me his card.

At that, John Mulronney, the ME, finally arrived. He stood at the bottom of the incline where Hutton lay and looked up to the body. Puffing out his cheeks and using his black medical bag for balance, he began his ascent. Halfway up, his feet gave out under him and he landed face down in the mud, his arms out to his side, one managing to hold his bag an inch off the ground.

'Fuck!' he yelled, while Nicell and I slid our way down to him to help him up as the others around us bent double with laughter.

Mulronney gave Hutton a cursory examination, signed the death certificate and left again with little conversation. Hutton's body was not to be touched until the state pathologist arrived and did his initial examination. For my part, I had promised Caroline Williams that I would be at Peter's funeral. I wanted to get home and showered before Debbie and I headed down. Before that, someone had to visit Lorcan Hutton's parents and inform them of his death. I suggested to Patterson that he might want to do it.

'Lifford is your station, Devlin. You can handle it.'

'In that case, I need you to send a Forensics team to the house in Rolston Court. I also want a team to check Ian Hamill's car. We found it last night on Barnesmore Gap.'

'Yes, Inspector,' he drawled. 'Lucky I have you to tell me my job.'

*

Hutton's father and mother sat together on their leather set-tee while I informed them that their son's remains had been discovered and invited them to officially identify his body in Letterkenny Hospital.

Both had been doctors, which may have accounted for the clinical, professional manner in which they received news of their son's death. Or perhaps, aware of the lifestyle he had been living, they had always expected such a visit.

'How did he die?' Mr Hutton asked, leaning back on the seat, stretching his arms across the back, crossing his legs as he did so.

'That has yet to be established,' I said.

'You must have some idea,' he snapped.

'It would appear that he was shot, Dr Hutton. The post-mortem will be more conclusive.'

Hutton nodded as if I had confirmed something for him.

'I am very sorry. Would you have any idea of anyone who might want to hurt Lorcan?'

His mother looked at me, slightly bleary-eyed. His father, however, snuffed his indignation at the question.

'Who *didn't* want him dead would be easier to answer.'

'You were aware of what your son did for a living?'

'We're not thick, you know,' Hutton barked, only to be silenced by his wife laying her hand on his knee.

She looked at me plaintively. 'I don't know where we went wrong,' she said.

I silently considered the fact that, for the past decade, they had bankrolled Lorcan's activities and paid for the best legal representation for him every time he was arrested. Yet they were just another set of grieving parents, no different from Caroline Williams.

'There was nothing you could have done to prevent this, Mrs Hutton,' I said, truthfully.

Chapter Eighteen

The church in which Peter Williams's Funeral Mass was conducted was huge, yet there were few empty seats by the time we arrived. The entire left-hand side of the main aisle was awash with the navy blue of the school uniforms worn by several hundred of Peter's fellow students, who stood to attention as his coffin was carried past. A Celtic football shirt had been placed over the coffin. On a table in front of the altar was a framed picture of Peter sat with a soccer ball and a games console beside it.

The school's choir began the Mass and I watched as a number of the students wept openly, hugging their neighbours. At the front I could see Caroline and Simon Williams standing side by side in the front seat. Caroline's parents sat in the next pew.

During his homily, the priest spoke warmly of Peter and referred to the tragic loss of his young life. He encouraged the other students to be careful in all that they did, and to always appreciate the gift of life they had been entrusted with. I could tell from the tone of his oration that he himself was being careful. He did not explicitly say that there had been something untoward about Peter's death, or that it was anything other than an accident. Still, his admonition to the assembled children was evident.

As we processed from the church afterwards, marching silently behind Peter's coffin, I noticed that the rain had finally stopped and the sun had managed to break out from behind a thick cloud bank to the east.

Caroline and Simon Williams stood at the church door while the mourners offered them their condolences. Caroline appeared to be holding together reasonably well, though her eyes were puffed and red. She was bent over slightly, as if the events of the week had somehow physically sucked some of her vigour from her.

In contrast, Simon Williams stood ramrod straight. As he thanked people for coming and agreed with them that Peter's death had indeed been a waste, his gaze flicked towards Caroline, his hatred barely concealed.

After the burial, family and friends were invited back to a local hotel, for some lunch. We stayed long enough to see Caroline, having not had a chance outside the church. As we spoke to her, she seemed dazed. I couldn't work out whether it was simply her brain's manner of coping with the day's events or if, perhaps, her parents had given her something to help her manage. Either way, she looked at us a little blankly while we talked. She thanked us for coming, thanked us for everything we had ever done for her.

'Anything you need,' I said, 'just ask.'

'That Guard, McCready, came to see us last night,' she said. 'He told us they've decided Peter's death was suicide. Is that right?'

I nodded, unsure what to say. 'He . . . the pathologist thinks that it might have been. You had mentioned he was depressed. I thought . . .'

'Do you remember what I said about being punished? That's why he did it,' Caroline said earnestly. 'He's punishing me.'

'That's not true,' I said, placing my hand on her arm.

'The selfish little fucker did it to punish me. But he never thought about me, did he? He couldn't forgive me.'

I tried to think of some way to convince her that she had made no mistake, but I could find nothing to say that might penetrate the aura of detachment that surrounded her.

On the way home, I caught the end of Patterson's press conference on the radio. I recognized Rory Nicell's voice as he reassured the public that An Garda had a handle on the drugs trade around the border. It was possible that the deaths of Martin Kielty and Lorcan Hutton were connected but, at this stage, he said, we were not looking at the involvement of any other persons.

'That's bullshit,' I said to Debbie, turning down the volume slightly. 'Hutton was shot in the head. Kielty was stabbed in the chest and burnt. They couldn't have killed each—'

Debbie interrupted me, turning the sound on the radio back up. 'There's your friend,' she said.

The interviewer was now speaking to Vincent Morrison. Did he feel in any way guilty about the death of Lorcan Hutton? she asked.

'Not at all,' he replied. 'Why would I?'

'An Garda did suggest that vigilante actions from groups like The Rising would simply force dealers underground. Might the actions of The Rising not have contributed to Hutton's disappearance and death?'

Morrison responded that the group were simply 'voicing frustration', and led the interview in a different direction by taking umbrage with the 'vigilante' suggestion. He reminded the interviewer that he was a community activist, not a member of The Rising.

'That must make you happy,' Debbie said, turning the volume down. 'The chance for a public smack on the wrist for Morrison.'

I shook my head. 'Morrison's not responsible for Hutton's

death. He was killed weeks ago, judging by the state of the body.'

'I'm sure you'll find some way to pin it on him anyway,' she sniped, undoing her seat belt as we pulled into our driveway.

'What have I done now?' I asked, though the slamming of the door was the only response I got.

When I went into the house, Penny was sitting at the bottom of the stairs. My parents had been watching the kids for us so we could go to the funeral. I knew, from both the expression on her face and the fact that she was awaiting our arrival, she had a request to make.

'Daddy, can I go to the cinema tonight with my friends?' she blurted before I'd even managed to close the front door.

I knew that Debbie's anger with me was due in no small measure to my refusal to allow Penny to go to the disco.

'Of course, sweetie. I'll drop you round and collect you again, though.'

Penny flashed me a smile, then turned and thudded up the stairs to her room, from where, a few seconds later, we heard the bang of her wardrobe door being flung open and the first of many clothes hangers hitting the floor.

My father was putting on the kettle to make us some tea. Debbie tried hard to maintain her anger but had clearly overheard my conversation with Penny.

'Don't think this makes it all all right,' she muttered as I passed her.

'Not even if I pay for her popcorn too?'

I collected Penny's two friends from their respective homes and drove the three girls down to the cinema. The twilight sky was still an inky wash over the horizon. The girls chattered happily in the back seat, whispering conspiratorially to each other then erupting into gales of laughter when I glanced at them in the rearview mirror. On one such occasion I caught Penny's eye and she smiled mildly in a manner that reminded me of Debbie.

We stopped at the cinema and I gave Penny twenty euros to pay her way in and buy some popcorn and drinks for the three of them. When they got out of the car she waved in the window happily, though I noted that she did not give me her customary kiss on the cheek.

I watched until the girls had disappeared inside before pulling off. As I approached the car park exit, a large black 4x4 drove past me. The driver glanced in my direction as he drove by me, raising his hand in salute. In the seconds of his passing, I recognized Vincent Morrison. In the passenger seat sat his son.

I stopped at the exit, wondering whether to go back and collect Penny. I knew that, to do so, in front of her friends, would not improve my relationship with either her or Debbie. In the end, reluctantly, I drove on.

Chapter Nineteen

I reached Letterkenny before 8 p.m. and headed straight to the station. Irvine's rally was due at eight thirty in the town square. Patterson had arranged for two squad cars of Guards to be on site, ostensibly to marshal, though the numbers attending were unlikely to be high enough to justify such attention.

'Intelligence tells us The Rising has an active membership of only a dozen or so. Hangers-on might make the numbers up to twenty. Don't take any shit,' Patterson told me before we left the station. 'Bring Irvine in on anything. Be creative,' he added.

The rally had begun by the time we arrived in the town centre. Someone had brought along a small amplifier to which was attached a single microphone. Irvine stood on a set of concrete steps leading up to the cathedral. Intelligence may have suggested twenty in attendance: in reality the figure was closer to fifty, amongst whom I recognized a few faces from the protest at Hutton's.

Irvine was shouting into the microphone in order to be heard but held the mike so close to his mouth that his words were lost and fuzzy with static. Still, the sentiment behind them was fairly obvious: drug dealers deserved no mercy; someone had to protect the local community.

The crowd in front of him clapped at each statement, some more enthusiastically than others. Patterson's deployment seemed to be having some effect, for some of those gathered twisted their heads occasionally to see if we were still sitting on the roadway watching them. One or two of the younger fellas at the front pulled scarves over the lower halves of their faces.

Eventually, Irvine addressed our presence directly.

'It's good to see An Garda protecting the community. Maybe they're afraid someone's going to sell drugs here.'

The crowd laughed as required.

'They know what would happen to them if they did. We're not taking their shit any more. If the Guards won't do anything about them, we will. The Rising shows the people of Donegal aren't prepared to tolerate any more drugs on our streets. We have a voice, which is good. Sometimes, though, you need more than a voice to deal with the scum that sell drugs to our kids.'

Applause here. Some of the more militant turned towards us, slow clapping in our direction. Other members of the crowd, though, seemed less comfortable with Irvine's sentiments.

'The only good drug dealer is a dead one,' Irvine shouted, his front-row acolytes raising a cheer of approval.

'That's enough for us,' I said into the radio transmitter in my car. 'Incitement to violence. Let's bring him in.'

The two teams of Guards began to move up through the crowd, heading towards Irvine. I noticed some of the people at the back begin to peel away, sensing something was about to happen. Others not only stood their ground, but seemed to swell slightly, as if this was the real event of the evening, the reason they had come in the first place. I noticed one or two of the youths who had covered their faces reach into coat pockets. I whistled across to two of the uniforms on the far side of the grouping and pointed to the youths. 'Blades!' I shouted.

I saw Tony Armstrong prise one of the planks of wood off a park bench to his left and hold it above his head. Irvine stayed where he was, mike in hand, shouting encouragement to his followers to stand firm against aggression.

A boy of no more than thirteen or fourteen, lacking the self-control of the older men there, was the first to strike, lashing out at one of our uniforms with a penknife. His action, and the shout of protest it elicited from the uniform he lunged at, provided the catalyst for others to join in. I noticed a few of my own colleagues similarly swell with anticipation as they reached for their batons.

The boy with the knife was the first to feel the impact of their use. A second uniform approached him from the side, his baton raised high above his head and brought it down so sharply on the boy's wrist it must have broken.

Armstrong moved suddenly forward, swinging the plank of wood he'd lifted, hitting another Guard on the side of the head with enough force to knock him to the ground. Armstrong raised his foot to kick at the prone man but several of my colleagues lunged forward and brought him down.

I shoved my way through, shouting to the men to get Irvine and to get back to their cars. I saw fists, feet, batons all swinging, the dull thudding of flesh being struck accompanied by the grunting of twenty odd men, their breaths harsh and fogging in the chilled air. Taking out my phone I called through to the station for support, then moved into the centre of the fracas, trying to separate the more vicious of the Guards from the people they were attacking, but any efforts were ultimately futile.

Irvine was moving down now into the crowd, twisting up his shirtsleeves, as if preparing for manual labour. I shouted to the two uniforms closest to me and pointed towards Irvine. As the three of us moved towards him he turned and lifted the stand of the microphone he had been using and brandished it at us. The younger of the two uniforms removed his baton and moved forward, swinging it towards Irvine, despite the fact that Irvine himself had not yet attacked anyone. I became aware of lights flashing around us and at first assumed it was the blue lights of the squad cars I had called. Then I noticed Charlie Cunningham, standing up on the steps where Irvine had previously been speaking, camera in hand.

'Don't!' I shouted, too late, as the uniform brought his baton down on the side of Irvine's head, splitting the skin of his bald scalp. Irvine smiled broadly, even as he turned towards Cunningham to have his photograph taken, the left-hand side of his face badged now with his own blood, his arms outstretched, before the Garda who had hit him pummelled him to the ground.

A few hours later, Irvine was led into one of the interview rooms in Letterkenny station. He had forsworn the opportunity to go to the General Hospital first, preferring to have the wound on his scalp sealed with paper stitches in the back of the ambulance. Dried blood still streaked from the top of his head to his jaw line. He had called for his lawyer, Gerard Brown, who had duly arrived. I had encountered Brown many times before, normally when interviewing the more amoral inhabitants of the borderland region. In fact, having Brown as representation was virtually a mark of criminality.

Irvine hardly needed legal advice; clearly a veteran of police interviews, he had the routine down pat. He denied everything, said little and looked bored throughout our conversation. He had no recollection of where he was the night Kielty was murdered, he didn't own a white van and had never heard of Ian Hamill.

After Irvine had been cautioned, Brown immediately stated his intention to file charges against the Guard whose unprovoked attack on his client had been photographed. He placed the picture on the table between us to emphasize the point. In the fracas that followed, I had forgotten to tell Patterson that Cunningham had been taking photographs. He looked from the image to me and back again, shaking his head.

'You file whatever charges you want, Mr Brown. Your client was seen to raise a microphone stand against my officer. He encouraged vigilante behaviour in a public forum and incited violence against members of the community.'

'Drug dealers,' Brown corrected him.

'Your bread and butter, I'd have thought,' Patterson said. He continued before Brown could respond, 'While we're on the subject, two have turned up dead. Murdered. One of them your client threatened in a public house in Strabane a few weeks ago.'

'Allegedly.'

'We have a witness statement,' Patterson said, stretching the truth a little.

'You have the word of a barman,' Irvine said.

'We have a Mass card with your organization's name on it.'

Irvine looked at me blankly.

'We didn't send anyone a Mass card,' he said.

'Kielty's partner says otherwise.'

'Then she's lying,' Irvine stated. 'Where's the card? Let me see it.'

'We'll let you see nothing.' I was grateful for Patterson's

interruption for McEvoy had told me that Kielty had dumped the card.

'Now, what about Lorcan Hutton?' Patterson went on. 'Did you know him?'

'I knew *of* him,' Irvine said. 'Most people did.'

'You wouldn't have threatened him at some point too, would you?'

'That's a ridiculous question, Superintendent,' Brown said. 'And this whole thing seems spurious. You have the word of a barman that my client threatened Martin Kielty – that's it. We all know that that means nothing. You have some bullshit charge about inciting violence. Unless you have something concrete, my client is leaving.'

'We know you threatened Kielty, Mr Irvine: you said yourself tonight that the only good drug dealer is a dead one.'

'You were doing your job properly, I wouldn't have to say things like that,' Irvine began. He was interrupted by a knock at the door.

A uniform came into the room with a slim folder that he handed Patterson. He opened it and glanced at the contents.

'Perhaps you'd like to spend some time discussing all this with your solicitor,' Harry said, nodding to me that we should leave.

*

'You let yourselves get photographed?' he shouted when we were back in his office. 'Jesus Christ.'

'It went to shit, Harry. They had knives with them.'

'And a fucking camera. They *wanted* you to do it. We'll be splashed all over the front pages tomorrow. More shit to deal with.'

'I'm sorry, Harry. It just snowballed out of control.'

'What did you lift him *there* for?'

'You said be creative. I thought incitement to violence would give us something to hold him on.'

'You could have let him get in his car, smashed the tail lights, and pulled him over on the dual carriageway. Jesus, Devlin.'

I'd endured enough of Patterson's tirades over the past few years to know they were mostly bluster. Still, it would not look good for the force, especially with The Rising claiming we weren't dealing with the drugs problem properly.

'I'm sorry,' I repeated.

'You're always sorry,' Patterson said, dropping heavily into his chair. 'Just another balls-up.' His tone, though, had dropped too, and I knew the worst of his ire was spent. 'Forensics found nothing to tie Irvine to Kielty's house. Not a fucking thing.'

'That doesn't mean he didn't do it.'

'No, but it doesn't prove that he did, either, does it?' he snapped. 'Follow up on Hutton's house. Contact Forensics and see if they've managed to match Irvine's prints to any taken from Rolston Court. If we can connect him to even one of the murders, we'll have the fucker yet.'

Friday, 9 February

Chapter Twenty

The following morning I decided to go to early Mass alone. Although Irvine was being held pending charges for the murders of Hutton and Kielty, I was angry that Penny had most likely lied to me about her cinema trip. I was also angry that Morrison seemed to be using my daughter to get to me in some way. And I was angry that, having witnessed Caroline's loss, instead of it making me value my children even more, I had allowed my relationship with my daughter to deteriorate.

On the way home I stopped and bought some pastries. The local papers were already running copies of Cunningham's pictures, under headlines about 'Police Brutality'. One Northern paper with an extreme political leaning featured the picture of Irvine's bloody face twisted in a grin.

Christy Ward, the aged owner of the shop, had been on the Bloody Sunday march in Derry in 1972. He glanced at the papers lying on the counter between us.

'Reminds me of the bad old days, Ben,' he said, fumbling with my change.

'It's not quite how it looks, Christy,' I said.

'It's hard to see how it could be otherwise. When the police take to beating people up, we have to start worrying.'

'The group in question are not entirely innocent.'

'Maybe not,' he said, passing me a handful of coppers, cupped in the twisted claw arthritis had created of his hand. 'But this'll win them more support than they ever had. Bloody Sunday did the same for the Provos, and it had nothing to do with them.'

'They're not equivalent situations.'

'No, but the consequences are always the same,' he said. 'I'm surprised you don't see that.'

On my way home I tried to dismiss Ward's comments and my annoyance at Penny. The kids were still in their pyjamas when I got in and I made a pot of coffee and laid the pastries on a plate at the table. Shane lifted his with a perfunctory, 'Thank you, Daddy,' and retreated into the living room where he was watching *Jurassic Park*. Penny sat at the table with Debbie and me, her legs long enough now for her feet to touch the floor. She tore small pieces from her bun and ate them delicately.

'How was the film?' I asked.

'Great,' she said, without quite catching my eye. 'Thanks,' she added.

'Just the three of you there?'

Debbie fired me a warning look, though Penny answered innocently: 'There was a whole cinema full.'

'Don't be smart. Was that Morrison boy there?'

'No,' Penny said, even as her neck flushed red.

'Don't lie to me, Penny,' I said, managing to keep my voice calm. 'I saw him going in.'

'Were you spying on us?'

'Was he there with you?'

'There were loads of us there.'

'Was he there, Penny – yes or no?'

Finally she looked at me, popping a chunk of pastry in her mouth before answering.

'Yes.'

'I told you to stay away from him.'

'He's in my class. How am I meant to stay away from him? He sits beside me in science.' From the way she spoke, and the glance she threw at Debbie, I could tell that there was more to it than simply sitting beside her in class.

'Are you dating him?'

'Dad!' Penny exclaimed, the redness making its way right up to her face.

'Don't let him fool you, Penny. He's getting close to you for his father. It's about me.'

If I had slapped her across the face, I doubt I could have elicited such a pained expression as that sentence did, and I immediately regretted having said it.

'I didn't mean it like that,' I said, though she quietly slipped out of her seat and padded away. Though her back was to me as she left the room, I could hear the raggedness of her breathing as she tried not to cry.

'Well done,' Debbie hissed, glaring at me. 'What the hell is wrong with you?'

'I don't want her getting hurt by Morrison,' I reasoned.

'The only one hurting her is you. Stop being an asshole. She's almost a teenager – start treating her like one,' she said, getting up and following our daughter upstairs.

I finished my coffee in silence, then took the plates to the kitchen and scraped the uneaten remains of the pastries into the bin. My mobile started to ring.

'Patterson here,' Harry snapped when I answered. 'Get yourself up here. We have a problem.'

I made it to Letterkenny in ten minutes, grateful to get out of the house. I assumed the summons would be about the newspaper reports, an assumption seemingly confirmed when I arrived to find Charlie Cunningham sitting in the foyer. He smiled when I came in and offered a 'Good morning'. Having been directed to Interview Room 1, I discovered Harry Patterson interviewing Patsy McCann, the barman from Doherty's, accompanied by Gerard Brown, who was looking remarkably fresh considering the late hours he had spent in the station the night before.

Patsy blanched when I entered the room. Patterson announced my arrival for the benefit of the twin tape recorders which were running on the table. The atmosphere in the room was heavy, Patsy's sheepishness matched only by Patterson's anger.

'Here to make that statement, Patsy?' I said, sitting down. 'It's good to see you.'

'Mr McCann is making a statement all right,' Patterson said. 'He tells me that you were mistaken about what he said to you on Wednesday – which is, we're informed, inadmissible in any case. Furthermore, in the interests of fairness and justice, Mr McCann felt duty-bound to come in and tell us that Jimmy Irvine, Charlie Cunningham and Tony Armstrong were drinking in the bar where he works on the night of Friday the 2nd of February. He tells me that they were there from 7 p.m. until 2.30 a.m.'

'What?' I asked. 'Have you been forced into this, Patsy?'

'Seeing this morning's papers, Mr McCann felt it his civic duty to set matters straight, Inspector,' Brown smiled. 'The times in question mean that my client, and his associates, could not have been involved in the murder of Martin Kielty.'

'What about Lorcan Hutton's?' I countered.

'As you don't know yourself when Hutton was killed, you can hardly expect him to provide an alibi. You give me a date and I will, I have no doubt, be able to provide you with a suitable alibi.'

'No doubt,' I muttered.

'That business concluded, then,' Brown said, standing up, 'it remains only for you to release Mr Irvine.'

'We still have him on incitement to violence,' Patterson said weakly.

'For which he will be released on Gardai bail, if you really want to go through the motions.'

Twenty minutes later, Charlie Cunningham posted Jimmy Irvine's bail of three thousand euros and the two men, with Patsy McCann in tow, left the station. Before leaving, Irvine made a statement about the night before, stating his wish to press charges against the young Garda who had attacked him.

'I want that fucker,' Patterson spat, watching him leaving the station. 'If you don't get him for Kielty, get him for Hutton. Get Rory Nicell to focus on it too. He knows the druggies – some of them must know something. Search Hutton's house again yourself, do whatever you have to but get something to pin on him.'

I was leaving the station to head to Hutton's house to go through it myself, now that Forensics had finished with it, when Debbie called. Caroline Williams's father, John McCrudden, had phoned our house looking for me. He was sorry to disturb us so early in the day, he said, but he thought I should know: Caroline had been rushed to hospital.

Chapter Twenty-One

When I arrived, the McCruddens were waiting at the end of the corridor, while the nurses worked with Caroline. John explained what had happened. Caroline and Simon had argued at the meal following the funeral. He had accused her of being responsible for Peter's death and had told the other mourners that she had deliberately stopped Peter from seeing him.

She had become increasingly withdrawn during the rest of the afternoon and early evening. Her mother had given her a second Valium tablet, having already given her one before the funeral. They had asked her to sleep in their house that night, but she had insisted on going back to her own home.

At just after seven this morning she had phoned her mother and father to thank them for their support during the past weeks. She had told them she loved them.

'I just knew,' her father said. 'You know your own daughter.'

I nodded, uneasily.

'So, I got in the car and went over to her house. Straight

out of bed.' He gestured towards his neckline, where the collar of his pyjama top sat over the neckline of his jumper. 'She didn't answer the door, no matter how much I knocked. I had a spare key, so I let myself in. She was lying in the bath.'

He paused and raised his chin slightly, as if to hold back the tears which I could see welling in his eyes. He swallowed loudly, and sniffed, tugging at the hem of his jumper as he did so.

'I thought I was too late. She was just lying there, in the water. She was so cold. She was so . . .' He raised a trembling hand to his mouth to stop himself saying anything more, and his gaze seemed to settle on the middle distance.

'You saved her life,' I said.

'She'd already taken them. A full pack of paracetamol. They think she brought most of them back up, though they'll not know for a while the damage she's done to her liver.'

'She's still alive, John, because of you,' Rose whispered.

He nodded and muttered 'Aye' softly, almost to himself, while his wife smiled sadly and rubbed his upper arm with her hand.

We were eventually allowed into Caroline's room and I was surprised to see that she was awake, though she had turned almost the same colour as the sheet which covered the lower part of her body. I could see the black smears of charcoal still around her mouth, from where she had had her stomach pumped.

As soon as she saw her father she began to cry, heavy, wracking sobs that shook her whole body. He leant down towards her on the bed and hugged her tight against him, while his wife stood to the side, her hand on Caroline's back. I excused myself and headed out to have a smoke. I phoned home to let Debbie know how Caroline was and to check on Penny following our earlier conversation.

By the time I went back up to Caroline's ward, she had settled a little. Her mum sat on the chair by her bed, keeping herself busy by organizing a few of her daughter's possessions on the top of the cabinet.

Caroline nodded grimly, though she struggled to hold my gaze.

'How's your stomach?' I asked.

'Fine,' she said. 'I feel stupid. I've a really sore throat, actually.'

We all laughed lightly, glad of the excuse to relieve the tension in the room.

What the fuck were you thinking? I wanted to ask. *Why?*

Instead, I said, 'Can I get you anything?'

She shook her head. 'You shouldn't have come down, Ben. It's very good of you, but you have enough to bother you.'

'I couldn't not have come down, Caroline,' I said. 'Debbie sends her best wishes too.'

'I'm sorry for all the hassle,' she said, seemingly addressing the room in general.

'No hassle, love,' her father said.

Then her mother asked what we were all thinking.

'What made you do it, Car?'

Caroline looked at her, square in the face, but did not speak.

'This wouldn't bring Peter back,' her mother persisted.

'Peter dying was my fault,' Caroline stated.

'That not true, Caroline,' I said. 'You know that as well as anyone.'

'Well, who else did it? Who else brought him up? Who else let him go to a fucking beach camping in the middle of winter?' Her eyes shone brightly, wet with grief and defiance.

'Is that what Simon told you?' I asked.

'*Him,*' John McCrudden spat angrily. 'He's the one should be . . .' He prevented himself going any further as his wife shushed him.

'Is he still here?' I asked.

'He's going home this evening. He's staying out at the Rosses,' Rose McCrudden said.

'He should never have been here,' her husband stated.

I glanced at Caroline but she was slumped back on the bed. Though her eyes were open, she seemed to have difficulty focusing.

'I'm going to go to the shop,' I said. 'Would anyone like anything? Caroline?'

'I need some stuff from home,' she slurred. 'My stuff.' She tried, with little success, to turn her head towards her mother. 'From home.'

'I'll take you, if you like,' I offered. 'If you need to collect some things. If it would help.'

After some discussion, Rose McCrudden agreed to go with me to Caroline's house. I guessed Caroline needed clothes and underwear. And I knew that her father would not want to leave her side for some time to come.

At Caroline's house the curtains were still drawn. While her mother went upstairs to collect clothes, I tidied up a little downstairs, opening the curtains to allow some light in. Then I headed up to the bathroom. I guessed that the room would not have been touched since Caroline's discovery. True enough, the bath was still full of water, mixed with vomit, which had also spattered against the sides. An empty tablet bottle lay on the floor beside a discarded pile of Caroline's clothes. An empty wine bottle lay in the nest of her black trousers.

I became aware of a buzzing noise and realized that Caroline's phone was sitting on the windowsill. I picked it up and read the caller's number, though I did not recognize it. I called to Rose McCrudden to see if she wanted to answer the call for Caroline but by the time she came into the bathroom the phone had rung off. I was struck, though, to see that there had been thirty-two missed calls. The same number was listed over fifty times since the night previous, with one single break in numbers at 7.05 a.m., to MUM. Some of the calls from the other number had lasted fifteen minutes, some only a matter of seconds. The incoming call immediately prior to Caroline's call to her mother had lasted forty minutes. All the calls from the anonymous number were incoming. The fact that Caroline hadn't saved the number or added a name to her phone's address book suggested it was someone whose contact she didn't wish to retain. I had a fair idea who it was.

I dropped Rose McCrudden back at the hospital, then headed out of Sligo towards Rosses Point, a sandy beach area made famous by Yeats in his poetry. I knew of only one hotel in the area and hedged my bets.

I asked for Simon at the reception desk, telling them he was expecting me. The girl, Polish by her accent, gave me the room number and told me she'd call ahead and let him know that I was coming up.

'I'll call him on his mobile,' I said. 'Can I just check I've got the right number for him? I can't remember if this is his work or private phone.' I read the number off the display of Caroline's mobile.

'I can't give out details of a customer's phone,' she said.

'Yes, you can,' I said, taking out my ID.

She looked at the screen in front of her, her teeth digging into her lower lip, as if she might find the answer to her predicament there. She glanced around.

'It's not like I'm going to shoot him. You don't have to give me the number. I just need you to confirm that the number I have is the right one.'

Reluctantly, she agreed. I read the number off again and she followed it on her screen, her lips silently forming each number.

'That's the number we have for Mr Williams,' she said.

'Thanks,' I said. 'You've really helped me out.'

I knocked twice on the door, lightly, as if for room service, then stepped back out of view from the fish-eye lens. Finally I heard the clunk of the lock been flicked and the door opened.

Simon Williams wasn't wearing his glasses, which meant he was squinting into my fist when it broke his nose. He fell backwards into the room, tripping over his travel bag. The pale blue of his shirt darkened with blood. I stepped into the room, closing the door behind me while Williams scurried backwards away from me.

'I'll call the Guards,' he stammered.

I spat, then lunged for him and lifted him off the ground by his shirt front. I spun him against the wall, the buttons on his shirt ripping off with the force. His head thumped against a framed print on the wall, which shattered with the impact.

He tried to shout out, even as he began to grapple with me, his hands clawing at my neck. Without thinking, I jerked back my head, then smashed it full force into his face, feeling the cartilage of his nose flatten against my forehead.

'Jesus,' he squealed, falling to the floor.

'You made her do it, didn't you?'

He curled into a foetal position, looking up at me through the crook of his arm.

'You called her through the night. You goaded her into doing it, didn't you?'

'Doing what?' he asked, spitting blood onto the carpet.

'She overdosed this morning. Is that what you wanted?'

His entire demeanour changed and he looked at me almost with an expression of ecstasy. 'Is she dead?' he asked, the note of hope evident in his voice, though even as he asked he tensed himself and covered his face with his arms, expecting me to strike him again.

'Do you hate her *that* much?'

He seemed to believe that my anger had subsided and he relaxed a little, twisting his mouth in a bloodstained smile.

'Did she let you screw her?' he responded.

He had misjudged the level of my anger.

Saturday, 10 February

Chapter Twenty-Two

The sky the following morning hung leaden over the Donegal hills, a thick haze obscuring the upper peaks from view. My entire body ached and my head was numb.

Debbie had been in bed by the time I got back the night previous. During breakfast we spoke little. Penny ate quickly and went upstairs to get changed. Shane was watching something on the TV.

'How's my buddy?' I asked him, forcing a lightness of tone which I did not feel.

'Fine,' he said, spooning Frosties into his mouth and turning his attention immediately back to the television.

I wanted to talk to Debbie about what I had done, but found, for once, that I could not be sure how she'd respond. In the end, she brought up the topic herself.

'I never imagined I'd end up married to a man with bruised knuckles,' she said, as she cleared the dishes from the table. 'Who was on the receiving end of your latest mood?'

'Simon Williams,' I said, then waited for her reaction.

'Jumping to Caroline's defence again?' she retorted, walking away from me.

'He goaded her into attempting suicide. He phoned her almost fifty times after the funeral.'

Debbie stopped at the sink and let down the dishes. She leaned heavily on the counter, though did not turn towards me.

'He's a bully. He needed to meet someone his own size.'

'And how did Caroline feel about you beating her husband?'

'I haven't told her.'

'What about Patterson? What'll he do when Simon presses charges?'

'I'm not sure. Should I tell him?'

Finally she turned towards me. 'You can't not. Do you think Williams won't report it?'

I nodded my head. 'I'm sorry,' I said.

'What for?' Debbie asked.

'For all this shit. For all the stuff with Penny and that.'

She murmured something and turned from me again.

'What?' I asked. 'What is it now?'

'Nothing.'

She stood with her back to me.

Finally, I asked, 'Debs, this isn't about Caroline, is it?'

'You're rushing down the road to be with her every day,' she said, making no effort to disguise the hurt tone in her voice.

'It's not like that,' I said, coming towards her, but she raised her hands and stepped back from me.

'Of course it is,' she said simply. 'You're spending longer with her than with us these days.'

'She's lost her son, for God's sake,' I said.

'And you're losing a daughter,' Debbie replied quietly. 'You're losing your whole family. And you don't seem to care,' she added.

Her words played over in my mind as I drove to Letterkenny to discuss the outcome of Lorcan Hutton's post-mortem with Patterson, and to check what Forensics had found in Hutton's house and Hamill's car. I also knew that I would have to tell Patterson what had happened in Sligo. In fact I was a little unsettled that I hadn't already begun to witness some fallout from my actions.

Patterson was standing in reception when I arrived, being interviewed by a radio reporter on Hutton's death. I had to concede that, in the years since his promotion, he had become much more polished in his presentations to the media. When quizzed about The Rising, he suggested that, while An Garda welcomed public support, the public might be better served by reporting anything suspicious to their local officers, rather than taking to the streets.

When the interview was finished he summoned me into his office with a crooked finger.

'Where have you been?' he asked. 'I expected you to go out to Hutton's yesterday.'

I explained about Caroline's overdose, though I left out the incident with Simon Williams for now.

'Is she OK?' he asked, gruffly.

'Seems to be.'

He grunted something approximating sympathy. 'Anyway, the PM results are back on Hutton. And the Forensics reports you wanted too.'

'What's the news?'

He picked up a folder from his desk and handed it to me. 'Hamill's car was clean. Set alight with petrol, nothing useable found. Hutton's house was a mess, by all accounts. As for the man himself, he was shot in the head with a Colt .45. Probably beaten up before his death. Cigarette burns on his arms. Dead three weeks at least.'

'Different MO from Kielty then?' Kielty had been stabbed. No signs of beating or torture.

'Seems different, certainly,' Patterson agreed. 'Could still be the same killer.'

'I doubt it, Harry. Kielty was killed and set alight in his own barn. Even with the body destroyed, we were going to find it straight away. Hutton was killed a month ago and hidden. Whoever killed him didn't want him found, at all.'

'You're crediting these people with too much intelligence. Most of these fuckers are so addled on drugs they don't know what they're at. Work with Nicell in the Drugs Unit, see what you can come up with on these. I had uniforms do a quick check on the other houses in the Court, take statements and that; they're all in the file. Hutton's house was trashed, by the way – before the Forensics team got there. Might have been someone after the protest the other night. Or a looter maybe.'

'I'll need more help to work this, Harry. Nicell is Drugs Unit; a murder investigation isn't his area of expertise.'

'What about that fella Black you have down there?'

'He's a part-timer, Harry. Christ, he needed me to tell him to take a piss the other day.'

Patterson chuckled to himself. 'Who do you want then?'

'There's a Guard in Sligo – Joe McCready. He's young, but he's smart; thinks on his feet. We could second him for a few weeks.'

Patterson considered this. 'A uniform – murder is *his* area of expertise then, is it?'

'He's thorough. And he wants to do well.'

Patterson nodded, more to shut me up than in agreement. 'I'll speak to his Super; see what he says. Get cracking.'

I started to stand, then sat again. 'There is something else,' I said.

Patterson had already begun to read something on his desk and he looked up at me without raising his head. 'What?'

'Caroline Williams OD-ed because her ex-husband bullied her into it. He called her through the night, convincing her she was to blame.'

'Why are you telling me?'

'I went to see him.' I glanced down at my hands. I had been rubbing my thumb across the bruised knuckles of my left hand.

Patterson followed my gaze and started to chortle to himself. 'I thought you weren't sporting those yesterday.'

'I might have roughed him up a bit,' I said.

Patterson smirked at me, though he did not speak for a moment. Finally he leant back again and put his hands behind his head. 'So, why are you telling me?'

It wasn't the response I'd been expecting. 'I . . . I thought I should.'

'You want Confession; go see a priest. I don't give a shit what you did. You think you're the first to lift your hand to someone? My only surprise is that you had it in you,' he added, laughing to himself.

'What if he presses charges?' I asked.

'Then I'll have you arrested, same as anyone else,' Patterson replied, all laughing done now. 'Get the fuck out of here until then.'

I went outside for a smoke before I did anything else. I felt a little better for having told Patterson. At least this way there would be no surprises. Though I was also aware that he would happily allow me to face whatever I had coming to me alone. I tried not to think about it. I had wanted to speak to our technical officer, Josh Edwards, while I was in Letterkenny and so headed back into the station. I got as far as the front desk when I was stopped.

'Inspector Devlin,' the sergeant called. 'The car pound say

194

they have a motorbike belonging to one of yours. They want rid of it.'

It took me a moment to realize that the motorbike in question had been Martin Kielty's. 'I'll go see his partner today,' I said.

Josh Edwards was the only technical officer in Letterkenny, who had gained his position not through training but rather a simple love of computers. Over the years he'd made himself indispensable in working with any IT problems in the station and was eventually granted his own room, where he surrounded himself with machines in various stages of disrepair. He had made himself at home, and when I entered he was rooting through his mini fridge. He produced a bar of chocolate for himself and, seeing me, reached in and threw me one as well.

'To what do I owe the pleasure?' he asked through a mouthful of Snickers.

'Do you ever get bored in here?' I asked.

'Here? How could I? My work is so ... *valued*,' he said, straining to remain deadpan.

'How do you fancy helping me out with something?'

His response, muffled as it was by his mouthful of chocolate, approximated 'That depends.'

'An interview. We found a body in Rossnowlagh. He died on Sunday morning and someone used the boy's phone that night to text his mother and say he was all right.'

'Sick bastard.'

'I don't think the guy who did it was sick. I think he was scared.'

'So where do I come in?' Edwards asked.

'Let me check with the officer in charge. I might bring you in as a technical expert.'

'Typecasting again,' Edwards said. 'Story of my life.'

Chapter Twenty-Three

I called Rory Nicell on my way back to Lifford and arranged to meet him at Rolston Court. I sat outside Lorcan Hutton's house and had a smoke. Photographs of the house showed the considerable damage that someone had done to it prior to the Forensic team's arrival. I read through the statements the uniforms had taken from Hutton's neighbours. Most commented on the numbers of vehicles that had been arriving at and leaving the house over the past year or two. Several commented that they had reported Hutton's activities to the Guards but nothing had been done. One or two ventured that they were glad he had been killed, that maybe the house prices might start to recover now there wasn't a drugs den in the centre of the cul-de-sac.

Only one person, Hutton's immediate neighbour, was able to suggest a possible date for his death. In his statement, Ryan Allan said he had noticed Hutton's absence since the 15th of January. He was used to Hutton coming and going, and knew that days went past when he wasn't home, but Hutton had left with a friend on the 15th and had not returned since.

Mr Allan was at home when I called. He was in his late fifties, I reckoned, though looked significantly older. For the duration of our interview he punctuated each sentence by drawing deeply on the oxygen mask he held in his hand. Two large tanks sat beside his chair, which in turn sat facing both the small television in the corner and a window which afforded him a clear view of his neighbour's driveway where my car now sat.

'I appreciate your speaking to me, sir,' I said, sitting on the sofa to his right. 'I'll try to take as little of your time as possible.'

He waved away my comment and took a deep rasping pull on his mask. "S fine. Happy to talk.'

'I just wanted to follow up your statement about Lorcan Hutton, sir. You said you last saw him on the 15th of January.'

"S right.'

'That's very specific, sir. Are you sure of that date?'

He nodded and tapped the top of the tank beside him with the thickened fingernail of his index finger.

'Read the label,' he said.

I leant across him and glanced at the sticker on top of the tank. Written in pen under the 'Last Checked' area of the label was '15/1'.

'Man that leaves these was here that day. He was setting them up when Lorcan left.'

'Did you see the man with whom he left? His friend?'

Allan drew on the mask as he nodded. His eyes bulged slightly as he did so, his skin flushing red. He held the mask clamped to his face for perhaps thirty seconds before the fit seemed to pass.

'Thin fella. Grey hair cropped up.'

'Would you know him if you saw him again?' I asked.

'Course,' Allan said, as if I had offended him.

I took the three pictures of The Rising members from my pocket along with the image I had of Kielty.

Allan studied each of them, looking from one to the other carefully. He held up the picture of Kielty. 'He was there before but not that day.' He flicked through the pictures again and lifted the picture of Irvine. 'Him too. But not that day either.'

'Were they here together?'

He shook his head. 'That one,' he said, holding up Kielty's picture, 'was here with another fella. But none of these.' He flicked through the other two and held up the image of Tony Armstrong. 'He's the one I saw Lorcan with,' he said.

'On the 15th – he's the one you saw leaving with Lorcan?'

He nodded as he glanced out the window. 'And he was back since then himself.'

'You're sure about this?' I persevered.

He nodded again, his face obscured behind the oxygen mask.

'You didn't think to phone the Guards when you saw him back alone?'

He looked at me a little angrily. 'Would it have made any

difference? The number of people wandering in and out of that house?' His ire seemed to exhaust him and he lifted the oxygen mask to his face shakily and drew deeply on it. 'Plenty around here phoned youse about what went on in there.'

I knew he was right, of course.

'But you saw this man with Lorcan on the last day he was here?'

He nodded again, absent-mindedly though, his attention seemed to have been distracted by something happening outside, which I could not see from my angle.

He raised his hand shakily and pointed out the window. 'He was with that first one,' he said, then took another quick gasp from the mask. 'Him there.'

'What?' I got up quickly and went to the window. It was Rory Nicell getting out of his car.

'He was with that man?' I asked, grabbing the picture of Kielty from him and holding it up.

He nodded. 'I'm certain of it. Never forget a face. Spend me days looking out at them coming and going.'

'You're absolutely sure?'

Allan was unable to speak for a moment as he breathed heavily into his mask, but his vigorous nodding left little room for misinterpretation.

'Thank you, Mr Allan,' I said, standing up to leave. 'You've been very helpful.'

*

I was unsure what to say to Nicell when I met him outside Hutton's house and he seemed to sense my unease for he looked at me a little quizzically.

'I followed up your interest in Morrison,' he said finally as I unlocked Hutton's front door and entered the house.

'Anything?'

'Not at the moment. If he is involved in drugs, he's keeping his head down.'

'What about his links with The Rising?'

'It actually seems to be more a case of The Rising attaching themselves to a legitimate community group opportunistically. I'm not sure Morrison is connected beyond that.'

'Have you heard anything more about The Rising?'

He nodded. 'Bits and pieces. Apparently they've been picking on certain dealers for a reason. The word is that Irvine is trying to push his own stuff. He's forcing lower-level dealers to sell his stuff, then picking on those who refuse. He's clear on Kielty, though, isn't he?'

'Not on Hutton, though, because we don't know when he was killed.' I stopped myself from mentioning what Ryan Allan had told me about the 15th of January until I could establish Nicell's connection with Hutton. 'Might Irvine have taken out Hutton as a rival supplier?'

'Hutton was a dealer, not a supplier. They might have been trying to force him into selling for them. There was one big supplier for the border area – a guy who lived in Galliagh in Derry.'

'The one they tarred and feathered?'

'The very same.'

'What about Ian Hamill? Does his name ring any bells?'

'Never heard of him. Who is he?'

'I think he's connected in some way with Kielty's killing. His car was spotted at the scene. His house has been trashed. The PSNI are on lookout for him, but I've heard nothing from them.'

'Can't help you there, I'm afraid. Though by the looks of it, Hutton and Kielty were killed by different people. Maybe Hamill did Kielty, Irvine did Hutton?'

'Maybe.'

'Two dealers in a month. Makes you wonder if the killers are worth tracking, eh?' Nicell said, laughing lightly.

'Kielty had a baby,' I said.

'Plenty of other fathers were hurt by Kielty and his kind. I wouldn't be killing myself over it, you know.'

'We should take a look around,' I suggested, unwilling to continue the conversation further.

The house itself had been thoroughly checked by Forensics. In their initial report they had noted that the rooms had shown signs of ransacking. The mattresses in the rooms upstairs had been slashed, the wardrobes emptied of clothes.

The downstairs rooms had likewise been gone over. The suite of furniture in the living room had been upended and the cloth bottom ripped back. DVDs from the shelves to the left of the hearth had been scattered on the floor. The TV sitting on a wooden corner cabinet, a new LCD model, had been moved, the dust revealing its previous position.

'Someone was looking for his stash,' Nicell said. 'They've left behind the TV and stuff.'

I nodded my agreement. The walls and furniture in places still bore the grey dust of the finger-printing that had been conducted by Forensics. 'Patterson suggested a looter did it.'

'Not a chance – and leave all that shit? No, it's a clear search.'

'And a quiet one. I spoke to the man next door and he didn't mention anything. If there'd been noises in here, he'd have heard it.'

The rest of the house was similarly disarrayed. In the kitchen a box of washing powder had been emptied into the sink.

I lifted the powder box by the edge and noted that it had been dusted for prints.

'I wouldn't have taken Hutton for a man who'd wash his own clothes,' I said.

'Yeah.' Nicell laughed.

'Did you know him?' I ventured.

'Not well. Heard his name a few times. That was about it. Might've spoken to him once or twice – if we lifted him for shit.'

'What about Kielty?'

He pantomimed confusion. 'I told you; he never featured before this whole thing.'

Chapter Twenty-Four

I stopped off at the station on the way back from Letterkenny. I wanted time to think through all that I had learnt. Irvine had had contact with both Kielty and Hutton. His group was believed to be muscling in on the border drug dealers, forcing them to sell *their* stuff. Yet both Kielty and Hutton were dead, which, if Irvine had killed them both, might suggest that they had been reluctant to do as he wished. Hutton was last seen leaving his house with Tony Armstrong in mid-January. Armstrong had been back since and the house had been trashed in a fashion which suggested he'd been looking for something. Whether he had found it or not was a different matter. The cigarette burns and cuts on Hutton's body suggested he'd been tortured before he died, rather than simply executed. They had questioned him about something and he'd been unable to answer them – otherwise, why search his house? Why not just go back and retrieve whatever they were looking for?

Then, of course, what about Kielty? Was it possible that his killing was unconnected? Perhaps it was simply the result of a row with one of his users, Ian Hamill, who had since vanished and whose car we'd found burnt out in Barnesmore Gap. Then again, Irvine had publicly threatened Kielty and had, possibly, sent him a death threat.

And yet, none of that explained why Rory Nicell had been seen with both Hutton and Kielty, and had denied knowing them. Certainly it would not be unusual for a drugs cop to know dealers, but then why claim that he'd never heard of Kielty?

Ultimately, there was little I could do but follow up on Tony Armstrong for Hutton's killing. As for Nicell, I would have to wait and see what else was revealed. I silently decided to exclude him, as much as possible, from the investigation until I had a chance to work out what his involvement was.

When I got into the station, I found that Burgess had left the preliminary toxicology report on Peter Williams lying on my desk. I scanned the findings, looking for mention of alcohol or drugs. In fact, Peter had taken both. His blood/alcohol levels were high – 0.14 per cent, which, judging by his age and size, indicated up to six cans of lager. Certainly more than the one or two the boys had suggested. In addition to this, however, relatively high levels of cocaine were found.

I had just finished reading the report when my mobile rang. It was Joe McCready.

'I got the tox report, sir,' he said.

'I know, Joe. I've got a copy here.'

'He took cocaine.'

'So it seems.'

'We need to push those two boys again. I'm planning on bringing them in this evening.'

I checked my watch. I wanted to call with Elena McEvoy. I had not spoken to her since questioning Irvine about the Mass card. By the time I'd get that done, it would be late afternoon. Debbie's comment to me during breakfast had made me wary of heading back down to Sligo and missing the kids' bedtime yet again.

'Would you mind putting it off to tomorrow?' I asked. 'I'd like to be there, if that's OK. I'm also thinking of bringing a friend.'

McCready did not speak for a second, before replying, 'Oh. OK.'

I sensed that he thought he was being sidelined. 'We have a techie up here who is very good. I can't see any of those kids suddenly folding and admitting to bringing drugs with them. But we might be able to nail one of them for taking and using Peter's phone. If we have him on that, who knows what he'll admit.'

'That seems like a plan, sir,' McCready said.

'It's still your case, Joe. I'm just helping out for Caroline.'

'I was sorry to hear about her . . . what happened to her.'

'Yes,' I said. 'I think she's OK, though.'

'I know,' McCready said. 'I called in with her this morning. She's going out to her parents this afternoon, I believe.'

The more I spoke to McCready, the more I hoped Patterson would make good on his promise to organize a secondment.

I crossed the border in an unmarked car and drove out to Plumbridge to Elena McEvoy's house. It took me several attempts and a number of wrong turns before I found the right cul-de-sac. I decided that rather than bring up the topic of the Mass card immediately, I would claim I was calling to arrange for the collection of Kielty's bike. While I doubted Ms McEvoy would necessarily want to see the bike again, it was a valuable machine and, if she wanted to sell it, it could help her out financially for a few months. That done, I could broach the subject of the death threats her partner had received. While I had little doubt as to the veracity of her claim that Kielty had been threatened in the pub, Irvine's reaction to my question about the Mass card suggested that she might not have been entirely honest, especially considering she had been unable to produce any evidence.

However, when I got to her house, I discovered that it was empty. I checked several of the windows, but the place was deserted; even the furniture had been removed from the front room.

The old woman next door, whom I had noticed on my first visit here, was standing at her window again, glaring over at me. I gestured to her, asking her to open the window, but she simply walked away from it with a scowl. I went to her front door and knocked. Almost immediately a voice called, 'Who is it?'

'I'm a police officer,' I said, omitting to mention that my jurisdiction was on the other side of the border.

'Let me see some ID,' she called, flicking open the letter box.

I handed over my card and waited.

Sure enough, her voice, stronger than her appearance had suggested, snapped, 'You don't belong over here. You shouldn't be here.'

'I'm looking for Ms McEvoy next door,' I said. 'Do you know where she is?'

'She's not there,' the woman replied.

'Can you open the door?' I asked.

'No,' the woman replied. 'You're not even a proper police-man.'

I decided not to get into a discussion on the issue.

'Do you know where she's gone?'

'Good riddance to them, I say. Nothing but trouble.'

'So you don't know where she is then?' I asked, biting my tongue to keep from saying just the type of thing she'd expect from someone from my side of the border.

'She packed her stuff. A van came and took her and that ... *child.*'

'What type of van?' I asked, eager to keep her talking now that she had started.

'White. From your side.'

'Southern registration plates?' I asked, to clarify.

'Isn't that what I said? A right dirty-looking thing it was too. That shiny paper on the back window. What do you call it?'

'Foil?'

'Aye, that shiny stuff. Hanging off the window.'

'Do you mean it was peeling off?' I asked, squatting down level with the letter box. A pair of angry eyes glared at me through the slot.

'That's what I said, isn't it?'

'Did you notice anything else?'

'I'd have said if I did,' she replied, before the flap snapped shut in my face.

That evening, I went home early, in time for dinner. Penny talked gaily with Debbie about school and her friends' latest 'boyfriends'. Shane sat beside me throughout our meal, leaning against me happily, and I realized how much I missed spending time with my family. Afterwards we took Frank for a walk, though he struggled a little on the path and tired easily. It struck me again that my family, even my dog, had grown older without my noticing. The intervening time was composed of moments I knew I had lost and could never reclaim.

Sunday, 11 February

Chapter Twenty-Five

I collected Josh Edwards from Letterkenny at 8.30 a.m. and headed down towards Sligo. On the way, I explained to him what I wanted him to do during the interviews with Peter Williams's two camping partners. He seemed quite excited about being out of the station. After listening to him extolling the virtues of various gaming consoles I might want to buy for my children, I suspected that Edwards's hobbies were unlikely to bring him into contact with people in general either.

We reached Sligo before ten. Rather than going directly to the station, I told Edwards I had a call to make. Caroline had got out of hospital and I knew she was staying with her parents. Edwards sat in the car while I went up to the house. Caroline's father, John McCrudden, answered the door. He looked older than his years, no doubt as a result of the many recent traumas affecting his family. One of his eyes watered slightly while we spoke, and he continually rubbed at it with his index finger. He invited me in, closing the door behind me, before

213

telling me that Caroline was resting upstairs. I suggested I call back later, but he insisted on my seeing her. She was awake, he said.

As I began to climb the stairs, he seemed to think of something and called me down towards him. Standing on the lowest step, looking up at me, he offered me his hand.

'I've wanted to do what you did to Simon for fifteen years. You did a good thing, son.'

I took his comment without response. At least I knew now that Caroline would have heard about the incident too.

She was sitting up in bed when I went in. On the cabinet beside her stood a half full cup of tea and some toast crusts on a plate.

'You're being looked after,' I said, nodding towards the remains of her breakfast.

She smiled mildly. 'You went to Simon, I believe.'

'Who told you?' I sat on the edge of her bed. I noticed on her lap lay a pair of glasses. 'I didn't know you wore glasses,' I added.

'I don't. I usually wear contacts.'

'I didn't know that,' I repeated. 'Isn't that funny?'

'So you went to Simon,' she said again.

I glanced down at my hands, which were clasped in my lap. 'Yeah.'

'Why?'

'You know why, Caroline. I saw your phone. I know you were talking to him. It wasn't hard to work out.'

She nodded, then lifted her glasses and began to fidget with them. 'Am I supposed to be grateful?'

'I didn't do it for you,' I said. 'I did it because he's a bully. I did it because people like him get away with their shit and nobody does anything about it.'

She listened but did not respond.

'I half expected to be suspended by now, to be honest,' I said. 'Maybe he's accepted it and has disappeared again.'

This time she shook her head. 'He knows you're waiting for him to do something. He's got you now. He'll decide when you get suspended. You've given him control. He'll want to enjoy it for a while. But he'll not let it drop.'

Our conversation lapsed into an uneasy silence again for a few moments. Then Caroline said, 'He was right though, Ben. It was my fault that Peter died. I drove him to it.'

'Caroline, the toxicology results have come back.'

She glanced at me, her face blanching. She swallowed dryly before speaking again. 'Did they find anything?'

'Peter had a high level of both alcohol and cocaine in his system. You didn't drive him into anything.'

Caroline's demeanour changed completely. She shifted in the bed, stopped playing with her glasses and instead put them on.

'Are you sure?' she asked.

'Certain,' I said. 'Had he taken drugs before, that you know of?'

She shook her head. 'I'd have known. I know the signs.'

'We're interviewing the other two kids who were with him that night. We'll find out from them where it came from. If you want someone to blame for Peter's death, blame the person who sold him cocaine.'

'They'll say nothing. Murphy's a bad wee shite. The other one, Adam, is a good kid but he's spineless. He'll be too scared to grass up anyone. The two of them will deny everything.'

'I have an idea on that,' I said. 'I wanted to run something past you. One of the kids must have taken Peter's phone after he died. You got a text message from him on the Sunday night, telling you he was in Dublin. We know he had actually been dead since that morning. One of them must have lifted his phone and sent that message. If I can get one of them to admit to that, I was thinking of offering them a get-out from a charge of perverting the course of justice, on condition they tell us where the drugs came from. If you're happy enough not to press charges.'

She considered the idea, angling her head slightly. Her glasses suited her, accentuated the sharp lines of her jaws and the prominence of her cheekbones. Finally she nodded her head curtly.

'Find me whoever did this to Peter.'

'I will,' I said, getting up and leaning towards her.

She moved back from me slightly. 'And as for Simon. I can fight my own battles.'

'We all can do with some help sometimes, Caroline,' I said, and kissed her lightly on the top of her head.

THE RISING

She reached up and put her arm around my neck, drawing my head level with hers. We hugged, awkwardly, for a second, then she let me go.

Chapter Twenty-Six

Edwards and I headed out to Sligo Garda station. McCready had already arranged an interview with the boys and their parents. The first to come in was Cahir Murphy, the more confident of the two on the night of Peter's disappearance. His father accompanied him, though they had not chosen to bring a solicitor; McCready had told the boys that he simply needed them to clarify a few points about the circumstances surrounding Peter's death.

'It was an accident, I understand,' Mr Murphy stated when they came into the interview room.

'We're still considering several possibilities,' McCready said. 'That is one of them.'

'An accident or suicide. Either way, I don't see how my boy can help you with anything.'

Cahir Murphy sat quietly beside his father. I could imagine the conversation they must have had on the way in. *'Just say*

*nothing, son. Don't you worry; I'll not let them push you around.
I know my rights.'*

'This is Detective Inspector Benedict Devlin,' McCready said.
Only two officers at a time were permitted to conduct interviews,
so Josh Edwards was sitting up in the canteen, waiting until
he was needed.

'Why is he here?' Mr Murphy asked.

'He's a friend of Peter's mum,' Cahir Murphy told his father.
'He was there the night of the search.'

'So this is a personal inquiry, is it?' Mr Murphy asked.

'I'm assisting Garda McCready with his investigation, Mr
Murphy,' I explained, then turned to his son. 'Cahir, do you
want a smoke before we start?'

Cahir Murphy blushed and dipped his head slightly.

'My son doesn't smoke,' his father said.

'I think there are a few things that might surprise you, Mr
Murphy. Perhaps you'd like to explain to us what happened the
night Peter died, Cahir.'

'I've told you already,' Cahir scowled. 'He went to go to the
toilet and didn't come back.'

'He'd been drinking. Isn't that right?'

'You already know this.'

'A can or two?'

'That's right.'

'Boys will be boys, Inspector,' Murphy said. 'Peter brought
a few cans with him, apparently.'

'Fourteen,' McCready said. 'And he had drunk maybe six or seven of them. Is that right, Cahir?'

'I only saw him take one or two.'

'What about drugs, Cahir?'

The boy feigned surprise. 'I didn't see any,' he said, though I knew he was lying.

'Peter had significant quantities of cocaine in his system when he was found,' McCready said. 'Where did he get it?'

'I already told you,' Cahir said, tilting his head nonchalantly, 'I didn't see any.'

'That doesn't answer the question,' I said. 'You weren't asked if you saw any. We know he had drugs with him. You were asked where he got them.'

'My son already told you he didn't see any drugs, and I believe him. If he didn't see any, how would he know where they came from?' his father said, leaning forward and clasping his hands on the table in front of him.

'Did Peter bring his own stash?'

'I already told you,' Cahir repeated, tutting and rolling his eyes.

'What about his phone?'

'What?' If Cahir Murphy was feigning innocence this time, it was a good performance.

'We know now that Peter died on Sunday morning. On Sunday evening, someone sent his mother a message from his phone. That was the day Garda McCready here last spoke with you. We believe that one of you took Peter's phone and sent his mother a message in the hope that it would stop us searching the beach area where he died. I suspect that was done because someone was afraid we would discover that Peter had taken drugs.'

'I know nothing about that. Besides, that's stupid. Once his body turned up you'd have found out anyway.'

'That's very true,' I agreed. 'So you don't know who might have taken it then?'

'No idea. I'd say it's the kind of stupid thing Heaney would do.'

Adam Heaney arrived with both his parents. His mother was sitting in the reception area, a brown handbag clutched on her lap. His father paced nearby, reading the posters on the walls repeatedly to keep himself occupied. Adam himself sat two seats down from his mother, his hands dangling between his legs. McCready called his name and he looked up. His face paled when he saw me.

McCready informed him that only one member of his family was allowed to accompany him into the interview room. Heaney blanched, his eyes welling with tears as he turned and asked for his mother to come in, much to the annoyance of his father who began to insist that he should be there.

'It might be better if Mr Heaney comes,' I said. 'There are details you might be better not hearing,' I added, looking at the boy's mother. I remembered that Heaney had hidden the night of the search in case his father found out he was there.

Mrs Heaney acquiesced and Adam walked slowly into the interview room, his father's hand clasped on his shoulder. His whitened knuckles told me that this was not a gesture of paternal solidarity.

We asked Heaney the same questions we had asked Murphy regarding the drinking.

'They were both drinking,' he said, then added quickly to his father. 'I wasn't though.'

'You'd better not have been,' his father said pointedly.

'What about drugs?' I asked.

'You'd really better not have been,' his father said. Even across the table, I could see his jaw muscles clenching.

'I didn't do any,' Heaney said, turning to his father.

'Adam,' I said. 'I need you to speak to *me*. Was anyone else taking drugs?'

'Peter might have taken something,' he admitted. 'I'm not sure.'

'Who brought them? The drugs?' McCready asked.

'I . . . I don't know.'

He was lying but I was prepared to let it slide for now.

'Let's talk about Peter's phone,' I said.

Heaney swallowed and looked askance at his father.

'What phone?' Mr Heaney asked.

'I'll let my colleague explain,' I said, opening my phone and calling Josh Edwards.

Josh arrived a few moments later, swapping places with McCready.

Firstly, he explained about the signals transmitted by mobile phones. Even when a phone was not in use, it was possible, he said, to pinpoint its position. When the phone was used – for example, to send a text message – its precise location could be discerned to within a few feet. He threw in some comments about triangulating transmission coordinates.

I could tell his spiel was having the desired effect; both Heaney and his father seemed lost in the increasingly technical jargon. Adam Heaney struggled for a few moments to retain an expression of innocence, though it soon became apparent, from the fearful looks he gave his father, that he had taken the phone.

Eventually, I interrupted Josh.

'Cutting through all the techno babble, Adam, it comes down to this. We know you have Peter's phone. You can lie about it and, when it goes to court, Garda Edwards will tell the judge the same thing he's just told us here. Or you can come clean about it now.' I nodded to Josh, letting him know I no longer needed him. He left the room quietly, McCready re-entering as he did so.

Heaney's father stared at him. 'Do you know anything about this?'

The boy struggled to swallow. When he finally answered, the response died in the dryness of his throat and he had to take a sip of water from the glass on the table.

He coughed once, into his fist, clearing his throat. 'I didn't steal it. He left it behind. I lifted it for him.'

His father glanced at us and shrugged, as if the response exonerated his son from any wrongdoing.

'I'm sure that's probably true, Adam,' I said. 'That doesn't explain why you sent Peter's mother a message telling her he was in Dublin.'

'I didn't . . .' he began, then stopped.

'You didn't what?'

He looked again at his father.

'Tell them the truth, whatever it is,' his father growled.

'I didn't want her to find out Peter was high.'

'What?'

He gestured across the desk at McCready. 'He told me that they'd find out if Peter had taken anything. I didn't want his mother to know that he'd taken drugs.'

'Why?'

'I thought she'd be annoyed,' he explained quickly. 'I thought if I told her he was in Dublin she'd . . .'

'She'd what?' I asked, incredulously. 'She'd stop looking for him?'

'I . . . I didn't think it through, I suppose,' Heaney said, his eyes welling with tears.

'You stupid fucker,' his father spat, then lifted his hand and smacked the boy hard across the side of the face, knocking him onto the floor.

McCready was out of his seat instantly.

I raised a placatory hand towards Heaney's father. 'Please, Mr Heaney; we need to get to the bottom of this.'

He stood from his seat and raised both hands. He moved away from where his son lay on the floor and stood at the far side of the room while McCready helped Adam back into his seat.

When the boy had settled again, I continued. 'You thought Peter's mother would be more upset about her son taking drugs than him falling to his death?'

Adam Heaney, embarrassed perhaps by our witnessing of his father striking him, responded quickly, 'But he didn't fall – he jumped.'

I straightened in my seat. 'Maybe you ought to tell us what happened that night.'

This was the story that he told.

The three boys arrived at Rossnowlagh around six thirty. They pitched their tent, then headed to a nearby van for fish and chips. Someone had brought a carry-out of cans – probably fourteen, he agreed – and they ate their dinner and drank beer. He didn't have any, he claimed, though the presence of his father was, doubtless, colouring his description.

The boys sat talking as they drank. Peter was agitated; he said he'd been arguing with his mother. He felt she was controlling him, bossing him about. He wanted to move out – had asked about going to live with his dad. His mother had refused.

Adam had gone out to go to the toilet around ten. When he came back, one of them had produced several small folded paper packages. He didn't know who had brought them or from whom they had been bought. Cahir and Peter snorted some – but, he was careful to stress, he didn't. Over the course of the next hour, they alternated drink with coke. The more Peter took, the happier he became. At one stage he got a fit of the giggles, which lasted over a quarter of an hour. He began to run round the tent, telling the others that he could not feel his legs any more. Finally, at around one thirty, he snorted a score by himself. Almost immediately, he announced that he could fly. Cahir was well on himself, and he shared the joke. But Heaney realized that Peter didn't mean it as a joke. He stated with intensity that he could fly. He began to get aggressive, suggesting that the boys didn't believe him. He'd prove it, he said.

'I'll show every one of those fuckers that I can do whatever I want,' he shouted at them. Then he ran from the tent.

The other two spilled out after him. Heaney tried to catch up with him, to stop him, but Peter was too far ahead. He ran towards the edge of the cliff, his arms flailing. Just before he reached the edge, when Heaney felt sure he would stop, he turned his head towards them and smiled. He climbed up onto the handrail and stretched out his arms.

'Geronimo!' he shouted, then launched himself into the darkness.

*

'He didn't scream, the whole way down,' Adam Heaney said, his face wet with tears. 'It was so quiet. It was eerie. Then Cahir started laughing, like it was all a joke. It took him a while to come down and realize what had happened.'

'Why didn't you tell us this on the night?'

'I didn't want to get into trouble,' he said pleadingly, as if trouble might yet be avoided.

'Who brought the drugs?'

He shook his head. 'I don't know, I swear.'

'Tell him if you know,' his father said gruffly.

'I said I don't know,' Heaney said, a little petulantly.

'I spoke to Peter's mother this morning,' I said. 'I told her about the phone. She was very upset by the message, Adam. You gave her false hope. You sent her to Dublin to look for her son when you already knew he was dead.'

'I didn't think!' he cried, his tears streaming again.

'She blamed herself for what happened to Peter. She attempted to take her own life, because she believed that she was responsible for Peter's death. You could have saved her all that pain.'

'I'm sorry,' he said, rubbing his face.

'If she had died, you'd have been partially to blame,' I continued.

'Jesus,' his father groaned. He made a sudden lunge towards his son but McCready was on him, pushing him back against the wall, and warning him that he'd be removed from the interview room.

'As it is,' I continued, 'you're facing a charge of perverting the course of justice, because of your trick with the phone.'

'Are you listening to this?' his father spat at him. 'Are you happy now?'

'There is a way out of it, though,' I said, as much to the father as to the son. 'Mrs Williams is prepared to let the matter of the phone and the fake message drop.'

Adam Heaney looked up at me, his face clouded with a mixture of emotions, knowing that there would be a price for such an offer.

'Tell us who gave Peter the drugs or where he got them from, and we'll not press any charges on your taking the phone.'

'I don't know who brought them,' he said.

'I don't believe you, Adam. That's our offer. I'm going to give you the night to think it over. By nine o'clock tomorrow morning, I want you to have contacted Garda McCready here and told him your decision.'

'But I don't know where he got them,' he protested.

'That's your choice, Adam,' I said, standing up and looking at my watch. 'You have just over twenty hours to find out. Or you're going away.'

His father straightened himself up, loosening his shoulders with a quick shrug. 'Don't worry,' he stated. 'He'll tell you. I'll make sure he does.'

I didn't doubt it for a second. Nor did I envy Adam Heaney the night that lay ahead for him.

Chapter Twenty-Seven

We made it back to Letterkenny by mid-afternoon. I dropped Josh Edwards off, thanking him for his help and declining the offer of a coffee, explaining that I had something to do.

I phoned Jim Hendry on my way into Lifford and asked him to find me an address for Martin Kielty's mother. I hoped that she might have some idea where Elena McEvoy had gone, which, in turn, might lead me to the white van. I mentioned the fact that it had been seen outside her house to Hendry.

'Let me see what I can do,' he said. 'You found young Lorcan, I believe?'

'I did indeed,' I said. 'Thanks to your info on The Rising, I might have his killer, too. Tony Armstrong.'

'Armstrong? He's a moron. Doesn't mean he wouldn't have killed him, I suppose. Bit extreme to score political brownie points with the locals, mind you.'

'Apparently it's more than that,' I said. 'Our Drugs Unit over here tell us that The Rising are trying to force their own supply on border dealers. Irvine must have invested in a stash he's looking to offload.'

'You're sure about that?' Hendry asked. 'Our intel is pretty good, Ben. Word here is that they were purely political.'

'We do have *some* intelligence of our own here, Jim,' I said light-heartedly, though I was conscious that it was Rory Nicell who was the source of that intelligence in this case. Nicell, who I had subsequently learned had been spotted with two dealers he denied knowing.

Hendry got back to me quickly with an address in Seven Oaks in Derry. He also mentioned that he had an idea on how to follow up the white van for me. Depending on which way the van had driven from Plumbridge, it may have had to drive past Sion Mills PSNI station, outside which were CCTV cameras, a legacy of the Troubles. He promised he'd let me know if they had picked anything up.

I headed on down to Derry, to speak to Kielty's mother. It was almost four thirty by the time I got there.

Dolores Kielty was alone when I arrived. She was smaller than I remembered from the funeral, only touching five feet two, perhaps, and she stooped slightly when she walked. She brought me into her sitting room, a newly furnished room with yellow wallpaper with an intricate frieze at the top. A large LCD TV dominated one corner of the room, on which a chat show host was shouting jokes at his audience. Mrs Kielty dragged deeply on the cigarette she held clamped in her hand. She hacked a cough into a tissue in response to my asking if I could join her in a smoke.

'Have you found who did it?' she asked, as I lit my own cigarette.

'I'm afraid not,' I admitted. 'We're following several lines of inquiry.'

'The radio said that that fella Hutton was being blamed. Is that right?'

I shook my head. 'I don't believe so. Not by us, at least.'

She nodded lightly, as if my response was one she had expected. 'I watch this every afternoon,' she said, gesturing towards the TV.

'Were you aware of what your son was doing, Mrs Kielty?' I asked. 'For a living.'

She coughed again, noisily. 'Well, I knew he wasn't buying this stuff with his brew money,' she said, pointing again at the TV.

'Martin bought you that?'

'Had the whole house decorated for me.'

I could formulate no response to her evident pride that her son had used his drugs profits to wallpaper her home.

'I'm afraid we have Martin's motorbike, still. I wasn't sure what to do with it. I tried contacting his partner, Elena McEvoy, but—'

Dolores Kielty tutted. 'Her,' she said.

'You didn't get on with Ms McEvoy?' I asked.

'She's a stuck-up bitch, that one.'

'You don't know where she might have gone?'

'No idea,' the woman said. 'She wouldn't tell me anyway.'

'But she has your granddaughter,' I said.

'If she even *is* my granddaughter. That slut was already pregnant by the time she got her claws into my Martin,' Dolores Kielty said, drawing another cigarette from the leather purse in which she kept the packet.

'So you have no idea where she is?'

'None,' she replied with finality. 'Good riddance to her, I say.'

So much for that, I thought. 'I'm sorry to mention it again,' I began, 'but what would you like us to do with Martin's bike?'

'I don't want that thing here. I hated those bikes of his. Hated the thought of him on them.'

I nodded. Dolores Kielty warmed to the subject.

'I used to lie awake at night if I knew he was out on that thing. In case he had an accident. His father died in a bike crash, when Martin was young.'

'I'm sorry to hear that,' I said.

'He had an accident himself when he was in his late teens,' she continued. 'Very bad. I thought I'd lost him.'

'That must have been difficult, after losing your husband that way.'

'It was,' she agreed, looking at me and nodded intently. 'He smashed up his leg. He had to have pins put into his ankle to hold it together. It took him months before he could walk again.'

'That's horrendous.'

'So you may keep the bike. Thanks, but no thanks.'

I stood to leave. 'We'll have the bike sold then, Mrs Kielty. I'll see that the money is sent on to you.'

Dolores Kielty rose from her seat and walked out to the hallway with me. As I reached the door she drew loudly on her cigarette, then coughed to clear her throat.

'I know what he did was wrong,' she said, as if feeling she had to explain herself. 'I know it hurt other people. I know that's what you think. But he was my son. Before any of that, he was good to me.'

I nodded, unsure what to say.

'I keep waiting for him to come into the house. "Ma," he'll shout. "Ma."'

She laughed sadly at the thought, her eyes betraying her pain.

Monday, 12 February

Chapter Twenty-Eight

My first port of call on Monday morning was Lorcan Hutton's funeral. It was poorly attended. He may have had many acquaintances in life but most were interested only in their next hit and, it seemed, had little sentimental attachment to their dealer.

Hutton's parents stood alone in the front pew. Both looked remarkably composed in the circumstances. Every so often, Hutton's father would rub at the back of his neck, then glance over his shoulder, as if hoping that a few more people would have arrived to bolster the twenty or so mourners.

Just after the Mass had started, Jim Hendry slid into the pew beside me.

'Thought you'd be here,' he said, glancing around the church. 'In the middle of all this papist idolatry,' he added, tutting and shaking his head.

'I'm surprised you didn't get burnt by the holy water when you came in,' I said.

'Is that what it was?' he whispered. 'I was wondering.'

'Did you just come in here to slag off the Catholic Church?'

'Oh ye of little faith,' he said. 'I come bearing gifts.'

He passed me an A5 sheet of paper. Turning it over I saw it was a CCTV image of the main roadway in Sion Mills. In the centre of the image was a white van, driving away from the camera, its back windows coated in silver foil, which had peeled off slightly on the left-hand pane. The Southern registration plate was obvious, though the numerals were a little difficult to decipher. Hendry saw I was trying to read the number and tapped the top of the sheet, where the number had been printed. It was a Dublin 08 plate.

'One of yours,' he said. 'I couldn't run the owner on this side.'

'Bit battered-looking for an 08 registration,' I observed.

'It might not be the same one, but it fits the description all right.'

'It's great, Jim,' I said. 'Thanks.'

After the funeral, having offered Hutton's parents our condolences, Hendry and I walked back down to the car park.

'I passed on your suspicions about The Rising to our people,' he said. 'They reckon you're half right. Someone is pushing drugs into the border but they say it's not Irvine. He might be muscle, but he's no genius. The surprise is that he's heading the whole Rising thing at all – he's not what you'd call a born leader.'

'What about Armstrong or Cunningham?'

He frowned. 'Unlikely. As best we can tell, neither of them have much disposable income. Armstrong's an idiot, but he's dangerous.'

'You told me he shot a policeman.'

'In broad daylight. He walked up to his car, shot him in the face then turned and ran off. Wasn't even wearing a mask. He's a bit simple, always used as an errand boy. But he wouldn't have the wherewithal to run a drugs business.'

'And Cunningham?'

'More likely, though again, he has no money. He only got out of jail last year for burglary. Stealing TVs and shit, nothing particularly high-end and certainly nothing that would bankroll a new career in dealing.'

'What about political donations, that sort of thing?'

Hendry shook his head. 'Naw. They're bottom feeders – low-level thugs. That's our reading of it.'

'Thanks, Jim,' I said.

'No problem,' he said. 'I live to serve.'

I was pulling out of the churchyard when something stuck me about my conversation with Kielty's mother. She had mentioned injuries he'd sustained in an accident, yet I could not recall there having been mention in the post-mortem report of surgical pins in the victim's legs. I phoned the pathologist Joe Long and asked him to check for me.

By the time I reached the station he called me back. He'd pulled his file on Kielty's post-mortem. X-rays had been taken due to the extent of surface burning. He'd double checked the images; the body on which he had conducted a post-mortem did not have pins in the ankles. Nor indeed did the victim's ankles display any thickening of the bones one would associate with a healed fracture. There were only two explanations: either Dolores Kielty was wrong about her son's injury; or else the body we found in the barn at Carrigans was not Martin Kielty. If the latter, how was it possible that the dental records I had obtained in Strabane matched the dead man?

I rang Jim Hendry again and asked him to contact Altnagelvin Hospital in Derry, which was out of my jurisdiction, to pull Martin Kielty's file for the purposes of formal identification. I guessed that any surgical treatment he had received would have been there. Sure enough, when I drove down to the hospital after lunch, they presented me with a thick beige medical file.

I flicked through his notes myself and, though most of them meant nothing to me, I came across a series of X-ray images of Kielty's leg following his accident, including several images of his newly pinned ankle.

I phoned Dr Long again from the road and asked him to

meet me in Letterkenny. An hour later, after comparing the notes from Altnagelvin with his own notes from the post-mortem, he concluded that the body we had recovered in the fire could not have been Martin Kielty.

Chapter Twenty-Nine

'Jesus,' Harry Patterson said when I told him. 'I mean . . . Jesus.'

'The dental notes I was given matched the dead body.'

'Then they weren't Kielty's notes.'

'Obviously,' I said.

'Don't get sarky with me. Have you contacted his relatives yet?'

I hadn't, dreading having to admit to Kielty's mother in particular that I had caused her several days of pointless suffering.

'Not yet. I want to find out how it happened first. I'm going to go back to the dentist, find out what the hell went on with their files.'

'It's too coincidental. Someone switched those files deliberately.'

'Do you think?' I asked. Patterson was developing quite a knack for stating the obvious.

*

The dentist, Roger Hughes, denied that the surgery was in any way responsible for the mix-up. He had given me sealed patient notes in good faith.

I explained that the notes matched the body we had found; it was just that they didn't belong to Martin Kielty, despite being in his file.

'I understand that,' Hughes said. 'But there's nothing further I can do to help. You asked for our notes on Martin Kielty. You were given the notes we had in Kielty's file.'

'Is there no way you can find out if his file has been mixed up with someone else's?'

Hughes looked at me as if I were mad. 'I have over five hundred patients in this practice. Without a patient's name, I can't help you.'

He showed me out to the reception area. After he had returned to his room, I asked the girl on the desk who was responsible for compiling notes and ensuring they went into the right files.

'I am,' she said. 'Why?'

As tactfully as possible, and without making her feel that she was being blamed, I explained the situation to her.

'That's impossible,' she claimed. 'You've made a mistake.'

'I have,' I conceded. 'But I'm not the only one. We have a dead body and no name.'

'There's nothing I can do,' she said. 'Without a name.'

I thanked her and turned to leave. Then, taking a chance, I went back to her.

'Was someone called Lorcan Hutton a patient here?'

'I'm not at liberty to say.'

'Can you ask Mr Hughes? Mr Hutton is dead so I'm sure he'll not mind.'

A few minutes after she buzzed him, Hughes emerged from his surgery wearing a blue paper facemask, which he tore off. 'I'm extremely busy. I'm up to my eyes in root treatments today.'

'I'm up to my eyes in dead bodies,' I retorted. 'I'd like some help.'

He conceded the point with a light wave of his hand. 'What?'

'Was Lorcan Hutton one of your patients?'

Hughes nodded to the receptionist – Karen – who tapped a couple of keys on the computer keyboard in front of her, then looked at the screen. She glanced up at Hughes and shook her head.

'No,' Hughes said.

'What about Ian Hamill?' I asked. Hamill was the only other name I had in connection with Kielty.

Before Karen even had a chance to check, Hughes grimaced and nodded his head. 'Yeah,' he said. 'Ian's one of mine.'

'Can I see his notes?'

'Don't you need a warrant or something?' Hughes asked.

I didn't bother pointing out that, as a Garda, I was out of my jurisdiction anyway; any warrant would have been worthless.

'I don't want to read them. I just want to know if they're in the right place.'

Hughes nodded to Karen who disappeared into a back room. While we waited in silence, I could hear the slide and metallic thud of a filing cabinet being opened and closed. Karen retuned with a thin brown envelope which she handed to Hughes.

He pulled out a sheaf of white A5 cards with scribbles on them, and glanced through them.

'These are Ian's,' Hughes said, handing them back to Karen. 'Sorry I can't be of any more help.'

'These are wrong,' I heard Karen mutter.

'I checked them myself,' Hughes stated with exasperation.

'No, the content is right. It's just all the notes for Mr Hamill have been written by the same person, going back years.'

'What's wrong with that?'

'Well, they've all been written by Elena. Except she didn't work here five years ago. She's rewritten Mr Hamill's notes.'

'Elena who?' I asked, my pulse quickening.

Elena McEvoy had worked in Hughes's dental surgery part-time for about seven months. During her time in the surgery, she had mostly carried out secretarial duties. Occasionally she would have updated patients' records.

'But she's rewritten every card, even the older ones she shouldn't have been working on,' Karen explained, showing me Ian Hamill's record cards.

'What's the story with Ian Hamill?' I asked. 'Mr Hughes remembered the name straight away.'

'Mr Hamill has a few problems,' Karen said, warming to the gossip. 'We've had to turn him away from the surgery on occasions because he was too drunk or stoned. Long straggly hair hanging over his face, unshaven, his breath stinking the place out. Mr Hughes sometimes had to pretend to be giving him treatment just to get rid of him. It was sad, really,' she concluded.

I phoned Patterson on my way back across the border.

'It looks like the body's Hamill's,' I said. 'We need an official request for his medical notes for comparison, but I think his dental notes were switched with Kielty's by Kielty's girl-friend.'

'Making the killing planned well in advance.'

'Absolutely. Best we get *his* medical notes too, though, to avoid a repeat fuck-up.'

'Can't you get that copper in Strabane to do it?' Patterson asked, presumably to avoid the five minutes' paperwork the request would entail.

'He's helped me out once with notes already – I don't want to push my luck.'

'You've made a career out of pushing your luck. One more time shouldn't make much difference,' Patterson said, though I suspected he'd put the request through anyway. A second mistaken identification of a corpse would really reflect badly on him as commanding officer.

'You'll need to organize an exhumation order as well,' I added.

'For fuck's sake, Devlin,' Patterson said, though I couldn't see why. He wasn't being asked to conduct the exhumation himself. 'Anything else while you're at it?'

'I think that should cover us,' I said.

'I've just had the Assistant Commissioner on the line, giving me a bollocking about this whole fiasco with The Rising rally. Pictures all over the fucking papers. I'm warning you, if a word of this latest balls-up gets out to the press, I'll pin this whole bloody thing on you. It's your mess.'

'I know that, sir,' I said. 'Which is why I'm the last person who's going to be telling the papers.'

He paused for a second, and I could hear his breath, ragged through the car speaker. 'So, what the fuck has happened here, then?' he asked at last. 'Is Irvine tied in with this or not?'

'Maybe The Rising were responsible for Hutton. We know from his neighbour that Tony Armstrong was with him the last day he was seen, and has been back at the house since. We know the house was ransacked. We could bring him in, put a bit of pressure on and see what happens.'

'No point,' Patterson stated. 'He'll lawyer up and say fuck all. Dig deeper. What's the connection with Kielty then?'

'There's the problem. If Kielty staged his own death, the focus is off The Rising. His case might not be connected here at all. Maybe he ran scared. The Rising were putting pressure on him so he took his chances somewhere else. Maybe he used the white van spotted at his house to shift his stash. Start fresh somewhere new.'

'Anything on the van we can use?'

'Jim Hendry managed to get a registration plate for me. I'm going to follow it up now.'

'So we have Kielty for the Hamill killing at least?'

'Looks that way.'

'And you have no idea where is he now?'

'I don't. But if we can find his partner, Kielty won't be too far behind,' I concluded, before telling Patterson I was on my way back to the station.

I'd just hung up when my mobile rang again. It was Joe McCready.

'What's happening, Joe?' I called into my hands-free set.

'Quite a lot, sir.' McCready's voice sounded tinny on the small speakers. 'I've some news on Adam Heaney.'

I'd been too distracted by recent developments to think about Heaney. 'What happened?'

'He arrived in this morning with a black eye and a busted lip. His father must have given him the hiding of a lifetime when he got him home.'

'I take it he gave us a name?'

'Murphy. He says Murphy has been selling stuff around their school, in the toilets and the playground at breaktime. Apparently he's making quite a profit from it.'

'Murphy's not dealing cocaine by himself. Someone is supplying him. Let's hear what he has to say for himself.'

'I'm going out to pick him up now. Heaney has just finished writing his statement. We should have Murphy in custody by the time you get here, sir.'

'I'll be with you soon,' I said. 'I have one other thing to do before I come down.'

I contacted An Garda traffic division and asked them to run the plate number on the white van. The chances were that it was Kielty's, but it was still a lead to be chased, not least because the van had Southern registration plates. They promised to have something for me within the hour.

I was making my way past Rossnowlagh when my phone rang. The caller introduced himself as a Superintendent Logue, which immediately struck me as strange, for I had placed the request with an unranked officer.

'Inspector, you placed a request on a white van, registered Dublin 2008. Can you confirm the number of the plate for me?'

I recited the numbers.

'With what is this connected?' Logue asked.

'It's an ongoing investigation, sir.'

'I guessed that, Inspector. What's the investigation?'

The man's tone made me suspicious.

'The van in question ran a red light, sir.'

Logue laughed quietly down the phone. 'Is that all? You have detectives in Donegal chasing up light jumpers?'

'It's a quiet month, sir.'

'It must be. Nothing to worry about, then. The van is one of ours, Inspector.'

'Ours, sir?'

'It's been seconded to the Drugs Unit up there for surveillance and the like.'

I felt the hair on my neck stand on end.

'That would be Inspector Nicell then, sir.'

'The very man,' Logue said, laughing. 'I think we can forgive him jumping the odd light, don't you?'

'Indeed I do, sir,' I said, cutting the connection.

Chapter Thirty

It was almost five by the time I made it to Sligo. Cahir Murphy sat again in the interview room where we had spoken the previous day, his father sitting upright beside him. When I asked Murphy did he understand why he had been brought in again for questioning, he shrugged.

'So you're dealing drugs?'

Murphy's father laughed, forcibly. 'Bullshit! Who told you that?'

'We know that your son took a quantity of cocaine on the camping trip. Peter Williams took a combination of that coke and alcohol. In all probability, the effects of the cocaine caused Peter to enter a psychotic state as a result of which he took his own life.'

'It was that wee shit Heaney, wasn't it?' Mr Murphy snapped.

'It's irrelevant who it was. Talk to us about it.'

'He has nothing to say,' Murphy continued. 'You have nothing to say, son. I want our lawyer.'

'That's fine, sir,' I said. 'So long as you understand the seriousness of what's happening here; we believe your son gave drugs to a boy who then died. That's manslaughter. He may not have meant to kill him – but he did. Plus we believe he's been dealing. In school, too, apparently.'

'It's bullshit,' the man said again. 'You can't touch him. I want my lawyer.'

His language, his manner, the clichés he used, all reflected the fact that Mr Murphy was wildly out of his depth.

'Of course, sir,' I said, standing up to indicate the interview was concluded, for now.

Joe McCready and I sat in the canteen, having a cup of tea while we waited for Murphy's solicitor to arrive.

'What do you think will happen?' McCready asked.

'He'll probably try to plea his way out. Either he'll blame Heaney, or else he'll offer the name of his supplier. His lawyer will know we'd be more interested in the next up the chain.'

'Is that good enough?'

'I suppose it depends how big a link in the chain it is.'

We sat in silence for a few minutes, waiting for the desk sergeant to call us. I had been considering all that Jim Hendry had told me, and Nicell's connection with the van that had been seen at Kielty's and McEvoy's.

'I want you to do me a favour, Joe. Charlie Cunningham. Member of The Rising. I want you to do a background check on him. I want to know everything we have on him: what he's done; who he associates with; when he served time; where; with who. Look in particular for any drug busts or for anything that looks irregular with his financial background.'

'Yes, sir, I'll do it today,' Joe said, just as we got the call to go back to the interview room.

Murphy's solicitor introduced himself as O'Hare. He complained about our having spoken to his client without legal representation, but this was no more than posturing – Murphy had not requested representation and had been allowed it when he finally asked.

'This whole thing seems to have been blown out of proportion,' O'Hare said, when I told him we had noted his complaint. 'I understand that the mother of the young man who died is a colleague of yours.'

'Was,' I said. 'The child's mother was a Guard.'

'The young man in question chose to take substances of his own volition. My client, if he did bring drugs with him, did so for personal use only. He tells me he did not supply.'

'Though we have a statement that he supplies in his school.'

'A statement from a young man who could just as easily be guilty, naming my client to spare himself.'

'We can apply for a warrant and search Mr Murphy's house, if that would make him feel better.'

'I hope that's not a threat,' O'Hare said.

'No. It's a suggestion to your client that we can, if needs be, pursue alternative, more intrusive methods to secure evidence. His cooperation at this stage in the investigation will spare his family and himself much public embarrassment.'

'Well, that's what I thought,' O'Hare said, and I could see where he was going. 'It seems to me that, whether my client or the other boy on the trip brought a small amount for recreational use, they are not responsible for the death of the Williams boy. I can fully understand that his mother may want someone to blame, but that's hardly fair.'

'I accept that,' I said, glancing towards Murphy and his father, who sat, tight-lipped, listening to the exchange. O'Hare had clearly advised them to say nothing. 'That doesn't mean that we are prepared to allow your client to continue selling drugs in a local school. That's a separate issue and one which I intend to pursue with full vigour. Your client will be charged with supplying and, without further assistance from him, I'll move on a warrant to search the family home and seize anything considered suspect.'

'You'll do no—' Mr Murphy snapped, rising from his seat, but he was cut short by O'Hare.

'It seems to me that the source – the supplier – is the person you should be pursuing.'

'And Cahir would be willing to give us this person, would he?' I asked.

'Without prejudice, in return for other minor charges being dropped. Alongside this nonsense about house searches and the like. Yes, my client would be prepared to offer An Garda information about where the drugs Peter Williams took were bought. That though is not an admission that he himself bought the drugs – rather that he is simply aware of where the drugs were bought.'

I considered the offer. I knew Caroline Williams needed someone to blame for her son's death. I also personally wanted to see Cahir Murphy held accountable for his actions. But I also knew that, even if I pursued a case against him, it would, in all probability, be dropped by the DPP. If Murphy was prepared to make a statement against a dealer, it would take out someone higher on the scale and would provide Caroline with some sense of justice.

'Your client will make a statement to that effect?'

'Obviously,' O'Hare stated.

I glanced at Joe McCready who shrugged his shoulders.

'OK,' I said. 'Who sold to you?'

Murphy glared at O'Hare, clearly unhappy about what he was being forced to do. His father, eager to avoid his son being charged with dealing, slapped his arm with the flat of his hand.

'Tell him,' he said.

'Some guy Hamill in Rossanure Avenue,' he muttered.

'What?' I asked, leaning across the table.

Murphy raised his chin. 'Rossanure Avenue, near the back. I don't know the number. The one with the green door.'

'No, the name,' I snapped. 'What was the name?'

'Hamill. Ian Hamill.'

'You're lying. Ian Hamill is dead,' I said. 'He died a few weeks ago.'

Murphy smiled and shook his head. 'Must be a different Ian Hamill then. The one I know was alive and well and selling coke two nights ago.'

A thought struck me and I retrieved the photograph of Martin Kielty from my coat pocket.

'Is this the man you're talking about?'

Murphy took the picture from me and looked at it. He nodded and held the image up to me, as if I were stupid.

'That's him,' he said. 'Ian Hamill.'

Tuesday, 13 February

Chapter Thirty-One

While Joe McCready took Murphy's statement, I called the Letterkenny station and had them fax me down a copy of Kielty's file. I recalled that he had had an address in Sligo and it took only a few moments to confirm that it was indeed in Rossanure Avenue. Kielty had clearly decided to use his house to keep dealing, albeit in Hamill's name rather than his own. And I guessed he had brought his stash with him – and presumably his girlfriend. And I could guess who had helped him move both.

'I want Rory Nicell arrested,' I told Patterson when I called at his house that morning. It was just past 6 a.m. and the sky was dark and clear, the stars bright, the first glimpse of false dawn barely a sliver on the horizon.

'Come in,' he shrugged, tramping from his front door into his kitchen. He wore leisure pants and a T-shirt under his towelling robe. Dirty dishes were piled in his sink and he rooted through them to find a cup which he rinsed as he waited for the coffee machine to begin percolating.

'I think I've found Martin Kielty and I believe that Rory Nicell had something to do with the events surrounding his disappearance.'

'Is this based on anything?' Patterson asked. 'Beyond your usual distrust of your colleagues.'

'The white van that was seen on two separate occasions – once when Kielty supposedly died and once when his girlfriend packed up house. Jim Hendry managed to get me a registration number. It traced back to An Garda, the Drugs Unit, specifically.'

'And?'

'Someone is operating out of Kielty's house in Sligo using Ian Hamill's name. I believe Kielty is alive and, for some reason, Rory Nicell has helped move him to Sligo from the border. More importantly, Nicell must have known about, or actually been involved in, the killing of Ian Hamill and the staging of Kielty's death. If we're lifting Kielty, we need to be sure that Nicell isn't going to fuck it up for us.'

Patterson placed a cup of coffee in front of me though I had not asked for one. The contents sloshed over the lip of the cup onto the white Formica of his breakfast bar.

'You lift Kielty, if it's him. I'll lead a team and bring Nicell in for questioning – *if* or *when* Kielty implicates him. You'd better be sure of your facts, though.'

'I am,' I said. 'Or as sure as I can be.'

'And don't mention this to anyone,' Patterson continued. 'We've been taking enough shit recently without adding this to it. I've told you I've had the Assistant Commissioner on the phone warning us to keep our noses clean. That bullshit at the rally the other night is hammering us. We need to be squeaky clean for the next few months, until this all blows over, so keep this whole thing between us, you hear?'

I was back in Sligo before nine that morning. McCready had agreed to gather a team of uniforms to support us in lifting Kielty. We drove in several unmarked cars into the Rossanure estate. Though it was almost 10 a.m., the morning air was fresh and the cars lining the streets washed with dew.

The streets of the estate were relatively quiet: a few mothers pushing prams; the odd truant schoolchild risking a sneaky smoke. There was a single corner shop which, by the looks of it, had closed down sometime earlier. The front window was boarded up and a metal grille hung on one hinge from the front door.

The housing in the estate was terraced in groups of five: squat, grey, pebble-dashed blocks. Kielty's house was the centre house in a row, located quite far back in the estate, the block itself bordered on both sides by alleyways running adjacent to the outer houses.

The car I was travelling in parked a hundred yards up the

street from the block, while McCready split the uniforms into two teams, one of which waited along the alleyway, while the other was positioned immediately behind Kielty's property, obscured by a hedge. I had a smoke and scanned the street. One of the houses looked deserted, though curtains still hung in the windows and children's toys were scattered on the small front lawn. I noticed that a pair of trainers hung from an overhead cable.

Kielty's house looked no different from the others, except for the fact that his front door looked newer; the other houses on the row had four panels on the door, Kielty's had two. It was PVC, whereas the doors of the other houses were painted wood.

Our plan was a relatively simple one. As I was not in uniform, I would approach the house on the pretence of delivering a parcel. The rest of the Gardai present would take positions on either side of the doorway. Once the door was opened, they would storm the house. While I hoped that no gunfire would be involved, we knew that Kielty had killed Hamill, so we had come armed and equipped with Kevlar vests.

I called McCready and gave him the go-ahead. His unit began to make their way across the gardens of the houses to the left of Kielty's, crouching low under the level of the windows, until they were positioned outside Kielty's, flush against the front of his house.

I got out of the car and shouldered a box we had taped up in the station, before making my way across to the house.

Rather than ringing the doorbell, I knocked on the door. The dull thud of my knocking confirmed my suspicion.

'It's reinforced,' I muttered to the man to my immediate left, Finn McCarron, who passed the word back. It simply meant we had to be quick.

I had to knock a third time before I saw any response from the house. The curtain covering the window above where our officers were hidden shifted slightly and a face peered out. Though it was only for a second, I saw Martin Kielty, bearded now, but still recognizable from the picture McEvoy had given me.

The curtain closed again and I heard the thud of a dead-bolt being snapped open. The door opened an inch or two, enough only to reveal the security chain still hanging in place and the soft features of Elena McEvoy.

'Yes?' she asked.

'I have a parcel here,' I said, shifting the box to try to conceal part of my face, but it was too late. I saw the flash of recognition, the exclamation caught in her throat as she struggled to shut the door on me.

I wedged my foot between the door and the jamb and shouted. The officers beside me moved quickly, throwing their weight against the door until McEvoy gave up and ran into the house screaming to Kielty. Finally the security chain snapped and we spilled into the hallway.

Ahead of us I could see McEvoy taking the turn on the stairs. Kielty was behind her, but facing us, the pistol in his hand already levelled in our direction. He fired off one shot which spun the man to my right sideways with its impact on his vest.

'Stay back!' I shouted, as the team behind me took cover on either side of the door. But Kielty was already moving on up the stairs.

I heard a crash from the rear of the house and three officers appeared from the kitchen, having broken in the back door.

'Check the rooms here,' I shouted. 'We have two upstairs.'

I started taking the stairs, cautiously. Kielty had tossed a child's walker across the top step in a vain attempt to impede our progress. Four rooms opened out from the landing. To my immediate right was a bathroom. I reached the door and glanced in. Empty. The room to the far left looked like a junk room. Again the door was open and I saw McCready move across and snatch a glimpse around the door. He looked at me and shook his head to indicate that it too was clear.

The doors to both middle rooms were closed. I approached the one closest to me and laid my hand on the handle. I depressed it and pushed lightly; the door offered no resistance.

'Martin!' I shouted. 'You're trapped. Give it up now. Peacefully.'

Nothing.

'No one wants this,' I said. 'No one wants to get hurt. Put down the gun and come out of the room.'

I pushed the door further open and stepped back.

Nothing.

Putting my face close to the jamb I stole a glance in through the gap at the hinges. The room was empty. One bed, made, a few pieces of furniture.

I glanced again at the walker lying at the top of the stairs. I hadn't seen a cot in the bedrooms we'd checked, which meant that Kielty was holed up in the remaining room with his girlfriend and their baby.

'His daughter is in there with him,' I hissed at the men standing with me.

'Should we move out?' McCready asked. We didn't want this degenerating into a hostage situation.

'Come out, Martin!' I shouted, desperately trying to remember the name of the child. 'I know your daughter is in there. Bring her out – none of you will be hurt. I give you my word.'

Kielty did not reply, though from the room I could hear a low murmuring, and the soft whimpering of a child.

'Elena!' I shouted. 'Even if you don't want to come out, hand us out your daughter. I promise you I'll keep her safe.'

The voices from the room now were more animated and I suspected that McEvoy wanted to give up but Kielty was holding out. Suddenly the name came to me.

'Elena. Think of Anna. Do what's right for Anna. Bring her out. Anna shouldn't be caught up in this.'

I heard movement in the room, then the click of the lock. The handle depressed as the men around me raised their guns. The door began to open and I saw Elena McEvoy, her face smeared with tears, her child bundled in her arms. I raised my weapon into the air to show that I meant no harm to them. She moved towards me, shuffling slowly, as the child in her arms began to mew.

At that moment, I saw Finn McCarron, who had been standing beside McCready, glancing towards the open door of the bedroom. Pushing past Elena McEvoy and the child, his gun raised, McCarron shoved his way into the bedroom. We all heard the pop of a pistol, echoing within the confines of the room, followed by a second, louder bang. The men on the landing scattered, some moving for cover, some moving into Kielty's room to support their colleague.

McEvoy held out her child to me, her expression changing as I saw the blood begin to seep through the front of her dress and mark the pink blanket her daughter had been wrapped in. McEvoy's gaze followed mine to the widening stain below her breast and she opened her mouth silently even as her body began to sag.

Supporting her, I frantically rummaged through the blanket, to check if the bullet which had hit her had passed through to her child. The baby seemed unharmed. McEvoy, however, swayed unsteadily for a second then collapsed onto the floor at the top of the stairs as the bloodstain between her shoulder blades widened.

Above her, Martin Kielty, cuffed now and himself bleeding profusely from a wound in his shoulder, looked down on her, uncomprehendingly.

Chapter Thirty-Two

Elena McEvoy was in surgery for less than thirty minutes before the medical staff officially pronounced her dead, though there had been little hope in my mind. Kielty had been rushed into surgery where doctors worked on the wound to his shoulder. There was nothing to do but wait for word that he was well enough to be interviewed.

I contacted Patterson as soon as we returned to the station. His only concern was that we discover as quickly as possible whether the bullet that killed McEvoy came from Kielty's own gun or from Finn McCarron's. I knew that McCarron was already in one of the interview rooms with his union representative, writing his statement.

I had just finished speaking with Patterson when Joe McCready came into the room, a manila folder in his hand.

'The information you asked for on Cunningham, sir,' he said.

'Great, Joe. Thanks.'

He stood to attention in front of the desk I was using.

'Anything up, Joe?'

He glanced around the room to see if anyone else was listening, then coughed quietly before he spoke. 'It was a bit rough this morning.'

I nodded. 'It was that.'

'Did we – could we have . . . you know?'

'Could we have prevented it?'

He nodded.

I considered my response. 'I don't think so. Kielty chose to pull a gun. He chose to hole up with his child. We did our best.'

I knew he was no more assured on the point than I was myself.

'I was wondering if I could take off for a while, sir. I didn't sleep much last night. I'd kinda like to have a shower and that.'

'Go home, Joe. Thanks for your work on this. Take a break for the day. This morning was taxing on all of us.'

He smiled expansively. 'Thank you, sir,' he said, wasting no time in leaving. Most new recruits spent time on traffic duties, so I had no doubt that McCready had seen a death before. Whether he had witnessed one so violent was a different matter.

The desk sergeant made me a pot of coffee while I read through Cunningham's file. A lot of it was straightforward, and simply fleshed out from information I already knew about him.

He had been a leading paramilitary for years, serving time for murder. During the Troubles he had been suspected of planning a number of attacks, including a roadside bomb which missed its intended victim and instead exploded under a minibus full of young fellas on their way to a stag weekend. Cunningham was also suspected to be the shooter in three other killings, though he had never been caught. When they eventually lifted him, it was on the word of one of the supergrasses of the eighties whom Special Branch recruited and paid for information.

Cunningham had made the most of his time inside to develop his academic record. He had studied politics and philosophy to degree level, graduating with first-class honours. During incarceration he had written to various humanitarian organizations, arguing that the manner of his conviction violated his civil rights.

He finally had been released under licence following the Good Friday Agreement, only to have his licence revoked just the previous year after he was accused of the attempted murder of the head of a rival political splinter group. Witnesses claimed that Cunningham had taken a machete to the man in the toilets of the Blackthorn Inn in Burndrum. Despite extensive injuries, the victim refused to name his attacker and would not press charges against Cunningham. The DPP in the North, though, clearly felt that Cunningham had a case to answer and he served eight months. During this time he submitted to regular drug testing, always being shown to be clean, which had helped him secure his release. However, perhaps due to him attacking a fellow ex-paramilitary in the Blackthorn, during this last stint in prison he had been refused permission to stay on the political wing by the other inmates and had been held in the general population. This in itself suggested that he was working on his own now, and that Cunningham's old comrades would not necessarily support The Rising – with the exception of Armstrong and Irvine, obviously.

I had almost finished skimming over the details of his incarceration, when I recognized a name I knew. During his eight months inside, Charlie Cunningham had shared a cell with a convict doing time for fuel laundering: Vincent Morrison.

It took me almost an hour to get back to Lifford. On the way there, I called through to Burgess and had him find out Vincent Morrison's new address for me.

The address he gave was a few miles down the road to Derry, outside Porthall. I knew the area, though I didn't recognize the house name. When I got there I realized why. The house was brand new, built within the past year or two at most. It squatted impressively in the middle of an estate comprising at least ten acres. The driveway to the house ran a quarter-mile up from the main road, alongside a field full of young colts, their breath steaming in the weak afternoon sunlight.

The house itself was a two-storey red-brick building, the heavy front doors sheltered beneath a porch held up by twin Doric columns. A pair of muddy wellington boots lay discarded beside the welcome mat. To my left, sitting in front of the double garage, sat the Range Rover in which I had seen Morrison that night near the cinema, and a second car, a new registration Citroën Picasso.

I rang the doorbell and stepped back, glancing around the estate. I heard the clunk of the lock and the door swung open. Vincent Morrison stood in the doorway, his trouser legs tucked into his socks.

'Inspector Devlin,' he said, his hand extended. 'What a pleasant surprise.' He glanced around the front of the house to see if I was alone. 'What brings you here?'

'I wanted to speak with you.'

He laughed lightly. 'Do I need my lawyer?'

'That depends on what you have to say.' He raised his eyebrows in mock surprise, then called behind him into the house. 'I'll be back in a moment.'

Over his shoulder, I could see his wife standing on a wooden chair in the hallway, taping a Happy Birthday banner to the wall. Various coloured balloons hung from the banister of the stairway.

Morrison followed my gaze. 'The young fella's birthday tomorrow,' he explained. 'A Valentine's Day baby,' he added as he closed the door and lifted the muddy boots to pull them back on his feet. 'C'mon. I'll show you around.'

We walked past the double garage I had seen and around the back of the house. 'You'll like the stables,' he said. 'The kids love it.'

'This is a fine place you've got,' I said. 'I'm amazed you could afford it. I thought you'd been declared bankrupt.'

Morrison smiled a pretence of embarrassment. 'A few wise investments before I got put away,' he said. 'Besides, I don't own this – it's the wife's. A gift from her father.'

'Rich father,' I said.

'And generous,' he added, laughing again.

'Does the Criminal Assets Bureau know about this?'

He shrugged his shoulders. 'Do you really think they'd care? My father-in-law looked after my wife while I was serving my time – nothing criminal in that.'

We rounded the corner to where a block of four stables backed onto the field I had seen as I drove up the main driveway. Three of the cubicles were empty; in the fourth a tall brown horse stood, its head hanging over the gate while Morrison's son brushed the white strip of its nose.

'You've met my son before, I believe. Haven't you?'

I had – the day in court when Morrison had been sent down. I had no doubt, from the flash of resentment in the child's face, that he remembered the occasion too.

'I'll finish up here, son,' he said to the boy, taking the brush from him. When he had gone, Morrison patted the horse on the nose, then led me outside. 'So, what can I do you for? I'm guessing this isn't a neighbourly visit,' he said.

'You know Charlie Cunningham,' I stated.

'That's right,' he agreed. 'I do. We were cellmates for a spell. So what?'

'It's handy that you've managed to convince your community group to support his Rising thing.'

'Nothing handy about it. I have children; I don't want them being exposed to that kind of stuff.'

'That's a bit hypocritical, isn't it?'

'Why?' he asked, perplexed. 'Because I did time? Move on, Devlin; I have.'

'I don't believe you,' I said.

'That's irrelevant,' Morrison said, smiling as he leant on the fence bordering the field, watching the horses cantering around its edges. 'The remission board believed me. To be honest, I don't give a shit what you think.'

'I'm told Cunningham's group are a front; instead of trying to drive dealers out, they're trying to force them to sell their produce.'

'You have evidence for all this, of course.'

'The thing is, our intelligence tells us that Cunningham's group wouldn't have the cash to start something like this. They would need someone with money. Someone rich.' I glanced around the expanse of his grounds. 'Someone generous, even.'

He laughed, though without humour. 'This is fascinating. If it's true, you can be sure that we'll not be supporting The Rising any more, Inspector. You're visiting all the local residents' groups and informing them of this personally, I take it.'

He extended his hand to shake, signalling that, to his mind at least, our conversation was over.

Chapter Thirty-Three

As I drove away from his house, watching the building recede in my rear-view mirror, I reflected on what Morrison had said to me the day I had seen him in court. He had boasted that he would be back on top in no time once he was released. He may well have been gifted his house from his father-in-law, but I suspected that he had more money at his disposal than he was admitting. Hendry had claimed that The Rising were linking themselves to Morrison's community group opportunistically. I suspected, now, that the relationship was symbiotic. With his money invested in their produce, and with Irvine and his cronies forcing the dealers in the area to sell the drugs for him, Morrison was himself rising back to power.

I contacted the desk sergeant in Sligo who told me that Kielty would not be available for questioning until the following morning. He had come through surgery on his shoulder, though was not yet well enough to speak to us. The sergeant had also received the findings from ballistics, which concluded that Elena McEvoy had been killed by a bullet from Kielty's own gun. There was, therefore, no need for me to go back down to Sligo until the following day.

I sat on the sofa with Debbie and the kids watching a movie that night. The schools were closed for mid-term the following day and we had promised them they could sit up later than usual.

'How was school?' I asked Shane who lay curled up beside me, his arm wrapped around my leg, my thigh muscle pillowing his head.

'Fine. I got my drawing on the best-work board.'

'What was the drawing?'

I could see the movement of his eyebrows as he rolled his eyes. 'A dinosaur. We had to draw something starting with the letter B.'

I frowned towards Debbie who shrugged. Penny sniggered into her mother's shoulder.

'Dinosaur doesn't start with a B, little man.'

'I drew a brachiosaurus,' he said with a sigh, reaching his hand around to the bowl of popcorn Penny balanced on her lap.

'What about you, Penny?' I asked, taking a handful of popcorn myself. 'How's school?'

'Fine,' she said.

'Penny has another disco tomorrow. For Valentine's Day. She can go, right?' Debbie said, the question phrased in such a manner as to brook no discussion.

'Of course,' I said. 'Long as your teacher's going to be there.'

Penny flashed a brief smile at me and nodded her head.

'I saw John Morrison today,' I said.

She stared at me horrified. 'You didn't say anything to him, did you?'

'Like what?'

'Anything.'

'I might have said "Hello".' I laughed. 'I was out with his father.'

'He says you hate his father.'

'I don't hate him,' I said.

'Then why do you keep harassing him? You don't like him.'

'It's not about liking him. I don't trust him,' I explained gently.

'You don't trust anyone!' my daughter retorted with a viciousness I wouldn't have considered her capable of.

'That's enough,' Debbie snapped at her. 'Don't speak to your father like that.'

Penny looked at me from under the fringe of her hair. 'Sorry,' she mumbled, sullenly lifting a piece of popcorn to her mouth.

'Forget about it,' I said, though I found it impossible to follow my own advice.

After the kids went to bed, Debbie and I spoke about the exchange.

'What were you thinking, bringing up Morrison, Ben? I swear, sometimes you can be so obtuse.'

'It's the boy's birthday tomorrow. When I was at the house they were getting ready for a party. I hope that's not where Penny is going for Valentine's Day.'

'She says the school has organized a disco. I'm taking her at her word.'

'What if she's lying?' I asked.

'After what she said tonight, you have no choice but to trust her, Ben. Otherwise, you'll just have proved her right.'

'I trust her. I don't trust Morrison.'

'Why were you out with him?'

'He served time with the leader of this crowd, The Rising. I'm fairly certain they're behind the killings of the two drug dealers.'

'Two dead drug dealers? Now that's worth investigating,' she said.

'They're killing them so they can flood the place with their own drugs. Except apparently they haven't got any money. Someone else is bankrolling them, and I'm fairly certain it's Morrison.'

'Penny's right,' Debbie said, changing the channel on the TV. 'You do hate him.'

Wednesday, 14 February

Chapter Thirty-Four

Kielty was brought from Sligo General under armed guard and, a little after 11 a.m., was led in cuffs into the interview room, where Joe McCready and I were waiting. His face was gaunt and yellowed, his eyes bloodless, his chin sandpapered with stubble so light in colour, it appeared grey.

His left shoulder was bulky with the dressing beneath his T-shirt, his arm still suspended in a sling. I smelled hospital disinfectant as he took the seat opposite. Looking at him, I instinctively reached up to my own shoulder where the burn wound seemed to have settled.

I turned on the twin recorders on the table in front of us and introduced myself and Joe McCready, then Kielty and the duty solicitor.

'I'm sorry about Ms McEvoy,' I said, after cautioning Kielty.

He nodded.

'It's a pity it came to this,' I said.

He straightened himself in the chair, wincing as he moved his left arm.

'Came to what?'

'Let's start with Ian Hamill, shall we?'

'I don't know what you're talking about.'

I took out the pictures we had on file of the three leaders of The Rising. 'Do you know anyone here?'

I had expected him to stonewall me, but after a short pause, Kielty decided to do himself a favour, and thumped his index finger onto the picture of Armstrong.

'I know him.'

'How?'

'He approached me before Christmas, asked me to sell some stuff for him,' Kielty said. Vague enough not to incriminate himself – detailed enough to incriminate Armstrong.

'What stuff? Drugs?'

Kielty nodded, a gesture I described for the benefit of the tapes.

'He said they had produce they wanted sold.'

'Who was they?'

'He didn't say. I guessed he meant one of the paramilitary groups.'

'And did you sell it?'

'Not initially,' Kielty said. 'I said I had to speak to my supplier.'

'Lorcan Hutton?'

Kielty didn't speak for a moment.

'Elena McEvoy told us,' I said.

Finally he nodded. 'Yes,' he said. 'Lorcan Hutton. I contacted him and he said they had come to him. Given him a load of produce to shift. Sort of forced themselves into the chain.'

'Why did Lorcan let them do it?' I asked.

Kielty glanced at the solicitor beside him who had said virtually nothing since his arrival.

'He thought they were a joke. He took a load of produce off them and split it between a few of us. We were to shift it and he was going to lie to them about the price he got.'

It didn't surprise me that Lorcan would imagine he could stiff Armstrong. Hutton had controlled drugs in the area for years and had become arrogant.

'They didn't take it well?'

Kielty shook his head. 'They got wind of it from one of Hutton's other clients. Kicked the shit out of me in Doherty's pub one night. Told me to get them the money they were owed. I told them Hutton had it.'

'What did they say?'

'"We've taken care of Hutton," they said. "You just make sure you have your bit sorted out."'

'Do you know what they did to Hutton?'

Kielty shook his head. 'I could guess, though. He disappeared one evening. They were able to start picking on all of us, all the ones he'd supplied. I guessed they must have beaten it out of him. He never appeared again.'

I nodded my head. 'He was found shot dead in an old grave-yard in Lifford,' I explained.

Despite the heat of the room, Kielty shuddered.

'So, what happened?'

'I didn't have the money,' he said. 'Elena had her kid and that. Things were a bit tight. I had some of the stash left, but not much, but I knew where Lorcan had the rest of his stash hidden. I couldn't be seen to be dealing too much around the border or they'd have known, so I came down here.'

'Calling yourself Ian Hamill? Why?'

'It just came to mind. He was one of my buyers.'

'Was,' I repeated. Kielty swallowed dryly. 'Go on.'

'They started threatening a bit more. Sent a Mass card and that.'

'So you decided to fake your own death?'

'It wasn't like that,' Kielty protested animatedly. 'I went to someone for help. Someone I could trust.'

'Who?' I asked, though I already knew the answer.

'A Garda,' Kielty said, his chin raised a little defiantly.

'Rory Nicell,' I stated.

He nodded, deflated by his trump card's failure to have the desired effect. He shifted in his seat slightly, glanced at his solicitor who watched him impassively. Kielty had clearly decided to talk; his brief was there only to witness what he wanted to say. Why he was being so forthcoming was another matter, though.

'What did you tell Garda Nicell?'

'I explained to him what had happened. About Hutton and his stash and that.'

'How did you know Nicell?' I asked.

'I was an informant for him,' Kielty said. 'We helped each other out, you know.' As if we were all part of the same battle.

'And what happened?'

'I don't remember,' Kielty said, rubbing at his beard with his knuckles. 'It wasn't planned or anything. Hamill came out to the house looking for stuff. He was a regular, so I knew I could trust him. But he had a bad reaction to whatever he'd taken. Went mental. Something in it fucked with his head. He started trashing the place. Attacked me.'

I recalled Kielty's stash house. It was hardly the type of place you'd worry about having trashed.

'So you killed him?'

Kielty stared at me, as if realizing for the first time what he was admitting to.

'Not like that. It was an accident. He grabbed a knife and went for me. We got into a scuffle and somehow the knife ended up in his chest; he may have fallen on it himself.'

'Where were you taking drugs?'

'In the back room,' he said slowly, wondering the relevance of the question.

'And the knife block was in the kitchen. He ran out into the kitchen and grabbed it, did he?'

Kielty glanced again at the lawyer who shrugged lightly.

'I don't remember all the details. I feared for my life.'

'Regardless, Ian Hamill was killed.'

'I did report it,' Kielty said and I began to realize why he was telling me this. He was going to implicate Nicell as deeply as himself.

'To who?'

'Nicell,' he said exasperatedly. 'He arrived after two. He was the one suggested we leave Hamill in the shed and torch the place. Make it look like someone had got to me first. Burn the place down to make it look like the stash was gone. He loaded his van with our stuff then he set fire to the place.'

Our stuff. And yet, previously, Kielty had been completely passive – it was all on Nicell.

'How did you think you'd get away with it?'

'Elena went into work early the next day and swapped our dental records,' he said. 'We thought you'd find out. Check with the hospital or something. But no one did. No one checked.'

'Then what?'

'When it looked like things were being dropped, Nicell went up and collected the rest of Hutton's stuff and brought it and Elena down with him.'

'Hutton's stuff? His stash you mean? The stuff that sent Hamill over the edge?'

Kielty nodded. 'He was a schizo anyway,' he said.

'Stuff that you sold in Sligo, to a teenager. A boy who jumped off a cliff after taking it.'

Kielty looked at me blankly. I knew he would feel no culpability. Like Lorcan Hutton, Kielty viewed himself merely as

part of a chain of supply and demand, like the arms manufac-
turer who contents himself that the use to which his product
will be put is not his responsibility, or the bartender who feels
no compunction about selling just one more drink to the man
whose car keys lie on the bar in front of him.

'I don't know anything about that,' Kielty said.

'Is it relevant?' his solicitor offered, slouching in his seat
while doodling on a yellow legal pad.

'Does your mother know you're alive?' I asked, reluctant to
believe that the woman had deceived me.

Kielty shook his head. 'Not yet,' he said, lowering his head.
'I have to call her.'

At that moment, the door opened and the desk sergeant
peered in.

'The Super wants to speak to you, sir. Urgently.'

'Maybe you should phone her now,' I suggested to Kielty.
'Why don't we take a break?'

I stopped the tape machines and stood up from my seat.
Kielty likewise stood and stretched his back again, as if clicking
his spine into place.

'Between us,' I said, conversationally, though not casually
enough to stop the solicitor from staring at me sharply, 'why
are you being so forthcoming? Is it because of Elena?'

He stared at me and I willed him to display some response
to her death, to convince me that he was capable of remorse.

'Kind of. Mostly it's Nicell. You can't touch me without putting Nicell away, too. I'm one of his touts. I'm too valuable to

have off the streets. And you'll hardly want it known that one of the Drugs Unit was involved in all this shit, will you?'

I called Patterson and began to explain what Kielty had told us about Nicell, but he cut me short.

'Your missus has been looking for you. She's rung a couple of times. You'd better phone her.'

Something about his final sentence unnerved me and as soon as I hung up I checked my mobile. I'd put it on silent before the interview and hadn't felt it vibrate in my pocket. The display showed that I had missed over a dozen calls from Debbie. The small tape symbol showed I had a voice message, but I direct-dialled her number.

'Where the hell are you?' she snapped when she answered, though I could hear her breath catch in her throat as she spoke.

I began to explain about the interview, but she interrupted. 'You need to come back,' she said. 'Penny's been in an accident. She's in Letterkenny General.'

'Is she all right?' I asked.

'We're here now,' Debbie replied, non-committally. 'You need to get here now, Ben. Please hurry.'

Chapter Thirty-Five

With siren going, it took me less than three-quarters of an hour to make the drive back to Letterkenny. When I got into the hospital I was directed straight through to A&E. Penny lay on a trolley in one of the cubicles. Her head was held steady by a neck brace, the side of her face visibly grazed. Her features were covered for the most part by an oxygen mask. I approached her, fearfully, and laid a single kiss on her forehead.

Debbie sat beside the trolley, her hand holding Penny's, her thumb rubbing the softness of the back of our daughter's hand. Her own features were pale, her eyes red with tears.

'How is she?'

'They need to operate on her straight away,' she managed, her tongue clicking in her mouth as she spoke. 'There's pressure on her brain, they said.'

'What the fuck happened?'

Debbie swallowed hard, took Penny's hand in both of hers, turned herself away slightly from me. 'She fell.'

'Where?'

Finally she turned and looked at me. 'She was at Morrison's home—'

'Jesus!' I shouted, kicking out at a table of instruments beside the trolley which fell over and clattered onto the floor.

A nurse tugged back the curtain sharply. I glared at her. She returned my stare angrily, then looked at Penny lying on the trolley. I righted the table and began to lift the fallen implements. When I straightened up again she had drawn the curtain closed again and was gone.

'She said she was going to the disco,' Debbie explained. 'One of her friends, Emma – her father collected her, took the two of them. She told me it was a school thing. They all went to Morrison's. For the young boy's party.'

'I warned her to keep away from him,' I snapped.

Debbie stood, seemingly reluctant to let go of Penny, but approached me, hand outheld.

'It was an accident. They all took turns horse riding, apparently. Penny fell off.'

'Bullshit,' I spat. 'Morrison's behind this.'

Debbie shook her head, though this simply made me more vehement in my anger.

'I warned you,' I said, emphasizing the comment with a pointed finger. 'I told you this would happen.'

'It wasn't Morrison. Emma's father was there. He said it was an accident. She fell off the horse. He said that Morrison rushed to her – he got her here so fast.'

'I don't believe it. I'll kill the fucker—'

My comment was cut short by the curtain being pulled back on the cubicle and a number of staff coming in. One, a young woman doctor in a white coat absurdly too big for her, spoke to Debbie, glancing at me as she did so.

'We're ready to take her into theatre. The anaesthetist will give her a little something now to prep her. You can help wheel her up if you want.' She smiled a brief, sympathetic smile, then stood back as her colleagues began to work with my daughter.

'Will she be OK?' I managed to ask.

'She's in good hands,' the doctor said, motioning towards the man standing by Penny's bed with a syringe, then leaving the cubicle before I asked her to be more direct.

As the butterfly was inserted into the back of her hand, I swore I could see Penny's eyes flutter beneath the lids, imagined I could hear a low moan escape from her pale lips – though the sound may have come from me. Then the clanging of bars as the sides of the trolley were raised and the orderly began to wheel Penny out.

Moving past Debbie, I took one side of the railings and held on to them as I walked my daughter into the theatre. The surgeon was already there, getting into his gown.

Debbie stood beside me, gripping my arm as I helped push the trolley into place and stepped back. The surgeon turned and smiled at us benignly.

'We'll call you when we're done,' he said.

Unsure what to do next, Debbie and I moved away from Penny.

'You can kiss her goodnight if you want to,' the man said so kindly that I had to swallow to prevent myself welling up. Beside me I could feel Debbie shudder as she began to cry.

We both went over and kissed Penny, as if she were indeed only going to sleep. Her skin felt unusually warm, the smell of her shampoo strong.

Debbie, unable to control herself any more, collapsed against me, racked with sobs. One of the orderlies helped me to support her as we led her out of the room. I glanced back one final time at my daughter, left alone in that room with strangers whose actions alone were to decide if she would live or die.

We were taken into a small room off the recovery ward where a nurse brought us tea and toast that we both ate but I am certain did not taste. Every quarter of an hour someone checked on us. I silently mouthed the rosary while we waited and I suspected that Debbie was doing something similar.

After what seemed hours she stood up and began to pace the room.

'What if something has gone wrong?'

'Nothing will go wrong,' I said, with more conviction than I felt. 'She's in good hands.'

'What if they can't fix her? What if she doesn't wake up?' She looked at me imploringly, as if I could dispel her fears.

'Don't think that way – she'll be fine.'

'What if she's not?' Debbie persisted.

'I'm going to go to Morrison,' I said. 'I don't believe this was an accident.'

'For Christ's sake, Ben, let it go, would you? Let it go. It was an accident. There's no crime – nothing to solve. No one to blame. Just let it go,' she said angrily.

'There's always someone to blame,' I said.

'Do you mean me?'

'I didn't say that.'

'Is that what you meant though? That it's my fault?'

Against my own wishes, I found myself being drawn into the argument. 'You were the one who wanted her to go to discos.'

'I didn't know she was going to Morrison's. She told me she was going to school. She wouldn't have lied if you'd let her be herself.'

I stood up, feeling the heat of the room intensely, loosening the collar of my shirt. 'Don't blame me. You let her go to these things. If you had said no, this wouldn't have happened.'

'Don't you blame me. I won't take the blame for this, do you hear me? This wasn't my fault.'

'You keep telling yourself that,' I snapped and saw, finally, the fear in her eyes that she was, in some way, to blame for what had happened. I went to move towards her, to apologize, but she moved away, rushing to the toilet at the far end of the room and locking the door behind her.

I slumped into my seat, angry and frustrated that despite

a burning need to apportion blame, I knew that it would do nothing to improve Penny's condition.

Debbie came out of the toilet a few moments later and sat on the edge of the sofa opposite me.

I moved and sat beside her, but she shied away from me, her arms crossed in front of her chest, her hand covering her mouth.

'I'm sorry,' I said. 'I didn't mean to say that.'

I reached across to her, laid a hand on her shoulder which she shuddered away.

'You think it, though,' she whispered. 'You blame me.'

'I . . . I don't blame you, Debs,' I said. 'I know it wasn't your fault.'

'But you're right,' she said. 'I did let her go. That night that you told her she couldn't go to the first disco, then you headed out yourself? I took her anyway.'

She turned her head to face me, glaring defiantly, as if attempting to provoke me into saying something, as if hoping that I would blame her again. And I realized that Debbie needed to blame someone too.

A figure appeared around the corner, removing the green gown which he had been wearing when we had last seen him.

'She's out of theatre now,' he said. 'There was a lot of swelling. We had to remove a clot.'

'Will she come out of it?' Debbie asked.

'She should,' the man replied, not quite looking either of us in the eye. I realized that I did not even know the name of this person into whose hands I had entrusted Penny's life. 'We'll have a better idea of the extent of her recovery over the next day or two.'

'Thank you,' I said, for I could think of nothing else appropriate.

He nodded and turned to leave, then seemed to think of something.

'She was lucky she got in here so fast. The bleeding in her brain could have been quite extensive. I hope we caught it in time.'

'Thank you,' Debbie echoed.

He nodded again, pursed his mouth slightly, turned and walked away.

'She *should* wake,' I thought. Not she *would*.

Chapter Thirty-Six

The young female doctor we had met in the Emergency Room earlier brought us into Penny's room. She lay attached to a drip now, an oxygen mask covering her face again, her skull wrapped in bandages, her forehead stained a dark yellow below the bandage line. Her face looked paler than I had ever seen it. Despite her age, despite her increasing maturity, she looked lost in that bed, surrounded with such equipment.

Her hand was cold, her nails, painted pink yet still ragged with biting, were smaller than I remembered. I stood to one side of the bed, her hand in mine, and touched her cheek with my index finger. Debbie stood on the opposite side of the bed, holding her other hand, on which a clip attached to her finger relayed her pulse and blood pressure to one of the monitors at the head of the bed.

'Penny,' Debbie said, her voice hushed. 'Penny, sweetheart? Mummy and Daddy are here.'

We both scrutinized her features for some flicker of recognition, but she remained impassive.

'She might take a while to come round,' the doctor explained, jotting something on the clipboard which she hung on the bedstead.

'How long?' Debbie asked.

The young woman grimaced slightly. 'It's hard to say. She hasn't woken since she was brought in, you see.'

'What does that mean?' I asked.

'Well, she *might* take a day or two to come round.'

None of us spoke.

'Maybe longer,' she added.

'Is she in a coma?' I asked incredulously.

'We don't know,' the young woman said, smiling apologetically. 'She's young and fit. She's got a good chance of coming through it OK. Plus she was very lucky she got here so fast.'

'The surgeon said,' Debbie commented absent-mindedly.

'Technicelly, the man who brought her probably shouldn't have lifted her, in case she had a neck injury,' she said. Looking around at the door as if she were telling us something she shouldn't, she added, 'But in this instance he did the right thing. He might have saved her life.'

The rest of the day passed as if in a dream. I constantly felt as if I were on the verge of moving out of myself, the feeling of derealization I had always associated with the panic attacks I had had a few years previous.

Debbie and I spoke little, making small talk as we waited for our daughter to waken.

Before visiting time ended, my parents arrived to visit Penny, staying only long enough to see that she was still asleep. Debbie's parents were looking after Shane and had decided it best not to bring him to see Penny as she was at the moment.

'Who is staying tonight?' my father asked, as they were leaving.

'I'm not sure,' I said, glancing at Debbie. 'One of us will need to get Shane.'

'You go home,' Debbie said. 'I'll stay with her tonight.'

'Are you sure?' I said. 'You look like you need sleep.'

'As if I'd sleep. She needs her mother beside her.'

I left soon after my parents, to go and collect Shane. Kissing Penny as softly as I could on the forehead, I felt the roughness of the gauze dressing against my skin. It struck me as strange that, despite wanting her to waken, we were all being as careful and as quiet as possible around her.

Debbie offered me a perfunctory kiss and told me to tell Shane that she would be home in the morning, when I would return and she could go home to shower and change.

'Though she might be awake in the morning,' Debbie offered. 'What do you think?'

'She might be,' I said.

Shane sat in the back of the car on the way home from his grandparents' house. He held a toy dinosaur in each fist, play-fighting with them for a few moments. Finally, his imagination temporarily exhausted, he lowered them onto the seat and leant forward to speak to me.

'Where's Penny?' he asked.

'She's with Mummy,' I answered.

'Is she sick?'

'Why, little man?'

'I heard Granny talking about it. Is she going to die?'

'Of course not,' I said. 'She'll be home in no time.'

'What's wrong with her, then?'

I looked at him in the rear-view mirror, the softness of his features, his brow lightly furrowed.

'She fell and hurt her head. The doctors have helped her feel better.'

The answer seemed to placate him and he sat back in his seat and turned his face to the window. In the passing illumination of the street lamps I could see his lips moving silently.

'What are you doing?' I asked, suspecting he was praying for his sister.

'I'm counting the lights,' he said.

'Why?'

'If the last one is twenty, Penny will be OK.'

'Who told you that?' I asked.

He shrugged. 'I just thought it is all,' he said, as if that explained everything.

By my count, the last light before our home was the nineteenth so I cheated and counted it twice.

After I got him into bed and he had said his prayers, I went into Penny's room. I half expected to see the familiar shape of her sleeping body, but the bed sat still made, her favourite teddy sitting on the pillow. Several items of clothing lay discarded on the floor, trousers bunched where she had stepped out of them in front of her mirror. I guessed she had been trying on different outfits for John Morrison's party.

I picked up the clothes and began to hang them in her wardrobe. One of her tops was slightly marked with a smudge of foundation. I placed it to my face and breathed in her smell as I fought back the growing fear that she might never see this room again.

I slept little that night, waking fitfully every time I drifted off, checking my mobile in case Debbie had called from the hospital. Around two, Shane woke to go to the toilet, then stumbled into my room and clambered into the bed beside me. In the dull illumination from the bathroom, his sleeping profile reminded me of his sister. Finally, rather than counting sheep, I recited the decades of the rosary over and over until I was no longer aware of the time.

Thursday, 15 February

Chapter Thirty-Seven

I called the hospital just after dawn to be told that Penny was critical but stable, which in reality meant there had been no change in her condition. Debbie was sleeping in the chair by her bed, I was told, having only managed to fall asleep an hour earlier. I asked the nurse not to waken her, but to tell her when she woke that I would be up before 9 a.m.

Debbie's parents arrived after seven, their drawn features showing that they too had slept little. We ate a light breakfast and they offered to stay in the house with Shane during the day. I left home at seven thirty, having a stop to make along the way.

A low mist drifted across the fields around Morrison's house, his horses shuffling softly in the dawn light, their breath condensing around their ears.

His house stood in darkness, a sheen of dew marking the

windscreen of his car. I glanced into the Range Rover as I passed it, and saw on the light upholstery of the back seat brown bloodstains where Penny's head had rested the day previous as Morrison had driven her to the hospital.

He evidently had heard my arrival for he opened the front door before I even had a chance to knock. He stood in his doorway in grey sweat pants and a T-shirt, over which he wore a white robe, untied at the waist.

'You're up early,' I said.

'Come in,' he replied, holding open the door, his face a mask of pity. 'John couldn't sleep.'

He turned and retreated into the darkness of his hallway and I followed him. He led me into the kitchen, a large bright room, all chromium-coated units and black granite surfaces. At the table a pot of coffee steamed beside a smouldering cigarette which was scarring brown the saucer of the cup he had been drinking from.

'Coffee?' he offered, lifting a second cup.

'Yes. Please.'

'How is she doing since?'

'She's still sleeping,' I said.

He nodded. 'I called the hospital but they wouldn't tell me.'

I began to object, but he spoke again.

'I had nothing to do with it, if that's what you think.'

I sat at the table, took the cup from him, couldn't trust myself to speak.

'It was an accident. She was given the hat to wear, but it must have slipped or something. I swear I had nothing to do with it.'

He made this as a simple statement of fact, without defensiveness, and seemingly not caring if I believed him or not.

'I don't hurt kids,' he concluded, then sat and, rubbing out his smouldering cigarette, lit a fresh one before tossing the pack across the table to me.

'I'm told you saved her life,' I managed finally. 'If you'd acted slower she might not have had as good a chance.'

Morrison lightly waved the smoke from in front of him and picked up his coffee. I noticed a flush of blood to his face and ears. He dragged deeply on his smoke, blew the stream towards the floor. 'Whatever's between us, that doesn't affect our kids. John really likes your girl. There's nothing more to it than that.'

We both finished our coffee in silence. I stared out the window at the stables in the distance as I smoked. Finally I stood to leave. 'I need to get back to the hospital.'

Morrison nodded, extended his hand, waited for me to respond. We shook and I opened the door and stepped out into the dawn.

'My son would like to visit Penny, if that's OK with you. I don't have to come in if you don't want me to, but he'd like to see her. He feels guilty as hell.'

I nodded, once. 'Thanks for the coffee,' I said. 'And thank you for saving my daughter.'

He smiled grimly, then stepped back and closed the door behind me.

I sat with Penny for most of the morning while Debbie went home and showered. Her condition had not improved, though the doctor assured me that it had not deteriorated.

'When she's ready, she'll wake up,' he said blithely, as if that assurance would assuage the pain I felt watching her impassive face, the almost imperceptible movement of the bedclothes that revealed the shallowness of her breathing.

Jim Hendry arrived before lunch, his face flustered with embarrassment, beneath his arm a large teddy bear and a few rolled magazines. He coughed as he entered the room, patted me awkwardly on the arm in sympathy.

'It was good of you to come,' I said.

'I heard it on the jungle drums, you know,' he said.

'I appreciate it, Jim.'

He gestured towards the teddy that he had placed on the chair in the corner of the room. 'I wasn't sure what age she was. Might be a little old for teddy bears.'

'It's very kind.'

'I brought her a few books too,' he said, handing me the magazines. The uppermost one was a women's magazine that Debbie read sometimes. The front cover boasted a strapline that it contained information on '50 ways to satisfy your lover'.

'That one might be a bit old for her, now I think about it,' he said.

He glanced at the figure on the bed. 'How's she doing?'

'We don't know. They're not saying much. Critical but stable.'

He nodded, as if this explained everything. 'Do you know how it happened?'

'She was horse riding, at Vincent Morrison's home. Fell off.'

Hendry looked at me quizzically. 'Do you need a hand taking care of him?'

I shook my head, smiled lightly. 'Thanks, Jim,' I said. 'He wasn't involved in it. In fact, he may well have saved her life.'

Hendry whistled low. 'I'll not ask.'

We chatted uneasily for a few moments until Debbie returned and Jim used her arrival to make his exit. I walked out with him, as much to give me a chance to have a smoke as out of courtesy.

As I stood outside, Caroline Williams arrived. She looked gaunt, her short-cropped hair serving only to accentuate the sharpness of her thinning features. She hugged me close, whispered words of consolation in my ear as she did so.

'I tried your mobile but it was off. I called the house and Debbie's parents told me what had happened,' she said as she stepped away from me.

'It was very good of you to come,' I said. 'Debbie will be pleased to see you.' I wasn't sure why I had added that, for Caroline was there more for me than for Debbie.

We walked slowly up to the room where Penny was being treated. Caroline asked about the circumstances that had led to Penny's fall.

'I understand how you're feeling,' she said, as we stepped into the elevator. She squeezed my hand reassuringly.

'I don't know how I'm feeling myself, to be honest,' I said. 'Empty, I suppose.'

She nodded as I spoke. 'I understand,' she repeated, looking me in the eyes.

'I'd almost rather it had been deliberate, rather than an accident. It would have been less . . . random – less frightening, I guess – if I could explain it, could blame someone.'

Caroline continued to nod but did not speak.

'I thought Vincent Morrison had been behind it, but apparently not. In fact he may have saved her.'

'Who's Vincent Morrison?' she asked, and I realized that she hadn't been partnered with me when I had first met Morrison.

The elevator reached Penny's floor and we moved into the heat of the ward.

'We'll see Penny and I'll explain it to you over coffee.'

Caroline was only permitted to stay for five minutes; the nurses were already annoyed at the number of people who had been in, complaining that visitors were meant to be confined to immediate family. She and Debbie chatted lightly about everything except Penny and Peter, as if each understood the other's pain without need for explication.

I told Debbie I'd walk Caroline downstairs to get something to eat. We sat in the cafe on the ground floor, near the hospital entrance. After I had bought a pot of coffee for us both, I sat down and explained my background with Vincent Morrison and the people-smuggling ring he was involved in.

'He reappeared a few weeks ago,' I said. 'He's a community leader; he threw his weight behind this Rising crew when they started protesting about drug dealers.'

'I've heard about them,' Caroline said grimly. 'It's about time someone did something, Ben.'

'Maybe,' I agreed. 'But The Rising isn't the group to be doing it. They're not trying to drive dealers out of the local communities, they're trying to pressurize the dealers into selling *their* produce. Their leader is a character called Charlie Cunningham who was a cellmate of Morrison's. Apparently, Cunningham and his crew don't have the money to start a drugs business. Morrison does though. He was bankrupt after that last business yet he's living in a huge house with stables in Portnee, up the side road past the Tavern.'

'Can you prove any of this?' Caroline asked.

I prevaricated. 'Maybe.'

'Depending on?'

Putting my cup down on the table, I laid my hand lightly on Caroline's. 'We've arrested someone we think was responsible for Peter's drugs,' I said.

A mixture of emotions blazed in Caroline's eyes.

'Which of them was it? That shit Murphy?'

I had not told Caroline how things had progressed since last we had spoken.

'Murphy claimed that Peter got the drugs himself. He gave us an address for a dealer in Rossanure estate.'

'He's lying. Peter was never near Rossanure. Besides, he wasn't doing drugs. I'd have known,' Caroline said vehemently. 'I know what to look for, Ben. I know my own son.'

She paused, reflecting on her final statement, swallowed the sentiment down.

'Murphy gave us a name that tied to another case I was working. A dealer from up here named Kielty.'

'What did you want him for?'

'We thought he was dead. You remember Lorcan Hutton?'

Caroline paused a second and grimaced.

'That's him,' I said. 'He and Kielty agreed to sell a stash for Cunningham, then tried stiffing him. We found Lorcan tortured and shot in the old Abbey graveyard. Kielty was setting himself up down in Sligo, selling off Cunningham's stash. Except there must have been something in it. One of Kielty's clients in the North took the stuff and went berserk. Kielty claims he killed him in self-defence, then used the corpse to stage his own death. He moved to Sligo full time, using the name of his dead client.'

Caroline listened as I spoke, her eyes following my mouth to ensure she was following what I was saying.

'Berserk?'

I nodded slowly.

'So what's going to happen to Kielty?'

'I'm not sure. He implicated one of the Drugs Unit, a guy by the name of Rory Nicell. Patterson was to lift Nicell. Then everything kicked off with Penny, so I don't know what's happened since.'

'But Kielty was the one who sold him the stuff?'

'Ultimately, yes. But it stretches back to Cunningham. Or further.' She raised her chin slightly, urging me to continue. 'Cunningham doesn't have the money to push drugs—'

'Morrison,' she said.

'Morrison,' I agreed. 'But that's not proven. Morrison claims he's clean. When I heard about Penny I thought he'd done it to take me off the case, but apparently he had nothing to do with it.'

'Do you believe that?'

'I think I do. Penny is in school with his son. I think the two of them had a thing for each other.'

'Jesus,' Caroline said.

'I know. I tried to stop her from seeing him.'

'You can't force your kids to do anything,' Caroline said quietly.

Unable to think of an appropriate response, I laid my hand again on hers. I glanced up at the entrance way to the hospital.

'Speaking of whom,' I said, nodding towards the man and child walking in through the doorway.

'Who's that?'

'Vincent Morrison,' I said, quietly.

'You let him come here?'

'His son wanted to see Penny. Maybe he might get through to her.'

Caroline looked me in the eyes, held my gaze and smiled lightly. 'That's unusually reasonable of you, Inspector Devlin.'

Morrison approached us warily. I introduced him to Caroline who, after a moment excused herself and left. Morrison and his son accompanied me in the elevator back up to the ward, though we did not speak until we reached Penny's room. Debbie stood and hugged him.

'Thank you,' she said.

Morrison blushed heavily. 'John wanted to see how she was doing.'

The boy looked from Debbie to me and then to where Penny lay. He moved up and stood at the head of the bed and looked down at her. Any doubts I had about the sincerity of his affection for her were dispelled when, of a sudden, he began to shudder with tears. He put his hand on top of hers, an apology spluttering on his lips.

'You're all right, son,' Vincent Morrison said, clearly embarrassed. 'She's going to do all right. She's going to pull through.'

'I'm sorry,' the boy repeated, this time to Debbie who was now starting to well up herself.

'It's OK, John,' I said, moving over towards where he stood. 'It's not your fault.'

'It's not my daddy's fault either,' he said, his face smeared with tears. 'Please don't put my daddy in jail again.'

I looked from the boy to his father. Vincent Morrison coughed lightly, put his hand on his son's shoulder.

'Time for us to go, wee man,' he said. He turned to Debbie. 'I hope Penny pulls through soon, Mrs Devlin,' he said.

He led the boy, still in tears, out of the room. As their footfalls echoed along the hospital corridor I could hear Morrison's voice, low and urgent, encouraging his son to stop crying.

I looked at Debbie who had taken her seat by Penny again, raised my eyebrows and released the breath I realized I had been holding since the boy spoke.

'He's a very nice man,' Debbie said.

'He may be involved in trafficking drugs,' I said.

'For Christ's sake, Ben,' Debbie snapped. 'When are you going to stop?' She glared at me for a second, then turned her attention to the unmoving figure of our daughter.

Friday, 16 February

Chapter Thirty-Eight

After spending the night on the armchair by Penny's bed, I went down to the dawn Mass in the hospital chapel and asked the priest to pray for her recovery. When Debbie arrived soon after and took her seat by the bed, I headed back home, showered and breakfasted, then brought Shane up with me to see his sister. He had been asking why she wasn't coming home. We had told him that she was in a very deep sleep, that she needed her rest for her brain to get better. That there was nothing to worry about.

When we arrived back in the ward, Shane carrying a bunch of flowers he had insisted on buying for his big sister, Harry Patterson was sitting in the room with Debbie. He offered his sympathies to me when I came in, then looked down at Shane who stared up at him openly.

'Do you think this was connected with . . .?' he trailed off.

'Apparently not,' I said. 'How did things end with Kielty? Did Nicell come clean?'

'Mmmm,' Patterson said, in a manner which made me immediately suspicious.

'He did come clean, didn't he? I mean we had his van at Kielty's house,' I persisted.

Patterson cleared his throat, glanced at Debbie.

'Let's go down and buy some sweets, Shane,' she said, leading Shane out of the room and closing the door behind her.

'What happened?' I asked.

'One or two things,' Patterson said. 'I thought you should know that Simon Williams has made a statement. He wants to press charges. He arrived yesterday morning at the station. Obviously, we'll not worry about it until all this ... unpleasantness is over.'

I had expected Williams to do something at some stage, though the timing couldn't have been worse.

'What about Kielty and Nicell?'

Patterson tugged at his ear, sniffing loudly as he focused on Penny.

'The Assistant Commissioner wants it dropped,' Patterson said quietly.

'What?' I said, leaning forward in my chair, as if I had misheard.

'After all this shit with The Rising people getting a beating, it's been open season on the Guards in the local rags. The AC is concerned how it would look nationally if one of the inspectors of the National Drugs Unit was implicated in a series of murders.'

'He can't do that,' I protested. 'Nicell has to answer for this.'

'And he already has,' said Patterson, and I realized that it had already been dealt with. 'He's resigned as of yesterday. Kielty was one of Nicell's touts, apparently; that was how they met. It was decided that he would be more useful outside, telling us what was going on.'

'Do you agree with this, Harry?' I asked. Patterson may have been difficult, but he was relatively solid.

'It doesn't matter whether I do or not, Devlin,' he said, his gaze shifting from my face to the window behind me. 'An order is an order.'

'Well, I'm afraid I can't agree to this, Harry,' I said. 'I can't just drop it.'

Patterson stood up, went to the window and looked out.

'Well, speaking of dropping things,' he began. 'It mightn't be surprising if Williams were to drop these battery charges he's placed. I'm sure he could be convinced. You could take a few weeks' paid leave while you wait for this wee woman to waken.'

'You'd convince Williams to drop the charges just to keep me quiet?' I asked.

'We are to avoid *any* bad press about the force,' he said. 'Orders from the top.'

'What about Joe McCready?' I asked. 'He sat in on the interview; he knows what happened, what was said.'

'You wanted him in Lifford, from what I remember,' Patter-son began. 'It's amazing how easily some of these new boys can get onto the ladder. He's getting married, isn't he?' he asked.

'Yes,' I said.

'He'll need every cent he can get his hands on,' Patterson said. 'We might be able to find a detective posting around the border.'

'It's not right, Harry,' I said, standing myself and approaching him. 'Kielty needs to pay for what he did.'

'Jesus, man,' Patterson hissed. 'He's lost his own woman; do you not think he's suffered enough?'

'Caroline Williams will want something more. Kielty's just going free?'

'I wouldn't call it free,' Patterson said.

'What would you call it?'

'He'll be monitored, limited in the amount he can shift.'

'He's going to keep selling?' I said, my voice high with incredulity.

'He's more useful to us in the game than out.'

'It's not a fucking game,' I snapped.

'Of course it is. And everyone wins in this one. The AC has agreed that Simon Williams will be convinced to drop any charges if you agree to this. McCready gets his promotion to Lifford, giving you a bit of support, keeping the station going. Nicell is out of the picture, Kielty is controlled by us, An Garda keeps its name out of the shit for another few days.'

'And if I don't agree?'

Patterson placed his hand on my shoulder, lowered his head to look me in the eye. 'You're not listening, Devlin,' he said calmly. 'Nicell has already resigned. It's already happened, whether you agree or not. Your girl's sick, God bless her, she needs you off to look after her. The AC has already agreed to your having a month compassionate leave, fully paid, to help get yourself and your family back on your feet.'

He stood, kneading my shoulder lightly. 'You're in all our thoughts, Ben,' he said. 'Give Debbie my best wishes when she comes back.'

He moved out of the room quietly, despite his bulk. I sat down again, for a moment in silence, staring at nothing, allowing all he had said to sink in. Gradually I became aware of the fact that I was looking at Penny. Her face looked impossibly young, her features small and neat.

I took her hand in mine, laid my head on the pillow beside her. Her breathing was shallow, her skin warm and supple as I placed a kiss against her cheek.

'You have to wake up, honey,' I said. 'I need you to wake up. I miss you. Shane and Mummy miss you so much too. We want you to come home.'

If I had expected any reaction, I was disappointed. Her eyes did not move beneath their lids, her mouth did not open any further under the mask she wore.

'I'm sorry, sweetheart,' I said. 'I'm so sorry for not being better. I'm sorry for not being better.'

I repeated the mantra over and over, in hope that she might

hear me, until my words grew indistinct among the first tears I had allowed myself to cry for my lost child.

I settled myself, as Debbie led Shane back into the room a few moments later. She looked at my face, the damp impression on the pillow where my head had been laid, and smiled sadly.

'I'm sorry, Debs,' I said.

'Shussh,' she whispered, glancing down at Shane. 'We're all together now. Penny will have to wake up if she knows we're all here, isn't that right, pet?' She ruffled Shane's hair and he beamed up at her.

'I brought her some sweets,' he said, laying the chocolate bar on the bed within reach of her hand. 'In case she wakes up hungry.'

I moved over to them and put my arms around Debbie who cried into the crook of my neck while Shane held his sister's hand and told her all the things she was missing.

Chapter Thirty-Nine

Caroline Williams called again early that evening. I had dreaded seeing her following my conversation with Patterson.

She and Debbie chatted lightly, and she played with Shane. His grandparents were due to visit to see Penny and take him home and, having spent the day around the hospital, he was getting bored as well as tired.

When they arrived, around seven, Caroline made her excuses and left. I offered to walk her down to her car, if only to free up some chairs.

Once we were outside I lit a cigarette.

'Things seem better today,' Caroline said. 'I'm glad you and Debbie have sorted yourselves out a bit.'

I smiled at her. 'How did you know?'

'I spent a lifetime hiding a strained marriage,' she said. 'I know when people aren't getting on. Plus, she told me the last day that she was blaming herself for what happened and you weren't disagreeing.'

I felt the need to defend myself, but couldn't truthfully do it.

'I was surprised at you,' she continued. 'Especially after all that happened with Simon. I thought you of all people would've known better.'

I coughed to cover my embarrassment.

'Anyway,' she said, 'I'm glad you've sorted it all out. Things happen, Ben, that are no one's fault. And you can't do anything about them.'

I drew deeply on my smoke, found myself flicking my cigarette so much the tip eventually fell with a hiss to the ground and I had to relight it.

'I have some bad news,' I began. 'About what happened with Peter.'

The benign smile on her face shrank into a tight line.

'Patterson called this morning. The AC has ordered him to drop the charges against Kielty and Nicell.'

'What?' Caroline's face, already drained of colour, seemed even paler under the street lamps.

'He's afraid of the bad press the force will take if it comes out that one of the Drugs Unit was involved. Nicell has resigned. Kielty is being kept on a leash.'

'Are they not charging him with anything?'

I flipped the butt of my smoke into the nearby bushes. 'Nothing. He's being forced into informing full time. Apparently he did some for Nicell anyway.'

'What about Morrison and Cunningham?'

I shook my head bitterly. 'There's nothing to connect them now. Unless Kielty can provide something the DPP wants to use. But it won't be on this – they couldn't charge them without revealing what happened with Kielty.'

'So that's it?'

I nodded. 'I'm sorry, Caroline. There's nothing I can do about it. It was all arranged while I was here with Penny. They're putting me off for a month – compassionate leave. By the time I get back, it'll all be forgotten.'

Caroline stopped at her car, searching through her bag for her keys. Eventually, flustered, she swore softly.

'You're holding them, Caroline,' I said.

She looked blankly at her hand, then flickered a smile.

'Stupid me,' she said.

I took her hand in mine. 'I am sorry, Caroline. I tried my best.'

'I know,' she said, her nose red with cold, her eyes beginning to water. 'Me with all my big talk about blame. I need to practise what I preach.'

'I understand how you feel, Caroline. You've a right to be angry.'

'Not with you, sir,' she said. 'Never with you.'

She stood lightly on her tiptoes, brought her face close to mine and hugged me tightly. I could feel the heat of her breath, the coldness of the tip of her nose against my cheek.

We stepped apart and she smiled at me, seemingly resolved to something.

'Thanks, Ben,' she said. 'I meant it when I said I was glad you two sorted things out.'

She pressed her keys and the indicator lights flickered alive as the locks shunted open. She climbed into the car without another word and waved out to me as she reversed from the space and drove away.

Saturday, 17 February

Chapter Forty

I slept at home that night. Just before nine the following morning, as I waited for Debbie's parents to arrive for Shane, the phone rang. I rushed for my mobile.

'Is that you, sir?' a male voice said. 'It's Joe McCready.'

'Yes, Joe,' I said. 'Is everything OK?'

'I've just heard on the radio and thought you'd want to know. Martin Kielty has been shot.'

'Is he dead?'

'I don't know, sir,' he replied. 'It's only just come through. I'm on my way to his house now.'

I called Debbie from the car to find out how Penny was and to explain that I had been called away urgently.

'I need a shower,' she hissed after telling me that there was no change to Penny's condition. 'I need a break.'

'I'll be up as soon as I can be,' I promised.

'I thought you were given time off,' she snapped. 'I need you here.'

'I'll be as quick as I can,' I said.

'Ask my parents to come down here with Shane,' she said grudgingly.

'I love you, Debs,' I said.

'Yeah,' she replied.

I reached Sligo around ten fifteen and drove straight to Rossanure. Outside Kielty's house, a number of squad cars were parked.

I nodded to the officer at the gate, explained who I was.

'Is he dead?' I asked, nodding towards the house.

'Oh yeah,' the man replied, smiling. 'A dealer.'

I grunted non-committally as I made my way past him, up the path and in through Kielty's front door. Boiler-suited Scene of Crime Officers were trudging up and down the stairs. As I mounted the staircase I was aware of a mewing sound from the living room and glanced down. A female Garda officer sat perched at the edge of a sofa, Elena McEvoy's baby daughter squirming slightly in her arms.

At the top of the stairs I went straight to Kielty's bedroom. On the floor, beside the child's empty Moses basket, Martin Kielty's body lay foetally curled. He wore only a pair of stained boxer shorts. He had been shot twice, once in the head, once in the chest, about half a foot below the puckered scar tissue from the incident a few days earlier.

Several SOCOs were working the room silently. One was taking photographs of the body and of the blood-spatter patterns which flecked the side of the basket.

He moved back to let me see the body more clearly. Kielty's arms had been tied behind his back, his wrists bound with piano wire. There were livid red scars like cigarette burns on his forearms, and his face was bruised on one side, the eye partially shut, the skin ballooning purple around the socket.

'How long are you here?'

I turned to see Harry Patterson standing in the doorway.

'I just arrived,' I said.

'This is handy,' he said, nodding towards the body as if I hadn't spoken. 'Ties up loose ends.'

'Any ideas who did it?'

'None,' he replied, shaking his head. 'These druggies take one another out; what can you do?'

I stared down at Kielty's body, the arms tense behind his back.

'The piano wire,' I said, pointing down at him. 'The same as Lorcan Hutton.'

Patterson considered what I had said for a second, puckered his lips as if he had tasted something bitter and unpalatable.

'How's Penny?'

'She's fine, sir,' I said.

'You're on leave,' he continued. 'Go home, Inspector. Spend some time with your family.'

'Is there nothing for me to do here?' I asked.

He shook his head. 'That Garda McCready is downstairs,

too, I see. The two of you have worked hard – you both deserve a break. Go home.'

His avuncular tone made it impossible to find offence in his closing me out of the conclusion of my own case.

I went downstairs to where McCready sat in the living room with the female Garda I had seen earlier with the child. She was shushing her to sleep in her arms.

'What's going to happen to her?' I asked.

'Social services are on their way,' the woman officer said. 'They'll take her into care.'

'The child's grandmother lives in the North,' I said. 'Someone should contact her.'

The officer looked around, as if for verification. 'I don't think anyone knows that, sir. Maybe you could contact her.'

I nodded.

'Can I get a lift back to the station, sir?' Joe said. 'My squad car's been commandeered for a bun run.'

Unable to speak, and feeling suddenly exhausted, I nodded.

As we negotiated our way out of Rossanure, the image of Martin Kielty's corpse played over in my head. I kept seeing his figure merge with Lorcan Hutton's in my mind. The wire around the wrists was troubling me. Why? Why not just shoot him? The state of his face and arms suggested he'd been given a going-over before they killed him. Had they tortured him for information? About his stash? If there was a link with Hutton, then it must have been The Rising behind it. And where was his stash? Nicell had helped him to move it. Nicell.

'Nicell,' I repeated, aloud this time.

'What?' McCready said.

'Rory Nicell. Kielty was tortured before he died. I've seen that MO before, when Lorcan Hutton was killed on the border. The Rising was behind that killing. I'd swear they're behind this one too. But why torture him? They were either looking for his stash or for revenge. They're looking for Rory Nicell.'

I tried ringing his mobile, but the phone rang out.

'Where does he live?' I asked McCready.

'I don't know, sir,' he said. 'I'll try Command and Control.'

He took out his own phone and dialled.

'Silverbirch Drive. Number 10,' he stated, once he'd hung up. 'Take a left up ahead.'

I twisted the steering wheel sharply, taking the corner too fast and having to overcompensate to correct the manoeuvre.

'"Popular man", she said,' he commented.

'Why?'

He looked at me blankly. 'I didn't ask,' he stated simply.

He directed me through traffic until finally we came to a quiet estate with, perhaps, a dozen houses, separated from the main road by a wall, above which the spindly arms of silver birches jutted into the sky.

We trawled slowly past each house until we reached number 10.

As we approached the door, a woman in her early forties opened it and stepped out. 'Yes?'

'Is Rory Nicell here?' I asked.

'Who are you?' she asked, raising her chin defiantly.

'Garda Inspector Benedict Devlin,' I said.

'Have you people not done enough to him?' she said, turning, her hand on the door to close it. 'Hounding him out of a job.'

I reached out, placed my hand against the closing door, earning a glare of anger from Nicell's wife.

'His life may be in danger, Mrs Nicell. I need to speak to him.'

The woman regarded me coolly, then cast a disparaging glance at McCready. 'He's gone to eleven o'clock Mass at St Mary's. He goes every morning.'

McCready drove, as he knew the way to the church. Even so, it still took us just over ten minutes to make it there due to the one-way system in the town centre.

As we approached the church, we realized that the roadway for a mile past it was being resurfaced, the traffic held up by temporary lights. We had to stop and start several times as we made our way towards Nicell, the car ahead skidding up loose gravel onto our bonnet each time it moved.

We drew level with St Mary's in time to see the last parishioners coming down the church steps, the priest standing at the doors, speaking with an elderly woman while, with one hand, he held down the hem of his soutane against the wind which threatened to lift it.

'There he is,' McCready said excitedly, pointing further up the road to where a blue Megane was pulling out from the kerb. Sure enough, in the driver's seat, his profile turned to check for oncoming traffic, I could see Rory Nicell.

He pulled out into the traffic three cars ahead of us, let out by someone looking for his parking space, so that we were held in the traffic as that driver reversed into the newly vacated spot. Meanwhile, Nicell had moved on ahead, back towards the town centre.

In the rear-view mirror I caught a movement, something red shifting quickly in and out of my sight. I twisted in my seat as best I could and saw that a motorcycle was driving down the centre of the road, weaving between the cars behind us.

'Try to pull out,' I said to McCready. 'Get past this queue.'

McCready twisted the steering, but the car ahead of us was too close. In the rear-view mirror, the motorcycle was closing in, the driving erratic. Finally it shot past us, weaving sharply past the angled bumper of our car, the pillion passenger twisting to watch the cars they were passing. Behind the plastic visor of his helmet, I could make out the sharp features of Tony Armstrong. The bulkiness of the rider suggested that it was Jimmy Irvine.

'That's them,' I shouted. 'Move it.'

The car ahead of us inched forward enough for McCready to push out past them, though not without hitting its bumper.

'You've no siren,' he cursed. 'We should have brought a squad car.'

We pulled out into the middle of the road, McCready hammering on his horn, his headlights blazing as he tried to push his way through the traffic. Up ahead I could see Nicell stopped at traffic lights. The motorcycle was pulling up alongside his car. McCready sped up, smashing off one wing mirror after another of the cars to our left.

I could see Armstrong ahead, stopped by Nicell's car, straighten up on the bike as his hand disappeared into his tunic. As we approached he withdrew his gun and pointed it towards the passenger window.

Irvine, though, must have seen us in his mirror. He pulled off, just as Armstrong shot, the bike lurching forward with such force that Armstrong was flung backwards onto the road.

Irvine's bike surged through the red light. There was a sickening crunch of metal as a car, cutting across the junction collided with the bike, smashing it sideways. The machine slid along the ground, Irvine beneath it, sparks flying.

McCready skidded to a stop in front of Armstrong, who was struggling to his feet. His arm hung useless by his side, his gun lost beneath Nicell's car in the fall.

He raised his other hand above his head, his crooked smile bloody clear behind the shattered visor of his helmet.

McCready ran to him and brought him to the ground, twisting his one good arm behind his back. To our left, Nicell's car sat, the engine still running. The side window was broken, the windscreen stippled with blood. I glanced in to see Nicell lying across his front seat, clutching his leg, from which blood was oozing, darkening his jeans.

I heard a shout and turned towards the junction. The man whose car had hit the bike must have gone over to help Irvine. But Irvine had managed to move the wreckage of his bike and was struggling to his feet, pawing inside his leather jacket and pulling out a handgun. With his free hand he pulled off his helmet.

He pointed the gun and fired. As I ducked, I heard the crack and shattering of the plate glass window of the newsagent's further along the pavement.

I didn't give Irvine a chance to find his range. Almost without thought, I pulled my gun and approached him.

'Drop it or I'll shoot,' I said. 'Drop it now.'

I was vaguely aware of passers-by stopping to watch. A few ducked nervously behind cover, others stood openly at the edge of the road as if the scene were provided solely for their entertainment.

Irvine looked at me, squinting slightly as if trying to remember where he had seen me before. Blood dripped down into his eyes from a gash on his forehead.

With a look of complete confusion he raised his gun again, pointed it at me.

My bullet caught him in the neck, spun his body around and knocked him back onto the road. He fell onto his side awkwardly and lay there, and did not attempt to correct his position.

I spun to my right, catching a figure out of the corner of my eye raising something and pointing it at me. A teenage boy swore as he cowered down, a mobile phone held aloft, filming all that had happened. He raised it in his hand to show what it was, then flung it to the ground as he covered his head with his arms.

I approached Irvine, my gun trained on him. His gun lay a few yards from his body and I kicked it further from him. He still lay on his side, his arm raised above his head, cushioning his face. Tiny bubbles of blood popped around his mouth. As I called for an ambulance, I noticed they had ceased.

Chapter Forty-One

'But you still haven't told me how you knew,' Patterson observed at the end of our interview.

We had been sitting in the office in Sligo station for over an hour while I talked through the events that had resulted in the death of Jimmy Irvine. Nicell was still in surgery as doctors attempted to stem the arterial bleeding. I knew that Tony Armstrong was being interviewed in a similar room further down the hall, after his busted arm had been plastered up in Sligo General.

'The wire they used to tie Kielty,' I said. 'The same MO as Hutton.'

'This is a fucking mess,' he said, his hands rubbing at the sides of his scalp. 'How the fuck did they know where Kielty and Nicell were living?'

'I have no idea, sir,' I lied. 'Someone would need to contact Kielty's mother and get her down to collect the child.'

He nodded, his hands in front of his face. I noticed he had

become jowly, his stomach flabby, since he had taken over as Super.

'Can I go, sir?' I asked. 'I want to get back to Penny.'

He rubbed his flushed face, tapped his hands on his desk. 'Of course, Ben,' he said. 'Good work today. Nicell owes you one. Not that the fucker deserves it.'

Caroline Williams answered the door on my second knock.

'Ben,' she said, smiling. She stood back, holding the door open. 'Come in.'

I stepped into the hallway.

'You look like shit,' she observed. 'What are you doing down here? Is everything OK with Penny?'

'Fine,' I managed, as she shut the door behind me and directed me towards the living room.

'My folks aren't in,' she said. 'Do you want tea?'

'Please,' I said, my throat so dry I had to repeat the word twice to be heard.

I followed her into the kitchen, watched as she lifted the kettle, filled it at the sink. She turned and looked at me where I stood, folded her arms across her chest, then unfolded them and leant back, her hands on the counter behind her.

Neither of us spoke for a moment.

Finally she said, 'I'm glad it's you.'

I swallowed hard. 'I'm not,' I said.

She smiled, turned and lifted two mugs off the tree to her left. 'Milk and sugar, right?'

I nodded.

She busied herself, placing tea bags into the two mugs, spooning out sugar, her hand shaking so much she spilt some on the counter which she then had to wipe up.

'How did you know?' she asked without turning.

'I didn't. I just guessed,' I said. 'Someone in Command and Control commented that Nicell was popular, when we called looking for his address. I checked back. You called an hour earlier, gave your name and officer number, to get his address.'

She nodded, continuing to make the tea.

'Which means that you knew you'd be caught, Caroline,' I said, moving towards her. 'You wanted to be caught. Why?'

'They killed Peter,' she said. 'They took my son from me. What else have I got left?'

'You have your parents,' I said, standing close behind her, only a foot or two separating us.

She smiled briefly. 'I lost everything, Ben. They took everything from me when they took Peter. I tried to be philosophical about it but I can't be. So I went to Morrison yesterday. The house was easy to find; I followed your directions to Porthall.'

'What did he say?'

'He remembered me from the hospital. I suppose he thought it was a set-up,' she said. 'He didn't say as much, but I could tell. I convinced him it wasn't, told him about Peter.'

'What did you tell him?'

'That I knew where Kielty was. That I had heard that he had taken their drugs. I told him that Kielty had been boasting to Peter's friends that he had stolen from The Rising. I told him that Kielty had staged his death, had sold drugs to my son and had killed him.'

'What happened?'

'He asked me why I was telling him all this, it had nothing to do with him. I told him I had thought he was connected with The Rising.'

The kettle switch clicked behind her. She brushed a strand of her hair from in front of her face. 'He gave me Charlie Cunningham's number. I called him and told him about Peter. I told him I wanted Martin Kielty dead, and the Drugs Unit man who had helped him steal their stash.'

'Why, Caroline?'

She smiled at me. 'Ben, you know why. I can't pretend I'm all right with them getting away with what happened to Peter. Why should I have to be the only one who suffered?'

'I tried my best, Caroline,' I said.

She put her hand on my forearm.

'I know you did, Ben. But they got away.'

'Kielty was killed this morning. In front of his infant daughter.'

Caroline grimaced slightly, then shrugged, before turning back to the mugs of tea. 'He deserved what happened to him. I'm not sorry for that.'

'Rory Nicell was shot too.'

She nodded, as if expecting this news all along. 'Is he dead?'

'No,' I said.

She stopped what she was doing and leaned forward on the worktop, her head bowed.

'You have Morrison now,' she explained. 'Charge me and I'll give evidence against him.'

I shook my head. Morrison had given her a phone number for The Rising, nothing more.

'Yes, you can connect him to the killings. I knew they wouldn't let it go. They couldn't have someone boasting about stealing from them. That's not how they work.'

'You don't understand, Caroline. I can't get Morrison,' I said. 'Or you.'

She turned to me again, took my hand in both of hers.

'They didn't know where Nicell lived. Kielty couldn't tell them. Cunningham called me this morning. I didn't even think my officer number would still be accepted, but no one asked any questions.' She paused. 'But I knew it would lead someone back to me. That's why I'm glad it was you.'

'I can't arrest you, Caroline,' I repeated.

She tugged lightly on my hand, lowered her gaze to look up into my eyes. 'If you don't, someone else will. They'll figure it out and come for me, Ben. I'm ready. This way I get to take down all of them, maybe right up to Morrison. I've nothing left here anyway.'

I could feel my eyes hot with tears. 'I can't, Caroline. I can't arrest you. I can't arrest Morrison; he saved Penny.'

'He killed Peter,' she said simply. 'I'm not afraid, Ben. I want you to do this for me. Please.'

I looked at her face. She placed her hand against my cheek and I could recall her doing something similar, years earlier. She smiled softly, her own eyes moist with tears.

'I want it to be you,' she said. 'It's my choice. I'm ready.'

I lowered my head and nodded.

I felt her hand on my chin. She raised my face slightly, brought her face close to mine, placed her mouth against mine softly. Her lips were warm, the kiss gentle and brief.

'Thank you,' she said, as I became aware of the first wailing of an approaching siren.

She turned off the kettle at the wall.

'You never got your tea,' she said.

I took her by the arm and we walked to the front door and out onto the street. She stumbled once, as we crossed over the threshold, and I could feel resistance in her movements, as if she had realized for the first time exactly what she had asked me to do. I stopped beside her, looked at her questioningly, hoping she would nod and go back into the house. There was still a chance she could disappear. However, after the briefest pause, she took a deep breath and moved forward again, her hand clasped in mine.

'Stay with me,' she asked as the first Garda car pulled up sharply in front of the house. I put my arm around her shoulder, hugged her tight against me, rubbed her upper arm to dispel the shivering which began to rack her body.

She placed her hand against my shoulder blade, where the burn wound now seemed suddenly raw and exposed once more.

Sunday, 25 March

Chapter Forty-Two

Around the time I was helping Caroline Williams into the back of the Garda car, Charlie Cunningham was being arrested at a checkpoint set up just south of Bundoran following the killings in Sligo. Two Gardai stopped his car and, searching it, found a handgun and a quantity of ammunition.

In the weeks that followed, Tony Armstrong was charged with the murders of Lorcan Hutton and Martin Kielty, as well as the attempted murder of Rory Nicell. Cunningham was charged with possession of a firearm which contravened his early release licence in the North and resulted in him returning to prison to complete his sentence.

Rory Nicell managed to salvage something, earning a reputation as a hero after the shooting. While still out of An Garda, he was publicly recognized by the Assistant Commissioner for being wounded in service, despite the fact he had resigned days before the incident.

Caroline Williams was charged with having information

likely to be of use to terrorists, incitement to murder and imper-
sonating a Garda officer. She was released on Garda bail of ten
thousand euros while she awaited trial.

I had promised I would be there on her first day in court.
As I stood outside the building, having a smoke, a small, squat
figure approached me, his face pasty behind his darkening
glasses. His nose was bent slightly out of shape, the crescent
shape of the scar my wedding ring had caused when I struck
him still clearly visible.

He stopped and looked at me with open hostility. A mixture of shame about what I had done, and fear that I would
repeat the attack if I spoke to him, stopped me from returning
his stare.

'I believe you were the one who arrested her,' he said, his
voice low and insinuating. 'And I thought *I* hated her.'

He shook his head and, tutting to himself, continued on
into the courthouse. He sat in court each day of the trial and
smiled when the verdict was announced and Caroline was led
down to the cells to begin her sentence.

Patterson forced me into taking the month's leave he had
given me, despite my objections. In all truth, I could not bare
the thought of sitting impotently by Penny's bedside each day,
watching her sleep. Her very state was a reminder of the futility
of my work, which I had always convinced myself was about
making the world a safer place for my children. I thought of

her, Peter Williams, John Morrison and Anna McEvoy, all of whom had been touched by the events of the previous month.

But as the month passed, and I spent day after day with her, I reached some sense of equilibrium. Debbie and I took turns to read to her, or play her favourite music, in the hope that it might bring her back to us.

Vincent Morrison returned once more with his son. The boy stood by Penny's side and told her all the news from school.

His father stood at the foot of the bed and spoke to me.

'I understand your old partner was sentenced to five years. That's tough going.'

'Cunningham and his cronies can expect more than that.'

Morrison nodded. 'They knew the risks when they started messing around with that nonsense.'

I turned and studied his profile. A thought struck me.

'The Rising took out all the dealers along the border and introduced their own supplies. Now that Cunningham and the rest have been put out of action, whoever bankrolled them can take charge of the whole operation.'

He looked at me. 'You know, now you mention it, you're right.'

'You're controlling drugs for the whole area,' I whispered, wary of his son's presence in the room. 'You rose right back on top again. You're running the borderlands, you son of a bitch.'

His jaw set slightly at the final insult, then softened. He smiled at me coldly.

'Prove it,' he said. Then he moved over and stood beside his son.

In the early hours of Easter Sunday, over a month after her accident, Penny's condition changed. I had left Debbie for an hour to go to the vigil Mass where I had lit my candle from the paschal candle and prayed that our daughter might come back to us.

I came back up to the hospital around 1 a.m. to let Debbie go home. The nurses came in and left a chocolate egg in the room, something which they did with all the children on the ward. One of them joked that she might waken to eat it.

Before she left, Debbie went over to kiss her goodnight as she always did. She leant on the bed, her hand resting on top of Penny's as she laid a kiss on her forehead and urged her in whispered tones to come back to us. Then she suddenly started, emitting a tiny shriek which pierced the silence of the room.

'She squeezed my hand,' she said urgently, turning to me, her eyes sparkling with tears.

I moved beside her. 'Are you sure?'

She nodded, her tears running freely. 'Oh, Ben. She squeezed my hand.'

'You might have imagined it,' I said. I had several times myself thought I had seen her eyes flickering.

'I didn't. I felt her squeeze my hand, Ben. I felt her.'

She looked around, then shouted louder to attract some of the staff. 'She squeezed my hand!' she called out again.

Finally one of the nurses came in.

'She's wakening,' Debbie said, smiling, her face smeared with tears.

'Let me get the doctor to check,' the nurse said cautiously. 'Keep talking to her, just in case.'

While we waited for the doctor to arrive, we spoke to Penny, loudly encouraging her to waken. I was beginning to doubt Debbie's claim when, of a sudden, I saw Penny flex one of her fingers, saw the ridge of her eyeball shift underneath the eyelid.

'She's wakening!' I shouted, rushing to the door of the room to be heard.

When the doctor arrived, he checked her eyes with a penlight, then tested her fingers one by one. As he did so, we heard, though barely audible, a soft moan escape her mouth. The young man turned to us, his face alight with his smile.

'I think you're right,' he said. 'She seems to be coming around. Congratulations.'

As dawn broke on Easter Sunday morning, Penny opened her eyes of her own accord and spoke her first words in over a month.

'Mummy,' she said dryly, the sound barely audible. 'Daddy.' She smiled benignly and moved her head to the side. On the bedside locker, Shane's T-rex sat looking down at her. 'Where's Shane?'

We sat with her through that day, Shane perched constantly on her bed, telling her all that she had missed, and how much he had missed her. She tired easily and slept through much of what he had to say, but he continued unperturbed.

That night, reluctantly, Debbie went home, having not slept properly for two nights. Neither of us wanted to leave Penny for a moment, in case we returned to find her gone from us again.

I sat awake by her until the dawn, watching her sleep. I recalled how, when both she and Shane were just babies, I would check on them at night, standing beside the cot, holding my own breath and listening in the darkness for the reassurance of their breathing. If I could not hear them, I would lower my face close to theirs in a panic, hoping I might feel the warmth of each exhalation against my cheek.

I found that I did so again now. I sat in silence by my daughter's hospital bed, and counted each breath she drew, their number measured by the dipping of the bedclothes above her heart, and the rising.

Acknowledgements

I have a number of people who deserve thanks for their help and support in the writing of *The Rising*. As always, thanks to my friends and colleagues in St Columb's who have been incredibly supportive of all the books. Particular thanks to Bob McKimm, who remains one of Devlin's staunchest supporters.

Thanks to a number of people who have supported the writing of the Devlin books in their own ways: Alex Mullan, Tara Vance, James Johnston, Eoghan Barr, Nuala McGonagle, Dessie Kelly, Susan Gill and Pawel in NWCLD, Margaret Giblin, Stephanie Swain, Belinda Mahaffey, Bobby McDaid and Rev. Edward Kilpatrick, and Harry Doherty. Thanks to Paddy McDaid and Carmel McGilloway for advice regarding legal procedures. All inaccuracies are my own.

Thanks to Peter and Jenny at RCW, Emily at The Agency, all at Dumont, Pete and Liz at St Martins and the fantastic team at Pan Macmillan; Cat, Ellen, Cormac, David, Sophie and Will.

Love and thanks to the McGilloways, Dohertys, O'Neills and

Kerlins. In particular, I'm hugely grateful for the support of my sister, Carmel, and brothers, Joe and Dermot, and, of course, of my parents, Laurence and Katrina.

Finally, my love and thanks to Tanya, Ben, Tom and David, as always, for putting up with me.

extracts reading groups
competitions books new events
books discounts extracts extracts reading groups
competitions extracts discounts
books new reading groups extracts discounts
events books extracts events reading groups
new extracts new titles reading groups
interviews events new
events extracts extracts books
discounts events interviews new books extracts
new books events events
events new interviews new books extracts
discounts extracts discounts
www.panmacmillan.com
extracts events reading groups
competitions books extracts new books